BEYOND THE
CONSEQUENCES

Book #5 of the bestselling Consequences Series

Aleatha Romig

New York Times and USA Today
bestselling author

BEYOND THE CONSEQUENCES

Copyright © 2014 Aleatha Romig

ISBN 13: 978-0-9863080-0-0
ISBN 10: 0986308005

Published by Romig Works
2014 Edition

Edited by Lisa Aurello

Interior design by Angela McLaurin, Fictional Formats

A Beginning Note from Aleatha

———◆———

Dear Readers,

As always, this is for you. BEYOND THE CONSEQUENCES began as a novella (A Peek Beyond the Consequences), which appeared in a limited-release anthology. After numerous requests, I decided to expand the novella and release it on its own. I was hoping to double it from its original 17 K word length. As I wrote, Tony, Claire, and Phil all decided they had more to say. I now introduce you to a 66 K+ word story. By definition this is no longer a novella, but a full-length novel. Welcome to the new and expanded BEYOND THE CONSEQUENCES, book five of the Consequences series.

Note that this story occurs after most events in CONVICTED and REVEALED take place. It's meant as a fun glimpse into the future of a family that had a very dark and unusual beginning.

As you know, Anthony Rawlings and Claire Nichols have taken the long road to get to this point in their lives and their relationship. I think they deserve some fun; there was enough angst in the beginning to last them both a lifetime.

Oh, who am I kidding? I enjoy giving you and them a little angst too.

Thank you for rejoining Tony and Claire for a look into their future. Please sit back and enjoy BEYOND THE CONSEQUENCES.

Sincerely,

~Aleatha

Disclaimer

The CONSEQUENCES series contains dark adult content. Although excessive description and detail are not used, the content contains innuendos of kidnapping, rape, and abuse—physical and mental. If you're unable to read this material, please do not purchase. If you can enter this world of fiction, welcome aboard and enjoy the ride!

BEYOND THE CONSEQUENCES

Book #5 of the bestselling Consequences Series

*We love life, not because
we are used to living but
because we are used to loving.*
—Friedrich Nietzsche

Aleatha Romig

Chapter 1

Late December 2016

Claire

———◆———

***Safety is something that happens between
your ears, not something you hold in your hands.***
—Jeff Cooper

CLAIRE GENTLY SMOOTHED back Nichol's fine dark hair, unable to break the connection with her daughter. The little girl was sound asleep with her head upon her mother's lap as the drone of the engines filled the cabin of their airplane. Claire sighed contentedly, taking in the unusually full cabin. Never could she remember their private plane being occupied by this many people. There was a time when this would never—could never—have happened. However, that was long ago, a distant memory. Now things were different, and their family and friends were together.

Though the trip back to Iowa from their South Pacific island was not complete, they'd been flying for what seemed like days. Sometime during the still of night, with Claire's patience and soothing, Nichol lost her valiant fight against sleep. Succumbing to the heavy lids, Nichol's dark brown eyes—those that matched her father's—disappeared behind thick lashes. Claire glanced toward her husband, seeing that his eyes too were uncharacteristically closed, and his chin bobbed near his chest. After all the turmoil that the Rawlings family had endured over the last few years, the serenity of the plane ride nearly brought Claire to tears.

Tony, Claire, and Nichol were sharing the flight home with their only family: Claire's sister, Emily, brother-in-law, John, and nephew, Michael. Michael's little body laid contentedly near Nichol's, their heads resting at each end of the long sofa-like seat, on each of their mother's laps. During their battle with sleep, the two children vied for their own space, often behaving more like siblings than cousins. Now, with the battle behind them, they rested peacefully, with the other near. Their closeness was to be expected after the way they'd grown up.

Sometimes, memories such as those would make Claire sad. The years lost were gone, never to be recaptured. However, she'd come to realize that she could spend her time mourning their loss or concentrate on the future. Seeing the children, hearing their excited squeals as they played together on the white sand in paradise, or watching their uncensored interaction, Claire decided the future was the best place to devote her energy: too much time had been lost in the past. She wasn't willing to grant it any more.

Before she could give it much more thought, her husband was beside her, his large hand covering hers as they both gently caressed their daughter's head. With her thoughts in paradise and its tropical beauty, and on the children, coupled with the distracting murmur of the engines, Claire hadn't noticed Tony awaken or move from his earlier reclined seat.

"She finally gave in? It was about time," he whispered, his deep baritone voice was low as to not awaken the others.

Despite her fatigue, Claire smiled as Tony's long legs knelt beside them bringing his eyes to hers. Also, keeping her voice low, she replied, "Well, she does seem to have a stubborn streak."

The dark brown of Tony's eyes glistened knowingly.

"But," Claire continued, "she did finally give in. She's been asleep for a few hours, just like someone else I know."

"Why don't you let me take your place, and you go lay a chair back and get some sleep?"

Claire shook her head. "I don't want to let her go, not even for a few hours."

Small lines appeared near the corner of Tony's eyes as his cheeks rose. "I think we know where she gets that stubborn streak. Don't worry, Nichol's not going anywhere and neither are you, except to get some much needed rest. This holiday in paradise has been great, but soon we'll all be home. You need rest too."

"Oh, Tony," Claire's whisper rose in volume. "It *was* wonderful having everyone together. I'm glad we were all there to celebrate Nichol's birthday as well as Christmas. It was everything I'd hoped and more." Tears teetered on her lids, threatening to coat her cheeks. "I can't believe our daughter's really three! I just wish—"

As she lowered her eyes, Tony lifted her chin. Kissing her lips, he interrupted her words. "I think we've learned that we can't wish away the past. Instead, we need to enjoy each moment we have."

Looking around the cabin, Claire confirmed their cloak of privacy. It was one created not by solitude, but by the sleeping state of the other passengers. Behind Emily, who was separated from Claire by the children, were John, Courtney, and Brent. The Simmonses's children, Caleb, Julia, and Maryn, had all taken a different plane, as had Meredith, Jerry, and their children. Nodding, Claire continued her thought. "I wasn't going to wish away our past.

3

I know there are more than a few people who think I should. I was going to wish for more times like we just had. The time on the island surrounded by family and friends was amazing. I've always loved the security of the island. There's something about being there that gives me peace."

"Could that something be Madeline and Francis?"

Claire thought about his question. The caretakers of the island were definitely unique, comforting people. From the first time she'd met them, she was lulled into their loving aura. "I don't know. I think it's more our memories there. Those months we shared on our island were some of the best of my life. Those were the memories I relived over and over after I..."

It wasn't Tony who interrupted her thoughts: it was Claire herself. She reached up and stroked Tony's scratchy, stubbly cheek. Momentarily, she imagined the abrasiveness on more sensitive skin. With a glint in her green eyes, she continued, "It was there that we learned to truly trust one another."

"Do you want to stay there? Did you not want to go home?"

"No!" Claire resumed her whisper. "I *do* want to go home. For the first time since I can remember, I want to be in Iowa in the winter. I want to build snowmen and make snow angels. I want to teach Nichol to love all the seasons: the warm and cold, the good and bad. They're all important. Ones we enjoy less make us appreciate the ones we adore more. I want to be there as she experiences each and every moment. Like when she saw the island and we explained that it was where she was born... and when she met Madeline and Francis. I'm excited to hold her mitten-covered hand as we see the lake covered with ice. Emily said that she's never ice skated. I've already ordered all of us skates."

The sides of Tony's lips moved upward. "All? Ha." He shook his head playfully from side to side.

Claire's brows rose in question.

Tony explained. "Though I recently lost my appreciation for winter, your excitement may help me learn to embrace the cold as well, but ice skate? I think you have more faith in my abilities than I do. I've never in my life ice skated."

"Then, Mr. Rawlings, I'd say it's time you learned."

Looking from his wife to his daughter and back, Tony shrugged. "I suppose it is."

Leaning closer, Claire's lips grazed his. "I like that."

Tony pressed forward and deepened their kiss. "I like that too," he said with a devilish grin.

"Not *that*... although, I'm not complaining."

"What then? What do you like?"

"The Anthony Rawlings who's willing to learn new things and see new perspectives." The emerald in Claire's eyes shone through the dimmed cabin.

"Oh, Mrs. Rawlings, it's true that I much prefer being the teacher, but I've learned many things since I brought you into my life. I'm up for learning more."

Claire snickered as she eyed their friends and family. "Now is not a good time to be *up*."

"No." He shook his head. "It's not. Now is a good time for you to get some rest. Let me sit with Nichol and you go lie back in one of the chairs."

Though Claire was about to protest, she realized that not only was Tony concerned about her well-being, he wanted to spend time with their daughter too. No longer were his dark eyes focused on her, but on Nichol, as the tips of his fingers lightly caressed her exposed pink sun-kissed cheek. When he once again looked up, Claire saw in his eyes the sadness she'd been feeling, the sense of time lost with no way to retrieve it. The look only lasted for a millisecond and then it was gone, replaced with a conscious expression of authority. He'd told her that he wanted her to switch places, to get some sleep. At first, it may have been phrased like a question, but that was only for her benefit. At one time, Tony's change in tenor and expression would have filled her with dread; that time, too, was long gone. Some memories were better left sleeping.

Claire concentrated on the micro-expression of sadness, the one she knew Tony wanted to hide. Not because he didn't want to be honest or share, but because he didn't want to feel the pain or add fuel to Claire's sense of loss; nevertheless, she took it in. The expression didn't make her pain worse. On the contrary, it eased it. They both had lost too much time. It was another one of their common bonds and shared goals. Together they'd work to fill the future with enough hope and love to overcome the past.

Summoning her smile, Claire nodded and acquiesced. "All right."

Lightly kissing Tony's lips, she lifted Nichol's head and they simultaneously moved, as they'd done so many times, instinctively knowing the other's action. This time they worked in unison not to disturb their sleeping daughter. Within moments, Tony was sitting with Nichol serenely snuggled into his lap. "She'll be fine," Tony whispered. "Now go—rest."

"I know she will." Stroking Tony's arm, Claire whispered, "There's nowhere that I feel safer than in your arms. She'll know that feeling too. The way she just sighed, I'm pretty sure she already does."

Tony's dark eyes shone, taking in both of his ladies. "I wish we were home in our big bed so I could hold both of you."

"Me too," Claire admitted. "But I'll settle for watching the two of you from over there, until I fall asleep."

Before Claire could walk away, Tony reached for her hand. "Mrs. Rawlings, we can go back to paradise anytime you need that feeling of security. You just say the word, and we'll be in the air."

"Thank you. I may take you up on that. But if I do, it's because I love the island, and I love Madeline and Francis, not because I need to be there to feel that way. Honestly, with you and Nichol, Eric and Phil, I know I'm safe. I know Nichol is safe. Besides," she added with a snicker, "it's difficult to make snowmen in the South Pacific."

Tony grinned. "Hmmm, I think sand angels sound more appealing than snow ones."

She squeezed his hand before making her way back to an empty seat beside John. As she buckled her seatbelt, Claire glanced back to see Tony's eyes close. No longer did she see sadness or even the need to control. She saw peace: a quiet, accepting peace, as his fingers brushed Nichol's fine hair. Contentedly, she followed suit and drifted off to sleep with visions of sand angels dancing through her dreams.

HOURS LATER WITH snow falling and coating the Iowa ground in a blanket of white, the tired friends bid each other goodbye as their luggage was loaded into various cars at the Rawlings Industries private airstrip. While Eric and Phil warmed the car, Claire helped Nichol secure her winter coat, hat, and gloves.

"Momma?" Nichol asked. "Do you like warm or cold better?"

Claire giggled. "Oh, honey, I like warm." Remembering her wish, she added, "But that doesn't mean I don't like cold." She lifted her face to the sky. "Look how beautiful these snowflakes are. See how they shine and glisten?"

"Yes, but I like bathing suits instead of winter coats."

"Look at your pretty pink coat. Don't you like it?"

"I guess." Nichol looked at her mother's coat and her small voice rose. "You need a pink coat too. Then we can be twins."

Just then, Emily came up behind Nichol. "A pink coat is definitely what you need, Claire."

"Only if all three of us can match?"

Looking down at her growing midsection, Emily laughed. "Oh, I'd be a sight in pink."

"Are you feeling all right? The travel wasn't too much for you, was it?"

"I'm fine. I'm just tired," Emily said. "I don't think that it's the pregnancy as much as the time difference. Thank you, sis, for this amazing getaway. We've had a fabulous time. The island was everything you said and more. I can't believe you left that paradise for John and me..." Her voice trailed away until she straightened her shoulders and went on, "I'm sorry. These stupid hormones are making me sentimental."

Reaching for her sister, Claire embraced Emily. Swallowing the growing lump in her throat, she replied, "We're both so happy you could be there with us. The children had so much fun."

Emily nodded. "I know we owe you both—"

"Stop that. We can never repay what you've done for us and for Nichol."

"Well, thanks anyway. The getaway was great, and for such a

long trip, traveling on your plane sure beats the heck out of flying commercially."

"Having everyone together made Nichol's birthday even that much more special."

Emily bent down and hugged her niece. "I love you, sweetheart. Be good for your mommy and daddy."

Nichol grinned. "I'm oways good."

Emily's brow rose as she peered up toward Claire.

"Mostly," Claire corrected.

Nichol blew kisses at Emily. "Bye-bye, Aunt Em. See you later. Momma, I'm cold," Nichol whined as she rushed toward Phil and the warm, waiting car.

"How about you?" Emily asked as the two women approached the cars. "Are you all right, being home? I know you don't like winter much."

Taking in the accumulating snow, Claire watched as white flakes melted upon the heads of Tony, Brent, and John as the three men shook hands and bid each other goodbye. Although the time away had been good for all of them, Claire was ready to be back to her intimate family. Two weeks in the presence of everyone had been a long time. Contemplating her sister's question, Claire replied, "I am. We've enjoyed being with everyone; however, I'm happy to be home with Tony and Nichol."

Emily smiled. "I understand. I'm ready for a little quiet time myself."

Just then, Michael ran toward his mom, sliding his tiny feet upon the snow-covered runway. "Wheeee!" he yelled, as he held on to Emily's leg for dear life.

Laughing, Claire said, "Good luck with that quiet time. You

better enjoy it now. Once my little niece arrives, you'll be pulled in every direction."

"Two children aren't that difficult," Emily replied wistfully, peering toward Nichol. "I miss having two."

The lump in Claire's throat made its presence known once again. Unsure how to respond, Claire was saved by the sound of Phil's voice.

"Claire, the car's ready."

Looking in his direction, she saw Tony sitting in the backseat, already talking on his phone, and Nichol beside him, her little booted feet swinging as she tended to the needs of her new doll. With full concentration she worked to wrap her prized possession in a blanket, protecting it from the frigid temperatures. Earlier, Nichol proclaimed that the doll was her favorite Christmas gift. Obviously she was concerned about its well-being. Claire had ordered the doll specially: the tiny replica looked identical to Nichol.

Turning back toward Emily, Claire gave her sister a parting hug, and, changing the subject, she said, "See, we've barely touched down and Tony's already back to work. I think I'll have plenty of that quiet time."

"I'm sure John's doing the same thing. His phone started vibrating the second he took it out of airplane mode."

"Thank you, Emily. I hope we can do more things together."

Emily nodded. "Me too."

"Mommy, we go home!" Michael proclaimed, as he tugged at Emily's hand. "Bye-bye, Aunt Care."

They said their goodbyes and moments later, Claire settled in the warmth of the waiting car and snuggled close to her daughter. "Are you cold, sweetie? Do you wish you were back on the island?"

Looking up to Tony and back to Claire, Nichol shook her head.

"Uh-uh. The island doesn't have pretty snowflakes, and I wanna be with you and Daddy."

The car eased forward with Eric driving and Phil riding shotgun. Claire glanced toward Tony, expecting to see his concentration on the phone call at hand. Instead, at their daughter's comment, their eyes met and he winked. Smiling, Claire helped Nichol with her doll's blanket and replied, "We like that too, sweetheart."

Chapter 2

Late December 2016

Claire

———◦◆◦———

Nothing can bring a real sense of security
into the home except true love.
—Billy Graham

THOUGH THE HOUSE on the island always seemed large and remote, it was nowhere near as big as their new home on the Rawlings estate. The fact that the island retreat had been occupied by four families with a total of seventeen people for the last two weeks helped to make the estate feel that much more secluded and private. Well, quiet, except for Nichol's happy glees at being reunited with her nanny, Shannon. It wasn't that Shannon hadn't been invited to the island: she had. Nichol's nanny had chosen to spend the Christmas holiday with her family. Claire completely understood; besides, Claire enjoyed spending more one-on-one time with her daughter.

After Shannon had retired to her suite, Nichol had been tucked into bed, and the rest of the staff had left the main house to go to their own apartments, Claire settled into the nice, large bed Tony had mentioned earlier on the plane. As she rested on the soft sheets, every muscle in her body began to unwind and relax. The quiet bliss of their suite filled her with peace while outside a growing blanket of white snow frosted the panes of glass that covered one wall of their bedroom suite.

Even in the nocturnal darkness, the freshly fallen snow reflected the sheen of the moonlight's brilliance, brightening the world beyond their bubble. The bare, leafless trees were a far cry from the palm trees of their paradise; nonetheless, as Claire stared toward the windows, she didn't miss the white sand and multicolored flowers that covered the lanai. No, as she stared outside and saw the flakes that continued to cascade from the sky, Claire relished her home and her family.

The radiating glow from the fireplace added to Claire's delight. Embers and remnants of fire, set earlier by the staff, filled the master bedroom suite with warmth while the sweet aroma of burning timbers permeated her senses. With the cold outside the windows, the roaring fire had been inviting and welcoming upon their arrival. As she relaxed against the soft pillows, Claire marveled at her reality. She was home. Suddenly, a childhood story—a favorite of generations—came to mind while simultaneously an unconscious smile came to her lips. Dorothy had definitely been right: there was no place like home.

Other than a break for dinner with his family, since their homecoming, Tony had been occupied with all things Rawlings Industries. Though the island was no longer hidden from the authorities, Internet service was less than stellar. Even with all of Phil's knowledge and connections—those that only money could buy—attempts at communication, in any manner other than email, were painfully slow. While they were away, Tony had been kept abreast of the happenings at Rawlings, but until this afternoon, his input had been limited. After dinner he was back in his home office.

Their home office was much different than it had been in the old estate. The new one lacked the dark cherry paneling and regal mahogany desk. Instead it was homier and lighter, containing two equally sized desks. Truly it was *their* home office. As lady of the house, Claire had the responsibility of the household staff and the daily operations of the estate. When Tony had the new house built, he could have easily had two offices constructed; however, he purposely chose to share the space that at one time had been declared his and his alone. Though Claire had complete access, on their first day and evening home, she chose not to spend her time catching up on her responsibilities. There would be plenty of time for that. Instead, she worked to help unpack and acclimate Nichol back to Iowa. Now, as she neared sleep, Claire pondered the length of the day. With crossing the international dateline, and in essence, going back in time, the day seemed to have lasted forever.

Though the heat of the flames lulled Claire toward the blissfulness of sleep, her mind spun with countless possibilities for fun, snow-filled activities. She knew that if she were excited about the snow and cold, Nichol would be also. Then, without warning, her consciousness filled not with the aroma of the burning wood, but the unmistakable scent of cologne. Without visual confirmation, every fiber in Claire's body let her know that she was no longer alone. Though she hadn't heard her husband enter their suite, the intensity of her suddenly rapid pulse confirmed that he was there.

Still not opening her eyes, Claire's lips moved to a slight grin as she listened and heard Tony moving quietly around the darkened suite. It wasn't until he settled into the big bed that she scooted closer and molded herself to his side. Immediately, his arm wrapped about her petite frame and his deep voice filled the suite, which moments earlier had contained only the crackling of the simmering fire.

"I thought you were asleep. Aren't you exhausted?"

"I am," she admitted, "but I'm also enjoying the peace and quiet."

"Next time we go to the island, it would be all right with me if we had fewer guests."

Claire nodded against his chest.

"Speaking of guests," Tony continued, "what were you and Emily talking about at the airport?"

She lifted her head. "What were you, John, and Brent talking about?"

"I believe I asked first."

Propping her chin on her fist, Claire replied, "She was thanking me for a wonderful getaway and saying how much they enjoyed it."

"Hmmm. That's pretty much what Brent and John were saying too."

"Tony?"

"What?" he answered, as he pulled her back to his chest.

"Did you hate it? I mean, you didn't seem like you did. Yet I know you didn't used to like to be around so many people."

"I didn't hate it. There were times I wanted to be alone with you and Nichol, but I didn't hate it." He sighed. "We've both been alone, and I know how much you enjoy having other people around. If that's what you want, I want it too."

Claire smiled against his warm skin, enjoying the tickling sensation of his soft chest hair against her cheek. "I do. I'm happy to be with people and with friends. I know the Meredith thing was strange at first, but no one knows how much she helped me. I love seeing her with Jerry and the kids. The risks she took for me... well, I can never thank her enough."

"I think you have. Just like you enjoy seeing her happy with her family, I think she feels the same way. Once in a while, I'd notice her watching you with a hopeful smile. I may have been skeptical when I first heard about her connection, but not anymore. I'm glad she and Jerry took us up on our offer and came with us."

"I also love this," Claire added.

"This?"

"Being alone, just the two of us, or three of us."

"Or six, if you include Eric, Phil, and Shannon," Tony corrected.

Claire sat up quickly, pulling the blanket dramatically around her nightgown-clad body, and mocked, "What? Eric, Phil, and Shannon are in *here*?"

With only the embers of the dying fire illuminating his devilish grin, Tony reached for his wife and pulled her close. Laughingly, he said, "Mrs. Rawlings, what have I said about that smart mouth of yours?"

Raining a trail of kisses from his chest toward his lips, Claire replied, "As I recall, you said you like it."

Suddenly, her world was reversed. No longer was she above him: now, with her head on her pillow, Tony hovered mere inches above her face. The weight of his chest pressed against her suddenly sensitive breasts.

Claire's insides tightened as she watched in amazement and wonder at the emotions swirling through her husband's chocolate-colored eyes. The suede of exhaustion mixed with the shimmer of amusement both faded into the darkened abyss of desire. How had there ever been a time when she couldn't read his every thought? His current thought—his current intention—was not only visible, but becoming more prominent by the moment. "Versatility?" she baited.

"Hmm, yes," Tony cooed, as he teased the slender strap of her nightgown. "Those amazing lips can not only spew smart comments and retorts, but I believe they're also capable of untold marvels." Kisses to her exposed shoulder interrupted his words. "I don't *believe*. I know."

With his continued encouragement, Claire's previous thoughts of sleep quickly morphed into a smoldering heat: one that possibly exceeded that of the one burning in the grate. As the tension within her continued to build, the seclusion of their private suite lifted any inhibitions they may have maintained during their crowded retreat. "You seem quite confident, Mr. Rawlings."

Easing her nightgown over Claire's head, Tony tossed it to the floor, creating a puddle of silk near their bed while his lips moved from her collarbone to her breasts. With deliberate precision and painstaking leisureliness, he moistened each nipple causing them to harden as his abrasive cheeks brushed the sensitive skin. Arching her back toward him, Claire's playfulness turned sultry. No longer did she want to offer bold retorts. The only thing on her mind was the man skillfully teasing and caressing her exposed body. Despite the warmth of the crackling fire, goose bumps formed on her arms and legs. Each move of his mouth, inch by inch downward, over her stomach, nearing the place she needed him most, helped to build the frenzy within her.

When his advances met the only remaining obstacle, Claire lifted her hips to help him remove her panties. Tony's deep voice pulled her from her endorphin-induced trance. "There were definite advantages to my previous rules."

At that moment, she couldn't have agreed more. Grinning,

Claire began to ease the lace panties from her hips.

"Wait," Tony commanded. Sitting upward on their large bed, Tony reached for Claire's hand. "You're so damn beautiful. I want to watch you take those off. I want to see you... all of you... as you give yourself to me."

Blood rushed to her cheeks as she tried to hide her gaze. Tony cupped her chin and pulled her green eyes towards him. "Don't look away. I love you. We're finally alone. I want to see all of you, including your beautiful eyes."

Watching the man before her, Claire smiled, accepted his hand, and stood. With the soles of her feet upon the soft satin puddle, Claire waited. It wasn't the warmth of the fire that filled her with the confidence to do as he'd asked. No, it was the sultry heat she witnessed in his dark eyes. The fire within him wasn't a reflection of the one burning across the room. It was the culmination of weeks surrounded by too many people, the need to connect to one another, and the desire that stems from a connection that surpasses all boundaries.

With the glowing embers inside and the reflection of snow outside illuminating their world, Tony led his wife to the rug in front of the giant fireplace, moved to the sofa, and sat before her. "Now, Mrs. Rawlings, let me see. Show me what's mine and mine alone."

Latching her thumbs beneath the lace, Claire slowly pulled her panties down her thighs. Letting go of the material, she allowed them to fall to the floor and stepped out of them. Resuming her stance, she again waited for her husband as invisible bonds from his gaze held her in place. Rising from the sofa, Tony moved gracefully toward her, each step predatory as he circled her form, his eyes glued on only her. From her round, soft globes and hard, taut nipples to her neatly trimmed sex, his eyes devoured as his erection tented the gym shorts he'd worn to bed.

"You are so damn beautiful," Tony growled as he stopped behind her. "I want you so much." Purposely keeping his erection away, he leaned near her neck and breathily asked, "Do you have any idea how fuck'n sexy you are right now?"

Tipping her head to the side and closing her eyes, Claire gave him full access. Inhaling his intoxicating scent of cologne and musk of desire, she replied, "I know how sexy you make me feel."

With his lips upon her skin, he continued to tease. "These last two weeks, I wanted to see you like this, so badly. I wanted you totally naked... in the pool, on the beach, in our suite with the doors open to the damn world, just like we used to do." He nipped her skin playfully, causing a gasp to resonate from her throat. "I wanted my wife to be available to just me, but..." He twisted a nipple then tenderly caressed it, creating the perfect combination of pain and pleasure. "...I couldn't have what I wanted. No, I had to share. I had—"

"You just said you didn't—" Claire began.

"Shhh," he whispered, putting his finger to her lips. "I'm not done."

With each word, each breath, her tension grew. Claire didn't want him to continue taunting; she wanted him. His demanding tone and suddenly possessive demeanor had her ready and on the verge of explosion. With nothing but words, he could twist her to the brink. This was the man who'd taken not only her body, but also her heart and fulfilled her every desire. "Tony, please," she begged.

Wrapping her in his arms, he pulled her back tightly against his chest. Claire wasn't sure when he'd taken off his gym shorts, but by the sensation of his hardness against her lower back, they were definitely gone. "Ohhh…" she mewed.

"What, Claire? Please, *what*? What do you want so badly you'll ask for it even after I tell you to shush?"

Melting against his chest, Claire replied, "You. I want you. I've wanted more of you than I've gotten in the last two weeks. We're home. I want to see you too."

"My dear, I'm right here." His hips moved slightly against her as his embrace pulled her closer. Resuming his CEO tone, Tony continued, "And I promise, you're going to see me; however, as I recall, I asked you to let me finish. Didn't I?"

Unsure if he wanted a verbal response, Claire nodded.

"That's a good girl," he replied, as he loosened his embrace and brushed the sides of her arms with the tips of his fingers.

Her lips parted, allowing the slightest sound to escape. Claire couldn't have stopped the whimper if she tried. Tony's gentle touch was almost painful. Claire wanted his arms around her, strong and sturdy. She needed to know he was there. The lightness of his touch had her body begging for more. She was ready to begin verbally pleading when Tony reached for her fingertips and led her to the sofa. Kneeling before her, gently spreading her legs, his darkened gaze continued to devour, as his lips moved up each thigh in preparation to do the same. Between taunting kisses, he said, "As I was saying, I had to share." With a devilish grin, he peered up her body until their eyes met. "I don't know if you've ever realized, but I'm not good at sharing."

With a gleam in her green ones, Claire nodded, still unsure if she should speak.

"Now, that doesn't mean I can't do it. For you, my dear, I'll do anything. However now… now that I have you all to myself, I plan on taking full advantage of you." He leaned back, taking in every exposed inch of his wife. "Full advantage. I don't only want to see you. I want to feel you, hear you, and taste you." Just before he reached his destination, his warm breath teased her sensitive skin as he said, "Now I'm done talking. I think this conversation has gone on long enough. There are much better things for both of our mouths to do. Do you agree, Mrs. Rawlings?"

Leaning back against the soft leather, Claire breathily replied, "Oh, God, yes, I agree."

Though more words did come forth, moans and sounds dominated their suite as they reconnected. No longer did the length of their day or the concerns of others fill their thoughts. Only the desires of pleasing and being pleased, filling and being filled, loving and being loved permeated their consciousness. It wasn't until later, after untold heights, that they made it back to the soft sheets and king-sized bed. Even then, sleep had to wait.

Finally, after they both were satiated, Claire nestled against her husband's chest, inhaled his intoxicating scent and drifted off to sleep.

There was no place like home.

Chapter 3

Late December 2016

Claire

———◆———

Surround yourself with good people:
people who are going to be honest with
you and look out for your best interests.
—Derek Jeter

THE STACK OF mail on Claire's desk looked daunting; nevertheless, she dove into it with renewed vigor. In all the previous years of their marriage and before, she hadn't been involved in the day-to-day operations of the estate. Now that it was hers, she wanted to do all she could and truly be hands on. In all honesty, she enjoyed the quiet time spent in their home office doing something productive. Although she was no longer forecasting life-threatening hurricanes—meteorology was more than likely gone from her future—Claire was doing more than she'd ever done before. Her work kept the estate running, which was a far cry from the idle hours she'd spent in the past. Besides, the name on the deed to the estate was hers: Claire Nichols Rawlings. She had every right to make the decisions, and it was one less thing for Tony to worry about.

Since last fall, her husband had been busy becoming re-acclimated to Rawlings Industries. His two-year absence from the daily operations of his multiple corporations and financial endeavors required quite a bit of catching up. Even so, whenever possible, Tony chose to work from home. His devotion and commitment to plunge back into his life was not limited to Rawlings Industries. Tony wanted to spend as much time as possible at home with his wife and daughter. That was why, when faced with a full return to Rawlings Industries, he decided to share the CEO position with Tim Bronson. Tim had handled things exceptionally well in Tony's absence; it only seemed right to keep him involved.

With Nichol and Shannon playing upstairs, Claire settled into her plush desk chair and took on the two weeks' accumulation of mail. Before she could make a dent, there was a knock on the door. Giggling to herself, Claire thought, it wasn't Nichol: she didn't knock. It was just another of her many father-like traits. "Come in," she called, expecting Shannon.

"Claire..." Phil's voice caused Claire to look up. "...I wanted to catch you before you went through the mail. I was just told that today's delivery was brought in here before I could go through it."

Phil wasn't only Claire's bodyguard and head of the estate's security: he was also her friend. With their long history, Claire recognized something in his tone that filled her with a sense of foreboding.

"Why?" she asked. "We haven't received any more threatening letters or packages since before the trip. Have we?"

Phil pressed his lips together. Golden flecks glistened in the hazel eyes that peered knowingly at her through squinted lids. With a furrowed brow, he replied, "I would've thought you knew. Haven't

23

you spoken to Rawlings? He said he was going to tell you."

Claire thought back to their time alone since coming home. It had only been one day, and honestly, last night there was very little talking. She worked to keep the blush from her cheeks as she remembered just how little talking they'd done the night before. Prior to that, they'd both been too busy doing other things or with Nichol. Discussions about the threatening mailings they'd received didn't exactly seem like good family-dinner conversation. "I've spoken with him, but I guess we didn't get a chance to talk about it, and he was gone this morning before I woke."

Phil took a deep breath and motioned toward one of the chairs opposite Claire's desk. "Do you mind?"

Straightening her shoulders, Claire shook her head. "I don't mind your taking a seat. I'm a little nervous that you think this conversation requires that." She feigned a smile. "Or maybe you just want to catch up? Tell me that's all it is. I'll have some coffee brought in and we can chat."

Phil shook his head. "Catching up sounds nice, but I have a lot to do right now. First thing after our *chat*, I need to go through that stack of mail—"

Claire leaned forward on her desk, and interrupted, "Fine, tell me. Tell me why you are concerned, and don't tell me you aren't. I hear it in your voice."

"Claire, I'm sure Rawlings wanted to be the one to tell you. I'll just take a quick look at that stack and leave you alone."

Claire eyed the large pile of letters. Most were regular sized; a few were larger. There were a couple of thicker envelopes. Squaring her shoulders she turned back. "Phil, the packages that we've received in the past have been addressed to me, or to *Claire Nichols-Rawls,* so I deserve to know what else has been delivered. I deserve to know what progress has been made. Just because Tony hasn't mentioned it—yet—doesn't negate my right to know. Besides," she added with a grin, "I thought you worked for me."

His shoulders relaxed as he exhaled. "You know I do."

Her emerald eyes sparkled, knowing she'd won. "Then tell me."

Claire watched the deliberation he wasn't voicing as Phil shifted slightly in his seat. Each second of silence added to her concern. Finally, he spoke. "You see, we've talked about it. I just don't want to upset you, not after everything you've been—"

"Stop," she said softly. "I'm not going to break. I'll admit, I came close, but it won't happen. Truly, Phil, I'm good. Not knowing scares me more than knowing. I honestly don't think that Tony intended to keep whatever this was from me. By the time we had a chance for some privacy last night, well, we were both exhausted. I mean, we all were and still are. We've only been home a little over twenty-four hours."

She pushed her chair back and stood, motioning toward the mail. "I'll make you a deal. I'll go get some coffee. You knock yourself out with the mail, but first, tell me about the last threatening mailing we received and what you know."

Phil nodded. "It came here, to the estate, while we were all in the South Pacific. Eric and I knew about it right away. We didn't say anything until after the FBI finished their tests. It was clean: no explosives, no chemicals."

Claire pondered. "While we were gone? When did you tell Tony?"

"After we had the results."

"Phil, *when* did you tell Tony?" She emphasized the word.

It was one thing for Tony not to mention it if he'd only learned about it yesterday. It was quite another thing if he'd known about it longer—a lot longer.

"It was right before Christmas." He hastened to add, "Everything was fine. There was no threat and no reason to worry you when you had so much going on. God, Claire, it was Christmas. Not exactly the time you want to hear about any of this."

"I don't care if it's my birthday—I deserve to know."

She walked to the front of the desk, stood before Phil and took a deep breath. This was definitely a matter she and Tony would be discussing. Softening her tone, she continued. "We—you and I— have been through a lot. I can't thank you enough for your devotion to me, Tony, and Nichol."

At the mention of her daughter's name, she saw Phil's expression momentarily change. It was almost too fast to discern. A second later it was gone. Claire's stomach turned. "Wait. Something was different about the last mailing, wasn't it? Oh, my God."

The temperature of the room fell; the hairs on the back of her neck stood to attention. "Tell me it wasn't addressed to Nichol."

Phil shook his head. "I can't."

The trembling came from nowhere. Suddenly, the cozy home office was a bleak frozen tundra.

His tone was more her friend than security. "This is why Rawlings wanted to be the one to tell you."

Claire nodded and sunk into the chair beside Phil. She had gotten used to being targeted by some psycho. She'd been to hell and back more than once. She could take it, but this was different. This was Nichol. As fast as the trembling came, it subsided, and Claire's protectiveness surged forward. In a voice stronger than she truly felt, Claire said, "Find this person. You said the DNA points to a woman, right?"

"Yes."

"She's not in the database of known offenders?"

"Correct."

Leaning forward, Claire reiterated, "If some bitch wants to come after me, fine. I'll take her on. But threaten my daughter, in any way? Hell no! I want her gone." Her eyes narrowed. "I don't care what you have to do. You have my total support. Whatever resources you need, no holds barred." Claire reached for Phil's arm. "Please, assure that she's no longer a threat to Nichol."

Phil's back straightened. "You don't need to ask. I'd rather you didn't. The less you know, the better."

Claire nodded and stood again. "I'm going to get some coffee. Help yourself to the mail, but if you find something, tell me."

Phil grinned.

"What?" she asked suspiciously.

"Well, Mrs. Alexander..."

Claire smiled at the reference from their past.

Phil continued, "...I believe that once again I've seriously underestimated you. Maybe someday I'll learn that you're tougher than I think."

"One more thing, Phil, what was in the mailing to Nichol?"

"There were two. The first was a card addressed to *Nichol Rawls*. The second was a gift, a birthday gift addressed to *Nichol Rawlings*."

Her brow wrinkled. "Why were they different and what kind of birthday gift?"

"We don't know. The gift was a doll. I didn't think much of it until I saw the one you gave her for Christmas. It looked very similar, very much like Nichol herself."

"I had that one made by a private company."

Phil nodded. "We've traced this one. It's a cheaper version, made by a company that takes online and mail orders. They advertise in magazines all over the world. The person who placed the order used your name and address. The credit card was a refillable card purchased in New York with cash."

Claire had researched some of the less expensive doll-makers. Even they required a picture. Through the years, Emily and John, and more recently, Tony and Claire, had done their best to keep Nichol's picture out of the public eye. "That still means they know what Nichol looks like, that they have her picture." Phil's words continued to process in her mind. "New York?" Claire asked. "Where in New York?"

"New York City."

"We're planning on taking Nichol there next month. We have tickets to see *The Lion King*."

"New York City is huge and filled with millions of people. Between Eric, me, and the rest of the security detail, no one will come near you or Nichol. Don't even concern yourself."

Standing taller, Claire assessed the situation. "Thank you."

"I haven't done anything."

Her green eyes shimmered. "You know that isn't true. You've done a lot, and I believe you're not done. I told Tony that I loved the feeling of security on the island. That's true. But in reality, it isn't just the island. It's him, it's you, it's Eric, and it's everyone. We're truly blessed to have so many people who sincerely care about our well-being. Whatever you need, ever, it's yours."

Phil nodded. "I need to look at your mail."

As Claire was about to leave the office, she asked, "Would you like some coffee? I was sincere when I said that we need to catch up. Things have been wild with the trip to the island."

"Maybe another time," Phil said. "I want to go through the mail, get out of your way, and go have a few words with the person who delivered today's mail to you before letting me see it. I think it would be better if I get to him before Rawlings."

Her smile broadened. "See, that's another reason why I trust you. You're always a step ahead."

———————◆◆———————

LATER THAT NIGHT, Claire glared at her husband as they made their way into their private suite.

"You know, you're not nearly as good at hiding your anger as you used to be," Tony said with a devilish grin.

"Well, maybe it's because I'm not trying to hide it."

"I've been home for hours. We've had dinner with Nichol and had a snowball fight in the backyard. I have no idea what you're upset about." He cocked his head to the side. "It's that you lost the snowball fight, isn't it?"

Claire put her hands on her hips. "No. It isn't about the snowball fight. Besides, I didn't lose. It isn't even what you've done. It's what you didn't do." She stood taller. "We promised to be honest. You haven't been honest."

Tony's brows knit together. "I believe I'm at a disadvantage in this conversation. I have no idea what you're talking about."

"Think, Tony. Did something happen while we were in paradise that you forgot to mention?"

It didn't take Tony long until he muttered under his breath, "Damn Roach."

"No, don't blame him. It's you who dropped the ball. Phil thought I already knew. He said that you said you'd tell me." Her volume rose. "Nichol is my daughter too. Tell me, Tony. Tell me why I didn't know about her birthday card and gift from the psycho person?"

He collapsed onto the soft leather sofa in front of the fireplace. The newfound tension in their suite was a completely different atmosphere than the one only the night before. "I was going to tell you, but the time was never right."

She paced the open space. "I agree. There's never a good time to say, 'Oh, by the way, the psycho lunatic who's sending you cards and packages is now addressing them to our daughter.' Nevertheless, just say it."

Tony reached for Claire's hand and tugged her toward him. "It was her birthday, Christmas, and as you may recall, we were almost constantly surrounded by people—lots of people." He pulled his wife down onto his lap.

"No, Tony." She stiffened as he held her near. "I'm mad at you. I don't want you to change the subject. I want you to be totally open with me. If you're not... Well, I don't know."

His arms wrapped around her as she yielded her position and settled against his chest. The rhythmic breathing and steady heartbeat against her back served as a constant drumming that relaxed her nerves and calmed her anxiety. His lips brushed her neck. "I'm being honest. I was going to say something. The time just wasn't right. We need more time like this, more time alone."

Claire turned in his embrace. She wanted to see his emotions: she needed to know he took this as seriously as she. "The doll, it was one of those twin ones. Tony, before I ordered Nichol's, I looked at all the different companies. They all require pictures. This person had a picture of Nichol. If she didn't, she couldn't have had the doll made."

With each word his eyes darkened.

Claire continued, "I know it can't be proven as a threat, but I think it was meant that way. This woman is telling us that she knows what Nichol looks like. She knows her birthday."

"I know all of that. Roach, Eric, and I've talked about it. Roach has been in contact with the FBI. They know all of this. We're doing all we can do. You aren't going anywhere without me or Roach; neither is Nichol."

"What about New York?" Claire asked.

"Roach told me that the credit card was purchased there," Tony replied as he looked deeply into her eyes. "If you don't want to go next month, we won't."

"We already have tickets—"

"I don't give a damn about a few tickets. Hell, we'll go back to paradise if that's what you want."

Exhaling, Claire lost her battle, allowing her anger to fade away and melting into her husband's embrace. Sighing, she said, "No. If we do that, this woman wins. That's not happening."

"I've been thinking about something, ever since that gift. I've talked a little to Roach about it, but I wanted to talk to you."

Claire turned back around to face her husband. She tried to read his expression and saw apprehension. "What?" she asked.

"I'm thinking about adding another member to our intimate security."

She shook her head. "No."

"You haven't even heard my idea."

"Tony, I want family time. I want it to be just us. I'm comfortable with Phil and Eric. We also have Shannon. I don't want anyone else."

"I was thinking about a woman. Roach has identified some

incredibly qualified female ex-military and ex-field agents who could be with you when he can't."

Claire shrugged. "When Phil can't, you can. I don't know if you remember, but I spent over a month alone with Phil. There aren't a lot of secrets."

Tony bristled. "I'm aware, and I'll be forever grateful that he kept you safe during that time. My thoughts were that this woman wouldn't replace him: she'd assist him."

"You've already made up your mind, haven't you?" Claire fell back onto her husband's chest in defeat. This openness was all for show. Anthony Rawlings was the same man he'd always been. His decision was the only one that mattered.

"No," Tony whispered. "I haven't. I've only discussed it with Roach. If you don't want this, we won't do it. I just thought there might be times when you and I and Nichol may all need to go in different directions. This woman could help with that too." His lips brushed her hair as the scent of his cologne wafted through the air. "I love you. I love Nichol. I worry about both of you. Your safety and security are my primary concerns."

The tension eased from her muscles as her body liquefied against him. "Really? You haven't already started hiring someone. You truly want my input?"

"Really," he whispered, as he nuzzled her collarbone. "I mentioned it to Roach. He's found a few viable candidates. No one has been contacted. I wanted your input first."

Allowing her husband more access, Claire tilted her head and closed her eyes. His prickly cheeks abraded her soft skin. The sensation was like a spark to dry kindling, warming her and infusing her with the fire of desire she'd purposely tried to subdue. "Can I think about it?" she asked.

He nodded, striking the match with each movement of his head. His intention grew as her internal flames intensified. "If that's what you want to do..." His words came breathily against her exposed skin. "...then by all means, my dear, think."

Thinking, however was not what she wanted to do at the moment.

Chapter 4

January 2017

Claire

Memories are the key not to the past, but to the future.
—Corrie Ten Boom

"SO WHAT DO you think of her?" Emily whispered as she and Claire stood on the shore of the frozen lake watching the mayhem of activity.

"I think she seems nice," Claire replied, glancing at Taylor, the new addition to their security detail.

Emily shrugged. "*Nice* doesn't seem like the best description of a bodyguard. That is her job description, isn't it? I mean, she looks awfully petite for a badass. Shouldn't she be like that knight lady on that TV show? You know the one who's about seven feet tall."

Claire laughed and shook her head. Taylor definitely wasn't seven feet tall. She was probably only a little taller than Claire, about five-foot-five or –six and physically fit. Her long, dark hair was usually wrapped in a low bun, and her clothes were professional. She'd only been working with the Rawlings family for a week, but she seemed to fit in well. The most important thing to

Claire was that she got along well with Nichol. "I don't know what she *should* be. She had the best references. Tony and I like her, and Phil was impressed with her resume. I guess that makes her worth a try."

"Well, I don't know how you deal with having all these other people around all the time."

It was Claire's turn to shrug. "They aren't *always* around and sometimes when they are, you don't even realize it. That's their job." She thought about how Phil had been watching and protecting Nichol without Emily or John's knowledge for years. That little secret brought a smile to Claire's face.

"I guess if you're all right with it." Emily leaned closer. "Did you even have a choice? Did you get any input in the matter? Or was it all decided for you?"

Claire turned indignantly. "Yes, Em, I had input. It was Tony's idea, and at first, I wasn't on board. But then I kept thinking about Nichol. I'll take a little less privacy to assure her safety any day of the week."

"But... like now... why are they here? We're on your property..." Emily looked around at the frozen lake, snow-covered ground, and bare trees. "...in the middle of nowhere."

Claire and Tony had agreed with law enforcement to keep all the information about the threatening mailings private. No one outside of their security and staff knew anything about them. The FBI explained that the fewer people in the know, the better chance they had of finding the culprit or culprits. Though they hadn't received any *Rawls-Nichols* mailings since Nichol's birthday, there had been some letters addressed to *Claire Rawlings*. After analysis, these new mailings were found to have male DNA. The writing was inconsistent, but the message was the same on each of these mailings: '*I will save you.*' Neither Claire nor Tony knew what that meant.

"Part of it is for Nichol," Claire explained. "The more she's used to them being around, the more comfortable she'll be if she ever needs their help or protection."

Emily shuffled her boot-clad feet. "Claire, I didn't know that she needed that kind of protection." Her voice softened. "I'm sorry. We did our best to keep her safe."

Claire reached for her sister's arm. "Stop that! You did great. You kept her out of the public eye. Look at her. She's perfect and she *is* safe. Things are just different now that Tony and I are with her. Tony's businesses and position puts him more into the limelight. You know we don't like that. We never have. And, well, with Meredith's book, there are still people who think they know us. Eric, Phil, and Taylor are our first line of defense. The more we include them in our activities, the more natural it is for Nichol."

"I get it," Emily admitted as the shrill expressions of glee came from the ice.

"Look, Momma!" Nichol yelled, as she and Michael performed their ice-skating wonders accompanied by their nannies and their fathers.

"I see, sweetie. You're doing great!" Claire replied.

"Claire, you should go back out there with them. I don't mind. I just don't think in my condition I should be on thin blades of metal."

"Of course you shouldn't." Claire looked down at her own skate-encased feet. "Can I tell you a secret?"

Emily leaned closer. "Sure. What?"

"I was so excited about this, about skating, but now that we've done it a few times, I'm totally over it. I want to spend my time here swimming, not skating."

Emily snickered. "Well, I think it's too late. I mean, look at our husbands! I can't believe you got them both out there on skates."

"I can't take all the credit. Nichol and Michael were pretty persuasive. The thing is... Tony's doing better at this than I am. I mean, seriously, I don't think there's anything he can't do. It makes me sick."

"That's because you're sitting here with me. Go on out there. Show them how it's really done."

When Claire looked back to the ice, she saw Tony's eyes looking directly at her. Turning back to Emily, she said, "If you're sure you're all right?"

Giving her sister a playful push, Emily replied, "I'm fine. Go!"

With each clumsy step on the snow with ice skates, Claire lost any pretense at grace. Honestly, walking in five-inch Jimmy Choo heels was easier than skates. However, once she reached the cleared ice, Claire easily glided toward her family.

"There's my beautiful wife," Tony declared as he reached for her hand. "I thought perhaps this was some grand scheme: get me out here on skates and then slip away."

"I wouldn't do that," Claire quipped. "I feel bad for Emily, not being able to participate."

"Don't," John said. "She's enjoying watching Michael—and seeing me make a fool out of myself."

Claire nodded.

"Aunt Care, wook at us," Michael shouted as he and Nichol held hands and tried to skate in a circle. Within seconds they were a giggling pile of snowsuit-covered arms and legs.

"I think we need to work on that," Shannon said as she helped the two children stand.

"The winter Olympics is probably not in their future," Tony whispered with a grin.

By the time they all made it back to the house, it was almost dark. After only a short distance, both children convinced their fathers they couldn't walk another step and needed to be carried. Claire was pretty sure that Nichol had even napped a little during the hike.

"Would you like to come in for something to eat?" Claire asked John and Emily.

"No, thanks. We need to get this little guy home," John replied. Then glancing toward his wife, he added, "I think we should've made Michael walk. He'll have more energy than either one of us."

After they'd all laughed and said their goodbyes, the Rawlingses made their way into the house. Shannon took Nichol to a warm bath as Taylor and Phil disappeared. In mere seconds, Tony and Claire were standing in the middle of the foyer all alone.

"Hmm, I like this," Tony cooed, as he kissed Claire's lips.

"This?"

"This... quiet."

Claire nodded. "Yes, me too. Emily was asking me how I liked having so many people around all the time."

Tony's back straightened. "It's really none of her business."

Claire feigned a grin. She knew that for her sake and the sake of their families, her husband and sister were trying to get along. Most of the time, they succeeded; however, once in a while...

Tony's tone hardened. "We're not getting rid—"

"No, we're not," Claire interrupted. "I told her that often we don't even realize they're there. I mean, like now. It isn't like they hover." She touched his arm. "I'm truly all right with it. Eric and Phil are part of our family. I'm sure that one day Taylor will be like that, too." She smiled reassuringly. "I'm fine."

"Are you still comfortable with going to New York?" Tony asked.

Nodding, Claire answered, "I am. This will be Nichol's first time in the city. I think that while you're working, we'll go to the museums. She'll like the Museum of Natural History, and she's already excited about the play."

"As long as you have Phil and Taylor with you, go wherever you want."

"Right now I want to go take a warm bath." With a sly grin, Claire asked, "Should I ask Phil or Taylor to join me?"

Tony's finger touched her lips. "Oh, Mrs. Rawlings, it's been what, two or three hours since I've heard that beautiful smart mouth of yours?"

"Well, you're the one who keeps emphasizing their presence. I just thought—"

His lips silenced hers as the temperature of the entry hall rose exponentially, and he swallowed her in his embrace. After a lingering kiss, Tony whispered, "Perhaps we could take this discussion upstairs? You, my dear, are excessively overdressed for a bath."

"You are so right. Let me go get Phil—"

Taking her hand, Tony led her to the stairs. "We don't need him." He leaned down to kiss her cheek. "I think I've got this."

"If you're up for the job, I guess you'll do," Claire said jokingly.

With a devilish grin, he replied, "Not yet, but I'm sure that can be arranged."

LATER THAT NIGHT, while in their suite, Claire settled into bed and reached for her Kindle. Not finding it, she realized she'd left her reader in their home office. Donning a robe, she slipped down the dimmed, quiet hallway. Unable to pass their daughter's door, Claire reached for the door handle.

With the opening of the door, the light from the hall spilled onto the carpet of Nichol's lavender room. The golden rays illuminated allowing Claire to peer beyond the light and see her daughter sleeping soundly on the large canopy bed with her doll on the pillow beside her. Tiptoeing to her daughter's side, Claire's smile grew, just being near her filled Claire's world with peace. It was obvious the ice skating had worn their daughter out. With her lips parted and eyes shut, she was lost in a dream world and oblivious to her mother's presence. Since they were leaving early in the morning for New York, Claire was glad that Nichol was already asleep. After a gentle kiss to Nichol's head, Claire made her way back toward the hallway, quietly closed Nichol's door, and eased down the back staircase toward their office. As she neared, she heard Tony's booming voice.

"...I don't care where they go, one of you needs to be with them at all times."

"Yes, Mr. Rawlings. They won't be alone."

Though she couldn't see, Claire recognized Taylor's voice as the person who'd responded.

"The last two mailings have had a connection to New York. If Claire weren't so damned determined not to allow this person to interrupt our lives, I'd insist that they stay home," Tony continued.

"With two of us," Phil began, "we'll keep them safe. One of us will be right with them and the other will stay back, watching the crowds. I'll keep Eric constantly updated. You'll know where they are at all times."

Claire stepped into the office, clad in her nightgown and bathrobe. "Don't mind me," she interrupted. "I feel like the president, overhearing his Secret Service agents. I wish you wouldn't all make such a big fuss out of this." She looked at Tony. "And you. I'll be honest. Your tone..." She pursed her lips. "...is a little intimidating. Give poor Taylor a break. You know they'll do their best."

Claire smiled in Taylor and Phil's direction.

Tony's eyes darkened. "Claire, my assistant bought the tickets for the play over a month ago. I didn't think about it at the time, but that's a red flag. We might as well have taken out a sign on Times Square and announced our arrival."

Finding her Kindle, Claire picked it up and walked toward Tony. Trying to lighten the conversation, she replied, "Wouldn't Nichol think that was special? Her name in lights on Times Square!"

"Claire," Phil warned, his gaze mimicking Tony's. "This is serious. Think about Patrick Chester—"

"I don't want to think about him," she snapped. "I don't want to think about the possibility that someone could be targeting Nichol or me. However, I will *not* let that someone hold my daughter captive inside of her own house. It's not happening." Her eyes met Tony's. Though she saw the darkness in his, Claire felt the fire in her own. Lifting her brow, she added, "She will *never* feel trapped in her own home. It's not debatable."

Her husband's lips formed a tight line as he forcibly retained his response.

"Mrs. Rawlings?" Taylor asked, breaking the couple's unspoken standoff.

They both turned toward Taylor's voice. "Yes?" Claire replied.

"May I suggest changing your tickets?"

Claire shook her head. "No. Absolutely not. Nichol's too excited about *The Lion King*."

"Not changing the show," Taylor continued, "just changing the performance. Your plans include being in the city for three nights. Could you go one of the other nights?"

Claire looked at her husband and tilted her head in question. "Can you change the tickets at this late of a date?"

His cheeks rose. "Hell yes. That's a great idea. Taylor, thank you."

"We'll get it all arranged and have the tickets put in another name," Phil interjected.

"There," Claire said. "It's settled. Now let's all get some sleep. Someone I know likes to wake up way too early for these business trips."

As Claire followed Phil and Taylor toward the door, Tony's voice rang through the office. "No, Mrs. Rawlings, I don't believe this conversation is finished."

Turning back, she took in Tony's demeanor. His tone and the piercing darkness of his gaze used to signal internal alarms. Not tonight. Tonight what caught her attention was the devilish grin he tried unsuccessfully to conceal.

When she turned back, Phil's questioning eyes asked what his lips couldn't. With a smile and a nod, Claire let Phil know that she was and would be fine. His shoulders relaxed as she said good night and closed the door. Looking again toward the dark eyes that filled her dreams, Claire walked back toward her husband.

"What do you possibly want to discuss that can't be discussed upstairs?"

Tony reached for the tie of her soft robe and tugged it open, exposing her satin nightgown. "Do you really think that this is appropriate staff-interaction clothing?" His hands caressed her hips, taking in the slippery material.

"I wasn't planning on seeing anyone but you," she replied. "I just came down for my Kindle." As she spoke, he stood. With each passing second, Tony's proximity gravitated closer until he hovered above her, and Claire's back arched over the desk. With a smirk to her voice, Claire continued, "You're the one having a big powwow in here. At this late hour, I thought you'd be alone."

"Now I'm alone." His tone morphed from business to sultry as the darkness too changed: his earlier visible concern swirled with desire. "What did you plan to do with me... alone?"

Warm bourbon-scented breath bathed her cheeks and mixed with the aroma of cologne as heat radiated from his chest. Parts of her body—ones which moments ago had been ready to sleep—were now suddenly awake and begging for attention.

With a giggle, she replied, "Nothing. I just wanted my Kindle."

Lifting her to his desk, Tony eased himself forward, spreading her legs and pulling her waist toward him. "Nothing?" he asked, as he eased her robe from her shoulder.

"Tony, we have a nice bed upstairs."

"You know," he spoke in bursts, kissing her neck as his fingers traced her collarbone. "I hate it when you make references... references to the past... I hope you know... how sorry I am... that you have those memories."

"It happened. I won't deny it."

"Hell no..." His volume increased and he stood straighter. Claire wondered how much bourbon he'd drunk. Tony continued his tone deeper. "It wouldn't do any good to deny it now. The whole damn world knows it."

While the world's knowledge was her fault, Claire refused to apologize. *My Life as It Didn't Appear* was a bestseller. Though she'd tried to stop its publication, she failed. Therefore, it just was. While Claire contemplated her response, Tony's fingers entwined with her loose hair. Tugging, he tipped her lips upward. With his mouth a mere whisper from hers, he said, "I hate it, but at the same time, your reference brought back memories." His head cocked to the side, and his brown eyes opened wide. "Those memories aren't all bad... for me at least."

Claire smiled. "No, Tony, they aren't all bad for me, either. If they were, we wouldn't be here right now."

"So..." Sultriness filled his tone as he continued to caress. "...it's been a while since we've had *that* kind of fun in the office." Peaking a brow, he added, "I seem to remember a few things."

Unable to shake her head, with his grip on her hair, Claire pursed her lips. "You, Mr. Rawlings, are incorrigible. Didn't you just help me with that bath before dinner?"

Again, his lips found her neck, sending goose bumps up and down her arms and legs. "That was me. However, as I recall, I wasn't your first choice."

When his grip upon her hair loosened she reached for his, running her fingers through his salt and pepper mane. "You, sir, are always my first choice." Kissing his neck and hearing the familiar growl, Claire knew her plans to read would never transpire. Within seconds, her husband seized her lips, swallowing the moans she didn't realize she was producing as their tongues intertwined. Finally, pulling back, she said, "But... I didn't lock that door."

Easing her legs farther apart, Tony lifted Claire's nightgown and pulled her hips toward his. "My dear, everyone else has gone to bed."

Claire couldn't think of any other arguments. She wasn't trying.

Honestly, she couldn't think of anything besides her husband and what he was doing, how he was twisting her body and mind merely with his words and tone. Though this hadn't been her plan, she consented. It had been a long time since they'd allowed themselves to do anything outside of the security of their bedroom. Being home did have its advantages. As Tony's large fingers roamed, Claire cared less and less about anyone else in the house. "Tony?" she managed, though forming words was becoming increasingly difficult.

"Hmm?" he asked, easing her panties down her legs with his gaze lingering on what he was unveiling.

Seeing him unbuckle his belt, her question no longer seemed important. "Let me help you," she offered. Not waiting for permission, she reached for his shirt and began to unfasten the buttons. His grin was enough reassurance as she continued to remove his shirt while he freed himself from the confines of his slacks.

Still sitting on his desk, with her nightgown bunched around her waist, and her robe forgotten, Claire ran her fingers through the softness of his chest hair. Leaning back, she unconsciously bit her bottom lip as she admired her view. Scanning her husband from head to toe, she took in his toned abs, which, even with age were still defined. As she peered lower, her eyes followed a trail of dark hair that led the way to his impressive erection. Rarely was she the one clothed, and he not. Moving her gaze back upward, their eyes met, and her cheeks flushed.

"Are you enjoying the view, Mrs. Rawlings?"

Freeing her lip, she grinned. "I am. Thank you for asking."

Stroking himself, he asked, "Perhaps you'd rather go upstairs?"

She shook her head. Watching his hands, she suddenly thought about how much she wanted to be doing what he was doing. "No, this feels a little scandalous... I think I like it."

"Oh, scandalous is the way I like you."

Kneeling before the desk, Tony reached for her legs and placed one on each of his shoulders. Planting a kiss on the inside of her leg, he slowly moved upward. His dark eyes peered up. "I like my view too."

Moments later, Claire's moans filled the office as his tongue and fingers consumed her thoughts. Lying back on the desk and closing her eyes, memories of similar scenarios filled Claire's mind. In time, their bodies became one, the good memories overpowered the bad, and for the second time in one day, she accepted all her husband had to offer and more. In the aftermath, as they walked hand in hand toward their suite, Claire squeezed his and whispered, "Those memories... they're not all bad, not at all."

His light chocolate eyes said more than words could ever convey.

Chapter 5

Late January 2017

Taylor

———◆———

Responsibility is the price of freedom.
—Elbert Hubbard

"IT DOESN'T MAKE sense. How could anyone know?" Taylor whispered to Phil.

He shook his head. "How did they know about the restaurant? I bagged these cards, just like the other one. The FBI will have them analyzed. All that matters is that the private viewing box is now clean. You stay with them in there, and I'll stay outside the door."

Taylor nodded. As the Rawlings family approached, she looked once again toward Phil. His headshake was almost indecipherable, but she saw it. With his unspoken statement, Taylor knew that telling Mr. or Mrs. Rawlings about the cards that had been left in Nichol and Claire's seat should and would wait until after the play.

Claire

NICHOL'S EXCITEMENT WAS contagious as she bounced beside her mother. Her little patent-leather shoes danced with anticipation, as her eyes widened and took in all the grandeur of the Broadway theater. "Look, Momma, look, Daddy, I see the music intruments!"

Claire smiled at Tony and back at Nichol. "In-stru-ments. Yes, honey, that's the orchestra. See the man with the wand in his hand?"

Nichol turned in amazement. "Like a magic one?"

"No, princess." Tony's words came through booming laughter.

"He's the conductor," Claire explained. "He'll tell the orchestra when to play the music. And when he does, he'll move the wand."

"I want to hear them." She turned toward Tony. "Daddy, make them start now."

Apparently Nichol believed there was no limit to her father's abilities.

"I could, princess." Tony replied.

Claire shook her head. Maybe Tony wasn't aware of his boundaries either.

Tony continued, "But see all the people who aren't in their seats yet? If I had the orchestra start playing, they'd miss the opening act."

Nichol pressed her lips together and wrinkled her forehead. "Then they should have gotten here sooner, like us."

"Yes, my princess, they should have."

Trying to distract their daughter, Claire said, "Honey, why don't you tell your daddy about our trip to the museum yesterday?"

Her brown eyes opened wide. "I lost Sophie!"

Tony reached for her doll and handed it to his daughter. "No, you didn't. Here she is."

"No, Daddy, I did lost her at the maseum. She was gone! Mr. Phil found her on a bench. I didn't mean to get her lost."

Claire put her arm around Nichol. "It's all right. You have her back, and yes, Mr. Phil was quite the hero. Just like the time we accidentally left her at that ice cream shop in Iowa City a few weeks ago."

Their daughter's dark eyes narrowed. "I didn't lost her at the ice cream shop. She was hiding."

Claire rubbed Nichol's shoulder. "It's all right. We found her there, and Mr. Phil found her yesterday."

Nichol smiled back at Taylor. "And Miss Taylor too."

"I'm glad you had all that help," Tony replied. "Sophie sure has a pretty dress. It looks just like yours!"

"Mommy did that. We have matching shoes, too. See." Nichol lifted her shoes near the doll's feet.

"I don't think I've asked you: how did you come up with that pretty name?"

"I named her for the lady who painted the pretty picture of Momma, the one of Momma in her beautiful princess dress."

"You did?" Claire asked.

"Yep," Nichol said. "I like her name, and she painted good. You look pretty in that picture."

Claire's eyes met Tony's, seeing a hint of sadness swirl below the surface. "You're right, princess," he said. "She did do a good job, and your mommy looked even prettier in real life than she does in that painting."

The theater darkened and the music began. It wasn't until Tony had had the chance to speak with Phil during intermission that Claire noticed his change in demeanor. When he looked her way, she silently questioned him. He only shook his head and mouthed, "Later."

Once they were back in the limousine after the show, the pieces of the puzzle began to slide into place. As Nichol snuggled against Claire's side and watched the lights through the window, Tony said, "We're going home tomorrow morning."

Lowering her voice, Claire replied, "Why? What happened?"

Shaking his head, he looked down at Nichol.

"But something happened, didn't it?" she whispered.

Tony pulled out his phone and opened up the camera application. Silently, he handed it to his wife. Adjusting her eyes to the small screen, Claire looked down at the image. The picture was of a plastic bag with an envelope with the name *Nichol Rawlings* printed on the outside. Claire's forehead furrowed.

"Swipe the screen," Tony commanded. Claire did. The next was a picture of a similar bag containing a similar envelope with the name *Claire Rawlings* on the outside.

"Where were these?" Claire asked, keeping her tone low.

"On our seats in the private box."

"On our seats?" she questioned, trying unsuccessfully to speak quietly. "But we just made these reservations."

"Roach is running leads. The reservations weren't in our name."

Claire looked closer at the screen and enlarged the image. "They're different, more like the recent *I'll save you* messages. The names are handwritten and it says Rawlings, not Rawls."

Tony nodded. "Roach contacted the FBI. They've taken the envelopes and will call as soon as they know anything. The fact that they're different worries me more than if they were the same."

Claire glanced at Nichol who appeared unfazed as she stared out the window, her little eyelids growing heavy as she struggled to watch all the sights just beyond her reach. "How could anyone know where we were?" With the light from the street and line of lights within, Claire saw Tony's jaw clench and unclench.

"I don't know," her husband replied. "That isn't all. There was another one, addressed to you, waiting at the restaurant."

Claire's stomach fell. "The restaurant? Where we just ate? It was waiting for *me*?"

Tony reached for her hand. "I'm not trying to scare you, but this is serious."

"I agree. What did they say?"

"We don't know. The FBI told us not to open anything. Once they do, we'll know more."

"Tony..." Claire peered down at Nichol, who, despite the chaos around her, had fallen asleep with her forehead against the window. "...I'm scared."

He scooted near and pulled her closer. "I'd feel better if we were home. I have a few early meetings, but then we're heading back to Iowa."

Claire nodded. "I promised Nichol one more trip to *FAO Schwarz* and *American Girl*. We'll do that first thing in the morning and then we'll be ready to go when you're done." Noticing his expression, she added, "Don't worry. We'll have Phil and Taylor with us the entire time."

When they arrived back to their building, Phil went up ahead to the apartment. Tony carried Nichol, Claire carried Sophie, and Taylor led the procession with Eric following closely behind. Once their apartment was declared safe, the Rawlingses were cleared to enter.

Dropping Sophie on the sofa, Claire sighed. "I know she won't remember all of this, but this wasn't how I envisioned Nichol's first trip to New York."

Tony laid their daughter on the sofa and undid her coat. "Look at her. She's blissfully unaware."

Claire smoothed Nichol's hair away from her face. "I don't know what I'd do if anything happened—" Tears threatened her painted lids.

"Stop," Tony interrupted, as his strong arms surrounded Claire. "Nothing will happen. We'll be home tomorrow."

Claire nodded against his Armani suit jacket and gained strength with each beat of his heart.

"Let's get Nichol into her bed. It's been a long day."

"All right," Claire replied. Her eyes widened as Tony picked up Nichol. "When do you expect to hear from the FBI?"

"Hopefully tomorrow." He started walking toward the front stairs.

"Oh, don't forget Sophie!" Claire said, as she picked up the doll. "You have no idea how traumatic it was when she went missing. We don't want Nichol waking in the middle of the night and not being able to find her."

EARLY THE NEXT morning, Claire and Tony woke to the thunder of running feet as their daughter launched herself onto their bed. "Momma, Daddy, I want to go to the doll store!"

Claire looked toward the red numbers on the bedside stand. "Honey, it's not even 6:00 AM. Look out the windows. It's still dark. Maybe you should go back—"

Her little forehead wrinkled. "Why? You said in the morning. It's morning."

"Honey, the store doesn't open—"

Not waiting for her mother to finish, Nichol asked, "When does it open?"

Claire was about to complete her suggestion that Nichol go back to sleep when Tony pulled himself up to a sitting position and tucked Nichol under his arm. "Come here, princess, let's look at what time the store opens."

As Tony turned on his phone, Claire shook her head. "I think that could wait until after—"

"Nichol? Where's Sophie?" Tony asked, interrupting Claire.

"Right here," she said, as she produced the doll from the foot of the bed.

"Oh, my. She's still wearing her dress from last night!" Tony said.

Nichol's eyes widened. "She is!"

"Doesn't she have a nightgown?"

"She does." Nichol climbed down from the big bed. "I'll go get her jammies."

Claire's brow furrowed. "Since when are you concerned about her doll's clothing?"

Instead of answering, Tony handed Claire his phone. It was open to a text message:

"MR. RAWLINGS. ALL THREE ENVELOPES AND CARDS TESTED CLEAR. THE MESSAGES WERE AS FOLLOWS: THE CARD FROM THE RESTAURANT, ADDRESSED TO MRS. RAWLINGS: **THIS IS THE PERFECT OPPORTUNITY FOR ME TO SAVE YOU. SO MANY PEOPLE IN THE CITY. SOON I WILL BE ABLE TO HELP YOU.'"**

"CARD FROM THEATER, ADDRESSED TO MRS. RAWLINGS: *'I UNDERSTAND THAT YOU CAN'T RESPOND, BUT TOMORROW. YOU WILL BE FREE TOMORROW.'*"

"CARD FROM THEATER, ADDRESSED TO NICHOL RAWLINGS: *'SOON YOU TOO WILL BE FREE.'*"

Claire read the text a second time. "What is it supposed to mean? I don't understand."

"I'll cancel my meetings. We'll leave right away."

Claire shook her head. "If we do that, this person wins. I almost felt better about the *Rawls-Nichols* mailings. At least they were consistent."

Nichol came rushing back, Sophie in tow. "I didn't put on her jammies. She's too excited about the doll store. She wanted to get dressed."

"*She's* excited?" Claire asked.

Nichol nodded. "Yep. Daddy, when does it open?"

Tony brushed the screen. "Just a minute. Oh, here it is. *American Girl* opens at 9:00 AM. Look at that, you silly: we have over three hours."

"I can't wait free hours." Her shoulders slumped. "That's forever! I want to go *now*."

Claire gave Nichol a big hug. "It's not quite forever, honey, but I understand. I'd like to go now too. However, we have to wait. I know, we can eat a big breakfast so we won't be hungry looking at all the toys. I bet Sophie would like some scrambled eggs."

"Nope," Nichol answered matter-of-factly. "She wants pancakes with lots of siwup."

"Of course she does," Tony laughed.

When 9:00 AM arrived, Claire, Tony, Nichol, Phil, and Taylor were all anxiously awaiting the opening of the *American Girl* store on Fifth Avenue. After a discussion with Eric, Phil, and Taylor, Tony decided to cancel his meetings and stay close to Claire and Nichol. Still blissfully unaware, Nichol bounced in her seat, excited to have her whole family see the store.

Phil watched the entrance for suspicious patrons while Taylor stayed by Nichol's side. Claire had arranged for a personal shopper to help guide Nichol to the areas of the store that interested her most, and the nice woman was waiting for their arrival. As she ushered Nichol about, Tony and Claire followed closely behind.

With each new section of the giant store, Claire began to relax. Nothing seemed out of the ordinary. Just before they were to leave, Nichol tugged on her mother's hand and whispered that she needed to use the restroom. They handed Sophie to Taylor who followed them into the restroom. As soon as Nichol and Claire entered a stall, the commotion began. It happened so fast that it was difficult to keep up.

The tile walls and floors only amplified the sounds as rants and crashes echoed throughout the bathroom. Nichol's brown eyes grew to the size of saucers when she looked to her mother and asked, "What's wrong?"

"Shush, honey," Claire whispered, hugging Nichol close to her thundering heart.

Saying a silent prayer, Claire moved her and her daughter to the back of the stall. Fighting the urge to close her eyes, she stared at the latch, held Nichol tighter, and listened as the commotion waxed and waned. Claire didn't know what or who had started the racket, but soon she heard not only Taylor's voice but also Phil's. Almost immediately, the chaos brought others. Though multiple people shouted, it wasn't until Claire heard the deep baritone voice that her world was made right and she even considered opening the stall door.

"Claire," Tony called. "Are you all right? Come out."

With trembling fingers, Claire opened the latch. Her heart found its steady beat as her gaze blended into the dark eyes. Walking to her husband, she turned just in time to see the back of a man being led away by store security, his wrists cuffed.

"...you don't understand," the man protested. "She needs me. I love her, and she loves me. I need to save her from him..." His words trailed away as Claire melted against Tony, who held Nichol tight.

"What happened?" Nichol's usually strong tone shook with uncertainty.

With a smile on his face and concern in his eyes, Phil joined the group. "Everything is fine, Nichol. Remember, Taylor and I are here to keep you safe?"

Nichol nodded.

"Well, Taylor has something of yours."

They all turned toward Taylor as she presented Sophie back to Nichol. "That man wanted to make a lot of noise. It's a good thing I was here, because he didn't get a chance to get near Sophie. But I think she needs you, don't you?"

Pursing her lips together, Nichol nodded and said, "Thank you, Miss Taylor." Reaching for Sophie, she held her tight, still safe within her parents' embrace.

Once they were back in the limousine and on their way to the apartment, Phil began to share the information they'd learned. Apparently, a man in his mid-thirties had been waiting in one of the stalls. He opened the door, as soon as Claire and Nichol entered another stall. Of course, Taylor saw him immediately and was on top of him. "The man's name is Rudolf. He has a history of delusional behavior. From his mutterings, it seems that he read Ms. Bank's book, *My Life As it Didn't Appear,* and has since devoted his time to an effort to *save* and *free* you, Claire."

Claire shook her head. "Save me? Free me from what... the book?"

Taylor shook her head. "As Phil said, Rudolf is delusional. He's been arrested before for celebrity stalking. They'll do more detailed psychological tests, but it seems that he believed the circumstances of the book are current, not past. He believed that you're currently in danger."

Through clenched teeth, Tony proclaimed, "I hate that damn book."

"What else did this Rudolf say?" Claire asked.

"He was very forthcoming," Phil replied. "He's been following you for a while. However, we still aren't sure how he knew your schedule. I know your phones and computers are clean. I check them daily."

"He had an earpiece in his ear." Taylor volunteered. "You know, like a Bluetooth." Her mind processed. "Phil, how long did he say he has he been following Mrs. Rawlings?"

"He said that he's been *with you...*" Phil looked to Claire. "...for weeks."

"I've never seen him before in my life."

Tony squeezed her hand.

"I still don't know how he knew where we'd be. And what did he mean, *with me*?"

Contemplating the earpiece, Phil asked, "Nichol, may I see Sophie?"

Shaking her head, Nichol hugged her doll tighter. "No, she's scared. That bad man scared her."

Taylor and Phil exchanged glances. "Honey," Taylor began, "you know that Mr. Phil and I are here to keep you safe, right?"

Nichol nodded.

"We also want to keep Sophie safe, just as I did in the bathroom. Can I please see her for a minute?"

Apprehensively, Nichol's dark eyes turned to her mom. Claire nodded, unsure of Phil and Taylor's new fascination with the doll. Nichol slowly held Sophie out to Taylor. "Mr. Phil, Sophie wants to go to Miss Taylor."

Phil smiled. "That's just fine, Nichol. Miss Taylor can make sure Sophie's safe."

"I'm going to look very closely at Sophie when we get back to your apartment. Is that okay, Nichol?"

"Don't let her get hurt again."

"Again?" Taylor asked.

"Yes, she got an ouchy on her back."

"I won't let anything happen to her," Taylor reassured.

Claire squeezed her daughter's hand and watched as Taylor's soft blue eyes gave Nichol the comfort she needed.

"I've called ahead; our things should be packed for us to head home," Tony declared.

No one disagreed.

A FEW DAYS later back in Iowa, Claire and Tony sat in their office as Phil and Taylor explained their findings. "There was a microphone, GPS, and transmitter hidden inside of Sophie. That's how Rudolf knew where you were or where you were going."

"Did it happen at the company?" Tony asked.

"We're confident that it was placed post-manufacturing," Taylor replied. "However, upon further inspection, a smaller, more sophisticated tracker was found in the doll sent for Nichol's birthday. The FBI didn't find it at first because it's made of a new polymer that is radiolucent. So it didn't show up in their initial tests and x-rays."

Phil interjected, "We suspect that the tracking software was placed when Nichol left Sophie at the ice cream shop in Iowa City. I remember thinking at the time that I hadn't seen the doll when we left the shop. If they still have their security footage we could confirm our suspicions, but I think Rudolf was there and stole the doll when Nichol and we weren't looking. I didn't recognize him at first, but now I'm beginning to think he seemed familiar. We believe he inserted the transmitter, GPS, and microphone and then left Sophie for us to find. When we retrieved her, we never thought to look."

"Yes, that *ouchy* that Nichol mentioned was a small incision sealed with clear glue," Taylor added. "I asked her when it happened and she said after Sophie got lost at the ice cream shop."

Claire shook her head. "I don't know if Nichol mentioned Sophie's injury before or not. I don't remember. I'd bet that if she did, I didn't think anything of it."

"The FBI confirmed that the DNA on the electronics in both dolls matched Rudolf's." Phil forced a reassuring smile. "There's no reason to think he was acting in conjunction with anyone else. His history is of lone stalking. The FBI is also confident that he isn't related to or involved with the sender of the *Rawls-Nichols* gifts. He never in any of his attempts at contact used the names *Rawls* or *Nichols*, always Rawlings."

"Great, so one psycho down and another to go," Claire said with a sigh.

"The most important thing is that you and Nichol are safe," Tony reiterated.

"And you," Phil added, looking directly toward Tony. "In Rudolf's delusions, he foresaw *saving* Claire and Nichol, and setting them *free*—by keeping them with him and assuring that you were permanently out of the picture."

Claire gasped. "Permanently? Does he have a history of violence?"

"No," Taylor answered. "However, it's well documented that criminals tend to escalate in their behavior. He was bolder with you than he'd been in his previously known cases. Taking Nichol's doll was quite the risk. His success undoubtedly fueled his confidence. Through the software he placed in Sophie, he had up to the minute updates of personal family matters. His intimate knowledge helped to perpetuate his delusion."

"Wouldn't that intimate knowledge have helped to refute his need to save Claire and Nichol?" Tony asked. "After all, he heard us interact. There was never anything that he would've heard to make him believe that either Claire or Nichol were in danger."

Phil cleared his throat. "As we've said, the man was delusional. Anything he heard, without visual confirmation, could be misconstrued in his mind. We know that the only real threat was from him, but he didn't see himself that way."

"I don't think I want to know any more about him, other than he's out of our lives," Claire said. "Tell me that there's no chance of him getting free and coming after us."

"It should be open and shut. After all, he was caught in the act," Tony added.

"It wasn't just what he did at the store; the FBI confirmed Rudolf had an unlicensed gun in his possession."

Claire shivered. "Thank God you two were there."

"With his history, at a minimum he's looking at being institutionalized. With the illegal audio surveillance and the firearms charge he's facing much stiffer penalties. Mr. Simmons has already petitioned for a restraining order. Don't worry. He's not coming near any of you," Phil replied.

"Confirm the timeline. When did Rudolf start his quest?" Tony asked.

"It seems as though it was near Nichol's birthday," Phil confirmed.

"That means that Nichol's birthday gift, the doll, was from him?"

Phil nodded toward Claire. "Yes. The doll was addressed to *Nichol Rawlings*. The card, no. It was addressed to *Nichol Rawls* and had the female DNA."

Tony wrapped his arm around Claire. "As you said, one down and one to go."

"Mrs. Rawlings," Taylor began, "it's an ongoing investigation. The FBI has been working with Phil closely. As a matter-of-fact..."

Phil's gaze shot toward Taylor.

"...we're hoping for more information anytime now," she continued.

"Is there anything else?" Tony asked, his gaze darkening as he looked from Phil to Taylor.

Phil and Taylor exchanged glances. "No, that about covers it," Phil responded, as the two of them stood to leave the office.

"I know I keep saying it. Somehow it seems insufficient, but thank you for everything," Claire said with a strained smile.

Taylor and Phil nodded as they both disappeared behind the door.

Once they were alone, Claire raised her brow and asked Tony, "Did you see that?"

"What? That they have something they're not saying?"

"No. The way they looked back and forth at one another, and the way Phil said *we*."

"Yes, I guess." Tony wrinkled his brow. "Why? I have no idea what you're asking."

"I think Phil's getting used to having someone else around. I mean, he's pretty much been in control of all things security, and although he was instrumental with our hiring Taylor, I got the feeling he felt like she was invading his turf. It just seems like after this, well, she was able to be in the bathroom with us when he couldn't. If she hadn't been there, and he'd been outside, who knows what would have happened."

"I don't even want to think about it."

Claire grinned. "I like it. It's good for him. I think he spends too much time alone."

Tony shrugged. "He's got Eric."

"I don't think it's the same thing," she said with a smirk.

Shaking his head, Tony pressed his lips together. "Mrs. Rawlings, don't play matchmaker. I want Phil and Taylor's attention on you and Nichol, not on one another."

"No one said they can't do both."

Chapter 6

Late January 2017

Phil

———◆———

Decision is the courageous facing of issues,
knowing that if they are not faced,
problems will remain forever unanswered.
—Wilfred A. Peterson

ONCE WITHIN THE hallway, Phil and Taylor moved silently away from the Rawlingses' office toward the security hub for the estate. As they approached their destination, Phil's gaze narrowed toward his new associate. Finally he voiced the question he'd been burning to ask, "What the hell did you almost say in there?"

Taylor's neck straightened. "I was going to mention the possible location of Mr. Rawlings' past assistant, Patricia Miles. She's the prime suspect, and in their last report the FBI said that she was recently suspected to reside in a small town in Minnesota under an alias."

"I didn't share that information with you. How do you know that?"

Taylor's hands found her hips as her voice dropped an octave.

"I'm part of this team." She motioned down the corridor toward the closed office doors. "Mr. and Mrs. Rawlings have accepted me. Eric has accepted my role. Maybe it's time you eased up on your one-man crusade and accept that I'm here to help."

"I never said you weren't here to help. Helping doesn't include scaring Claire or upsetting Rawlings with unsubstantiated information."

"What's unsubstantiated? I read the report. Patricia Miles is believed to be living as Melissa Garrison and working for a small law practice in Olivia, Minnesota. More definitive results are due back in a matter of weeks."

Phil bristled. "There are some things that are better left unsaid."

"Team, Mr. Roach, that's how this works. Teams talk; they share."

Phil reached out to grab Taylor's elbow. "You want to talk about it? Fine, talk to me. Talk to Eric. Do not take this to either Rawlings or Claire until we have definitive answers. Even then, talk to me first. Security for this family is *my* detail."

Taylor pulled her elbow free. "Excuse me, who was there when Rudolf came out of the stall? Who figured out the connection with Sophie?"

"I'm not saying that your assistance hasn't been valued. What you did in New York was, well, it was more than I could've done, but you don't understand all that they've been through, especially her."

"Her? Your employer? Mr. Rawlings's wife?"

Phil took a step back, assessing the meaning of Taylor's question. "Yes, her. Her last few years have been difficult. She doesn't need additional stress."

As Taylor began to speak, Phil's mind flashed with memories—snapshots in time—beginning when he received the call from Brent

Simmons: the first time he'd heard the name *Claire Nichols*. At the time, it seemed simple enough. Phil had done investigative work for Simmons in the past. This time he was asked if he could locate a lost woman and work temporary surveillance. That was almost four years ago. Four years. Phil hadn't spent four consecutive years with anyone since he left his parents' home and joined the military. Four years was a lifetime: more than Nichol's lifetime.

Not hearing Taylor's response, Phil went on, "She's all of those things. I've been with this family longer than anyone here, besides Eric. You don't understand all that's transpired."

"Really?" she asked, snapping her neck so that her blue eyes blazed toward Phil. "Do you think that poorly of my investigative skills that I'd walk into a job with a family like the Rawlingses with no information about them? Why the hell did you support my hiring if you'd assume such ignorance?"

Phil briefly closed his eyes. He had no desire to get into this with anyone, especially his new associate. "Did I ever say that I supported your hiring?"

"Mrs. Rawlings said that you did. Perhaps I shouldn't believe my employer?"

Damn. Claire always did talk too much, to everyone. "You had an impressive resume. I was particularly interested in your independent work since leaving the bureau."

Yes, Phil had done his research too. He would never allow someone open access to *his* family without it. Taylor Walters had all the right schooling, a double major in psychology and criminology. She worked local law enforcement for seven years before joining the FBI. Six years at the bureau had her working hostage negotiation. There's no doubt she had a way with diplomacy. Taylor excelled in her chosen field until she was shot in the line of duty. After rehab she was reassigned to a desk job: cybercrime. It only took a year of sitting behind the scenes until she left the FBI and pursued independent jobs, many not unlike some that Phil himself had done.

Taylor's eyes widened. "I don't recall that information being on my resume."

"Now whose turn is it to be offended? Do you think I'd support, as Claire informed you, a hire that I hadn't fully investigated? And if you think you learned all there is to know about this family by reading a book, you're sadly mistaken."

"I never said what research I did. Yes, the book was part of it; however, a very small part. I'm aware of more than you know. Since I've been here, I've also made it a point to know all I can about my coworkers."

Phil shook his head. "I'm not trying to have a pissing contest with you. You're here. I'm fine with that. Just don't give either of them information on this particular subject without first running it by me. And I can tell you right now, I'm not going to approve sharing."

"The FBI is already involved. They're zeroing in on Ms. Miles. If you think you're going to go in and remove the subject under their noses, you're mistaken."

"Am I now?"

Taylor leaned closer. "You want to keep the Rawlingses safe? Then don't do something stupid so that you're in prison and not here."

"I appreciate the warning, Ms. Walters."

Phil turned, leaving Taylor in the grand hall as he made his way toward the security office in the lower level. He half expected her to follow and equally as much didn't. He didn't really care. Women had always been unpredictable, even women as well trained as

Taylor Walters. She'd proven herself under pressure, yet she couldn't hide the fact she was missing a damn Y chromosome. He knew he should think of her like a partner, yet when they'd be sitting side by side going through footage or researching theories, he'd notice the sweet scent of perfume. It was different than Claire's, lighter. Yet even as he entered the security office, he sensed it lingering in the air, accentuating her absence.

Sighing, Phil sat at his desk. He'd never meant to think of Taylor in a personal way. Doing so was an insult to her professionalism. She was qualified to be part of this detail. Phil closed his eyes and massaged his temples. He needed to get his head on straight. Why had Taylor questioned his protectiveness of Claire? It was his job. Obviously, he was nothing more to her than an employee. That wasn't true. He and Claire were also friends.

Phil recalled the first time he saw Claire, his assignment, through the window in the Palo Alto condominium. A slight grin came to his lips as he remembered her smug expression in San Antonio when she knew she'd duped him. He still felt the heaviness in his chest as he ran toward her Palo Alto condominium, knowing that her life was in danger. Phil's fascination and sense of duty involving Claire Nichols should have ended then and there. After all, Rawlings fired him. Whenever Phil remembered that terrible day, the firing was the least of his concerns. It was his failure to protect. If he'd done his job, he would've known about Patrick Chester. Instead he'd been lulled into a sense of the mundane, and it was Claire who'd paid the price.

When Catherine London called and asked Phil to help Claire disappear, he could've said no; however, he'd thought of it as his opportunity to atone for his error in judgment. Ms. London explained that Claire wanted to get away from Rawlings. It made sense. Phil had witnessed Rawlings' intensity. Phil had failed to protect her from Chester; he wouldn't fail to protect her from her ex-husband. Though once again, things weren't as he'd been led to believe. Nothing with Claire ever was.

Phil remembered their time in Europe, running from Ms. London and outwitting the FBI. Scenes with historic backdrops replayed in the recesses of his mind. The woman who had been broken and mending in California was stronger than he'd ever imagined in Europe. No longer oppressed, as he'd later read about in her memoirs, *Mrs. Alexander* was determined to make a life for herself and her baby. Though it took many favors and promises, Phil secured the island for her. Nothing was too much to make her dream come true. However, it didn't take long for Phil to realize that Ms. London had lied about Claire's goal. She didn't want to be separated from Rawlings. Without coming out and saying it, Phil knew she wanted the opposite. He couldn't stand to see her sad— not in paradise. Therefore, instead of protecting her from Rawlings, Phil did what he needed to do to make Claire happy: he brought Rawlings to her.

That temporary surveillance job became something Phil had never known, ever. It became his life, his family. Though keeping Claire safe and happy was still his top priority, his sense of responsibility grew the evening he felt Nichol move within her mother. Nichol was an extension of Claire. Part of him wanted to hate the beautiful, brown-eyed girl for what she'd done to her mother upon her arrival. Never in all of his years of service had he felt so impotent. But once again, Claire's strength showed through, and Phil adored the child as much as he did her mother. How could he not? Nichol was the only baby he'd ever held.

The sense of family somehow over time even transferred to

Rawlings himself. The egotistical, narcissistic, hothead who'd originally hired him had morphed into a kindred spirit. Despite the Rawlingses' past history, Phil and Rawlings had a shared interest in keeping this family safe. On the tragic day at the estate, when faced with the inevitable, Rawlings looked into Phil's eyes and placed his infant daughter in his arms. Trust. After failing them in Palo Alto, Phil had earned it back.

Phil remembered holding Nichol inside of his jacket to keep her warm and protect her from the cold water of the sprinklers and the bitter Iowa spring temperature. However, after receiving the greatest gift he could imagine from Rawlings, Phil once again failed to protect Claire and all of their lives spiraled out of control.

During the next two years he could've walked away. No one would've blamed him. Hell, Brent Simmons told him to leave, for his own good. Phil didn't care about *his* own good. He never had. One doesn't do what he'd done throughout his life while being concerned about his own well-being. There had always been another reason.

Did his infatuation start that day in March of 2013 when he saw Claire through the fourth-floor window, or perhaps in San Antonio? Phil couldn't say. He'd foolishly shown his cards in San Diego when he sent Claire the note with her room service. No matter the time it began, Phil's sense of duty was too ingrained. The Rawlingses were his responsibility. He'd failed them before and he wouldn't do it now.

No matter how mixed up Phil's feelings were about Taylor, she'd saved Claire and Nichol from Rudolf. He should welcome her knowledge and assistance. However, that one act didn't give her the ability to share unsubstantiated information. Phil was still the go-to man on this *team*, as she called it. And he would do anything to keep Claire away from the dark place where she was unreachable, the place she'd been for two long years. It wasn't as simple as keeping her physically safe. It was keeping her mentally stable. The way he saw it, a sense of unwavering security was a strong component of that mental health.

Keeping his employers uninformed didn't only apply to Claire. From Phil's perspective, Rawlings didn't need the responsibility. Phil had plans for the sender of those gifts and cards. If things didn't go as he intended, the Rawlingses could honestly claim ignorance. Neither one of them needed a public and lengthy legal battle. They'd both had their share.

Early February

Claire

CLAIRE SIPPED HER warm coffee as Courtney's excitement bubbled forth with each word. "I'm not supposed to say anything, but I feel like I might burst! Brent and I are so excited about Caleb's call. Can you believe it? Can you honestly believe it?" She raised her chin and turned her profile to the left. "Come on, tell me the truth. Do I look like a grandmother?"

Claire giggled as she shook her head. "No, but if you stop going to those every-three-week salon appointments, you might."

"Nonsense. I don't need to be a white-haired, frail little thing to be a grandmother. I'm going to be the hottest grandma this side of the Mississippi."

Claire's laugh filled the restaurant. "Yes, Cort, you are! How's Julia feeling?"

"She's having morning sickness, or as Caleb said, morning, noon, and night sickness."

Claire scrunched her nose. "Poor thing. I remember that with Nichol. Mine didn't last too long, but even one bout is too many."

"I told her that it doesn't usually last past the first trimester. I mean, look at Emily. She's feeling well. Isn't she?"

Claire nodded, swallowing a bite of her salad. "She is. She's just starting the dreaded third trimester. You know, when you're ready to be done. I remember sleeping a lot. Em can't do that, not with Michael. I guess she can with Becca helping her, but it's still hard. She seems tired most of the time."

As Courtney continued to talk about Julia's pregnancy, Claire basked in the memories of her own. She tried to think of the good times, those of her and Tony on the island. A faint pinkness came to her cheeks as she recalled the difficulty and inventiveness of being together during those last few months. It would seem that in that enlarged state, sex would be the last thing she'd have wanted; however, Claire remembered it being the exact opposite. It wasn't a subject she wanted to ask Emily about or bring up to Courtney. Heaven knows, with Courtney's filter—or lack thereof—she might just say something to Julia, and Claire didn't want to be the source of that uncomfortable daughter- and mother-in-law conversation.

The noontime crowd had thinned by the time the two ladies finished their lunch and last cup of coffee. They'd had too much to talk about to rush. "It's been great to get some time to catch up," Courtney said as she squeezed Claire's hand.

With Claire's response on the tip of her tongue, she saw Phil looking her direction from a table away. "It has," she confirmed. "Are you ready for Phil to get the car?"

They both looked toward the large windows of the restaurant.

More snow had fallen while they'd lunched. "I wish he'd have joined us for lunch. I always feel bad when he's by himself."

Claire shook her head. "I asked him to join us. He said he didn't want to intrude. Besides..." A gleam came to Claire's emerald eyes. "...he isn't always alone. I'm kind of enjoying watching him and Taylor."

"Hmmm?"

"Well, I just get this feeling there's some unresolved tension." She raised her brows. "And I don't mean the bad kind either. They're both professional. However, the atmosphere is different when Taylor's working with Eric than it is when she's working with Phil. I doubt he even realizes how obvious it is."

Courtney laughed. "Probably not. After all, he's a man."

Both women giggled as Phil approached the table.

"Are you ladies ready for me to get the car? I can warm it up. Mother Nature isn't being too kind to us today."

"That'd be great, thank you. Unless..." Claire's expression sparkled. "...we could convince you to join us for one more cup of coffee?"

Phil shook his head. "Oh, no. I've been hearing your chatter from across the way. I think I'll stay out of all this girl talk. I don't have much to add to the conversation."

Both ladies laughed into their mugs as Phil walked away and secured his jacket and gloves. Once he was gone, Claire said, "I'm sorry we haven't done this more often. Since we returned from the South Pacific, things have been busy."

"Speaking of busy, I'm sorry your trip to New York was ruined. How's Nichol doing with all of it?"

"She's doing fine," Claire replied. "She really isn't having any problems. I wasn't sure how much to talk to her about it. I didn't want her repressing it and having issues with it later, and I didn't want to scare her by dwelling on it too much."

Courtney's lips pressed into a tight smile. "You can tell that you talk to your therapists a lot."

Claire's forehead rose. "Ha! Yes, I guess I'm starting to sound like them. Well, I do talk to them a lot. Between *my* twice weekly sessions at Everwood and *our* once a week family session with the child psychiatrist, I feel like there's very little that ever goes unsaid."

"I hope it doesn't make you uncomfortable by my asking, but do you think it helps?"

"I guess," Claire commented. "It's been our norm for the last few months. I just want to be done with it—and not have to schedule my weeks around therapy. I know everyone's worried, but I feel good."

"Good?" Courtney asked.

"Yes, good," Claire confirmed.

"Claire, I've been your friend for over seven years. I love you, and I know how you're fond of superlatives. Things are usually *the greatest, fantastic, etcetera*. I could go on. *Good* is never good. What's going on?"

Claire's eyes dropped to the table. "I haven't said anything to the therapists, but it's all the medicine they have me on. I know it helped me get to where I am. I just want to be totally me again."

"Have you talked to anyone about it?"

Her green eyes met Courtney's blue. "Do you mean Tony?"

Courtney nodded.

"No. I don't want to worry him. He's continually asking me how I am, how I feel, and if I'm all right." Tears threatened to fall. "I want to be all right. I want to be me. Instead of talking to therapists, I want to do this." She gestured to herself and then Courtney and her voice quieted. "I know it's stupid. The therapy and medications helped me confront my past. I've done that—over and over. Now I want my future."

"That doesn't sound stupid at all. Perhaps you should talk to your doctors. Tell them how you feel."

Claire stood and wrapped her arms around her friend. Stepping back, she smiled. "Thank you. Thank you for not telling me it's too soon, or that I don't know what's best for me. Thank you for listening."

Tilting her head, Courtney whispered, "Emily?"

"Yes," Claire admitted. "I started to broach the subject with her the other day and she was all over me." Reaching for Courtney's arm, Claire hurriedly continued, "I know how you all feel about her, but don't. She's trying. She just has this obsession with mothering me."

"Well, honey, after her little girl is born, she'll be too busy with Michael and the baby to worry about mothering you."

Claire sighed as they left the table. "It feels great to talk to someone who knows me, knows the real me and everyone around me. I can't say these things to my therapists or doctors. They don't get it. They'd want me to explore my feelings or my motivations. I just want to say, 'hey, I love my sister, but today she's driving me nuts' without delving into the psychology of why I feel that way."

Making their way through the tables, Courtney grinned knowingly and whispered, "You know I'm here anytime. My guess is that your husband isn't the best sounding board for your complaints about your sister."

Claire feigned a laugh. "That goes without saying. However, he's trying too. They both are. Very trying." She added with a giggle as her eyes lit up. "And I'm very happy that John decided to stay at Rawlings Industries. Even though it's still strained with Emily, when Tony talks about John, I sense a genuine admiration."

"I know that Brent thinks the world of John. If you're ever looking for reasons or positive outcomes that resulted from all that you've been through, John coming to Rawlings could be one. According to Brent, he's a wonderful asset to the company. They're all glad he's there."

Claire smirked. "Not a *good* asset?"

"No, a *fantastic* asset."

"Who's the one who's over the top—who's keen on superlatives?" Claire asked as they stepped into the Iowa winter wonderland and cold air bit their cheeks.

Courtney laughed as she settled into the backseat of the waiting SUV next to Claire. "So, maybe I'll be a hot, over-the-top grandma?"

"I have no doubt!" Claire replied.

"So are we still on for next Saturday night?" Courtney asked.

"Yes! I want Tony to have the best birthday celebration he's had in years."

"I don't think that'll be too difficult. And with our plan, I'm sure we'll succeed. I heard from Eli and Marianne, and they're flying in on Friday night."

Claire watched the flakes of snow swirl in funnels near the street. Neither she nor Tony had had much to celebrate in the last few years. She thought about Tony being alone in prison on his last two birthdays. Though Tony didn't talk about his prison experience much, Claire knew. She knew what it was like to be alone. She didn't want that for either one of them, ever again.

"Oh! Tony will be so excited to see them."

Courtney went on, "So that'll be Eli and Marianne, John and Emily, Tim and Sue, Jerry and Meredith, Caleb and Julia, and the four of us. Can you think of anyone else I should invite?"

"No, that sounds good."

"Good?"

Claire shrugged. It surprised her when memories would hit. For some reason, the thought of Derek Burke popped into her head. She'd only met him once and she'd never met Sophia, but nevertheless, Claire had a momentary flash of how nice it would be to have them among their circle of friends. Pretending the thought hadn't occurred, Claire replied, "I just realized I'll be seeing Julia and I can't say anything about her pregnancy. That'll be so hard."

"Tell me about it! I'd have one of those giant yard signs announcing my grandchild to all of our guests if Caleb and Julia would let me. They just want to wait until she's further along to tell people."

"I understand, besides..." Claire leaned closer. "...they might be afraid you may be a little over the top?"

"Me? Not at all!" Courtney laughed.

Chapter 7

February 2017

Claire

———◆———

Where there is love there is life.
—Mahatma Gandhi

TONY'S BIRTHDAY BASH was a huge success. Though he wasn't surprised to have a party, having Eli and Marianne there made it extra special. The next morning, Tony, Claire, Nichol, and Eric, Phil, Taylor, and Shannon, traveled to Phoenix. Tony had business there for a few days and since his actual birthday would fall during his trip, he wanted his family near. Claire couldn't have been happier. Not only was she thrilled to get a reprieve from the Iowa winter, she was happy to do her best to make his fifty-second birthday one he'd never forget.

It seemed that traveling with only the three of them was no longer a viable option. Having Eric, Phil, Taylor and Shannon with them was becoming a natural extension. Claire didn't long for the days of solo travel, with just her and Tony on their plane. She'd willingly come to terms with their new normal. Though Rudolf was no longer a threat, he proved to both Tony and Claire that they could never take their safety or Nichol's for granted.

Over the past few weeks, they'd also learned a little more about Rudolf. Everything they'd been told before proved to be true. He was indeed working alone—a quiet, strange man fixated on someone he perceived as being in need. It was a similar modus operandi to his previous arrests. According to the police reports, Rudolf truly believed it was his mission to save Claire Nichols Rawlings from the clutches of Anthony Rawlings. The psychological evaluations were still incomplete, but without a doubt, the man was a few cards short of a full deck. With the restraining order in place, the law stipulated that if released, Rudolf could never come within one hundred yards of Anthony, Claire, or Nichol Rawlings. According to Phil, he'd never come within ten times that close. Thankfully, Rudolf was currently residing in a state facility under lock and key. Being his third such arrest coupled with the additional charges, his chances at an early release were slim to none.

Now that the Rawlingses were back home in Iowa, they were once again facing another celebration. Truthfully, it wasn't Claire or Tony who was excited about the impending holiday: it was Nichol. She was absolutely beside herself at the idea of celebrating Valentine's Day with her parents, and of course, it didn't take a lot of convincing to have Claire totally on board. Thinking back over Valentine's Days spent together, Claire was certain this would be a Valentine's Day unlike any her husband had celebrated. The curiosity of seeing his reaction propelled her through the painstaking task of cutting out paper hearts and frosting cupcakes.

Late on the afternoon of the fourteenth, Nichol paced the lavish kitchen, scanning the paper hearts and flowers dangling from the ceiling and littering the floor. Her dark eyes searched desperately, double- and triple-checking all of their hard work. "Momma, I want it peufect." She peered up through her long lashes. "Do you think Daddy will like it?"

Claire stifled a giggle as she shook her head. Their daughter couldn't be more like her father if she tried. "Honey, I think he'll love it."

"Are you sure?"

Claire wrapped Nichol in a warm hug. "I'm sure, sweetie."

"But..." Nichol scrunched her eyebrows together. "...what if he doesn't like paper hearts?"

"I'm sure he'll love paper hearts, especially when they're made by his two favorite girls."

Nichol clapped her hands as the sound of voices traveled from the foyer. "Oh, Momma, he's home!"

Before Claire could respond, Nichol was gone, her small feet running hurriedly toward the front door. Claire took one last look around the kitchen dining area. Pink, red, and white construction paper lay everywhere. She shook her head, confident that Anthony Rawlings had never celebrated Valentine's Day with paper hearts and homemade cupcakes; nevertheless, that was Nichol's idea, and Claire was not about to discourage their daughter's creativity.

"Don't look, Daddy."

Claire turned to see their daughter leading Tony by the hand, his eyes squinted shut. By the way his lips turned upward in that mischievous grin, Claire was confident that he could see the colorful explosion all around him. Moments later, his wink confirmed her suspicions.

"May I open my eyes yet?" he asked.

Claire was sure she'd never tire of hearing him banter and play with their beautiful daughter.

"Not yet," Nichol responded. "Momma and I have somefing for

you." She led Tony to a waiting chair. "Sit down here."

Yes, thought Claire. Demanding just like her daddy, too.

"You do?" Tony asked as he sat. "What does your momma have for me?"

Claire's insides tightened as she brushed his cheek with a fleeting kiss and whispered, "Later."

Placing a paper crown on his thick salt and pepper mane, Nichol clapped her hands and shouted, "Open your eyes! Happy Valentine's Day, Daddy!"

Tony laughed as he pulled Nichol to his lap and kissed the top of her head. "Is this all for me?"

Her little pigtails swung back and forth as she nodded. "It's 'cause we love you! We made cupcakes too!"

"We did," Claire added as she grinned at Tony's paper crown. "However, I think we should eat dinner before cupcakes."

"No, Momma." Nichol pouted and looked pleadingly from Claire to Tony. "It's a special day." Her little fingers fumbled with the neckline of her top. "See, I even got to wear my great-grandma's necklace. That means it's *very* special. So we can eat cupcakes before dinner."

Tony shrugged and smiled at Claire. "My dear, your negotiating skills have been passed on to the next generation. I don't know how we could possibly argue with that reasoning."

Claire sighed. "All right, you two, but we have a wonderful dinner waiting, so after the cupcakes..."

"We'll eat dinner," Nichol and Tony said in unison.

AFTER DINNER AND a bedtime story, Tony and Claire tucked Nichol into bed and closed her door. Melting against her husband's side, Claire enjoyed his strong embrace as she let out an exaggerated breath.

"Are you tired of celebrating, my dear?"

"I think I am. You have no idea how long it took to cut out all of those hearts."

Leading her toward their suite, Tony opened the door to a candlelit surprise. Their private table was set with white linen, a bouquet of long-stemmed red roses, and covered dishes.

"Tony? What did you do?"

"Well, I may have been tipped off about the paper and confection celebration."

Claire raised a brow. "Who told you? It was supposed to be a surprise."

"Shannon may have said something—but don't be upset with her. When I told her that I wanted her to watch Nichol tonight while I took you out to celebrate, she explained the secret plan. She didn't want me to ruin Nichol's surprise."

Claire turned slowly, noticing the rose petals strewn across their turned-down sheets. "What is all of this?" she asked as she motioned toward the table. "We already ate."

With a devilish grin, he lifted one lid to reveal strawberries.

"Hmmm," she replied. "I think I could be persuaded—"

Before she could finish he lifted the second lid revealing chocolate sauce and whipped cream. Her eyes opened wide. "Tony?"

He gracefully moved toward her, his eyes darkening with each step, twisting her insides to a painful pitch. As Tony held her close, pressing her breasts against his strong chest, and seized her lips, tired was no longer part of Claire's thinking. Moments later, his skilled fingers began to unbutton her blouse.

Less of a protest than a question, Claire repeated, "Tony?"

His warm breath tickled her exposed shoulder as he whispered, "We don't want to get chocolate sauce or whipped cream on this beautiful blouse." Cocking a brow, he added, "Or your slacks, or any colorful lace you have underneath."

Holding his shoulders for support as her slacks joined her blouse in the puddle of silk on the floor, she replied, "We don't?"

"No, because, my dear, it's time for our own confection celebration, and if you think our kitchen was messy..." He grinned as his dark eyes sparkled in the candlelight. "...you haven't seen anything yet."

"Hmmm," she managed, words forming with some difficulty as Tony's lips followed a path from her ear to her shoulder. Before speech was totally out of reach, she asked, "W-What about you?"

"What about me?"

Her fingers fumbled with the buttons of his shirt. "I wouldn't want chocolate on this nice shirt either."

When she undid the last button, he seized her hand. "My dear, you and Nichol planned your surprise. This is *my* Valentine's surprise for *you*. Do you trust me?"

Claire nodded, allowing Tony to back her toward the bed, buckling her knees. Wearing only her pink lace bra and panties, Tony's dark admiring gaze scanned her from head to toe. Each second filled her with both vulnerability and anticipation. Finally, she answered, "I trust you."

A lust-filled grin radiated from ear to ear as he heatedly said, "Good. I have something I'd like you to wear. Remember... you said you trust me."

Claire's eyes widened, her breaths becoming shallow as she sucked her lower lip. "W-What do you want—"

Before she could finish, Tony opened the drawer of her bedside stand and removed her satin sleep mask. Claire's cheeks rose approvingly as she reached for the mask.

"No," he said, as he lifted her dark hair and kissed her neck. "Let me." Tenderly, he placed the mask over her emerald eyes and secured the elastic band behind her head. "Can you see?"

"No." She giggled.

Her amusement soon morphed to unbridled desire as his sensual caresses traced an invisible line from her cheek to her breasts, teasing the round globes from their lace enclosure. Each time she began to speak, his finger gently touched her lips. When his mouth retraced the path, Claire fell back upon their soft comforter, giving him access to her newly exposed breasts and enjoying the sensation of his warm breath on her sensitive skin.

Soft moans came from somewhere deep in Claire's throat as he moved slowly—painfully slowly—down her stomach, touching, caressing, and igniting the flames of her desire. Just before reaching the trim of her panties, Tony stopped. Gasping, Claire reached for him—finding only air in the darkness.

Before she could sit, she heard her husband. "God, you're so beautiful."

Blood flushed her cheeks as she listened to his sultry tone. Suddenly, she felt his presence on the bed behind her. Within moments, his strong embrace tenderly pulled her back, situating her in front of him. When she leaned back against his bare chest, Claire smiled, her green eyes gleaming under the mask. From what she could tell, they were now dressed—or more accurately, undressed—to match.

"Open your mouth," his deep baritone voice dripped with seduction.

Obediently, she did as he said. Her compliance was rewarded with the rich taste of warm chocolate. Immediately, Claire opened her mouth wider allowing him to place the strawberry upon her tongue. Quickly, she closed her lips, purposely licking the chocolate from his fingers. His chest vibrated with his resonating growl as she sucked each finger clean. All the while, her insides quivered at the sound. Sweet strawberry juice mingled with the decadent chocolate as Claire swallowed.

"Again," he commanded.

This time, cool whipped cream covered the berry and her lips. As she swallowed, Tony captured her chin, turning her toward him and tasted the cream from her lips. The loss of sight had her senses on high alert, making each move unexpected and erotic. Next, Tony gathered her hair and secured it on top of her head with a clip. Before Claire could decipher his intent, the alternating sensation of warm chocolate and cool whipped cream dribbled over her chest. She gasped as he laid her back, moved in front of her, and began to savor the contrasting culinary delights.

"Oh, Tony," Claire panted, as the alternating sensations found new and creative locations.

It wasn't until Claire's breathing became erratic and they were both a sticky mess that Tony removed the mask and they came together as one. No longer blinded, Claire's emerald eyes stared deep into the only chocolate she would ever crave. They moved as one until both of their worlds shattered in blissful ecstasy.

As they later stepped into the warm spray of the multiple showerheads, Tony kissed his wife and said, "Happy Valentine's Day, Mrs. Rawlings."

With a smile glistening with sparks of emerald, Claire replied, "Mr. Rawlings, not so fast—now it's my turn." Her husband's devilish grin was all the encouragement she needed.

When they finally settled into their bed for the night, Tony pulled Claire close and whispered, "To many more celebrations with Nichol..." He pulled her tighter against his side. "...and more with just the two of us."

"To many more..." Claire's words slipped away as the beat of Tony's heart lulled her to sleep.

Chapter 8

March 2017

Claire

———◆———

Courage is what it takes to stand up and speak; courage is also what it takes to sit down and listen.
—Winston Churchill

DR. CARLY BROWN leaned back in her chair and studied Claire Rawlings. "What makes you think you're ready for that?"

Claire sat taller. She'd been adjusting well to the decrease in medications. Coming off of them was the next logical step. "Don't you think that I am?"

"You seem to be avoiding my question. What makes you think you're ready to stop taking your medications?"

"Well, first, I don't think I need them anymore. I haven't had any problems since I was here at Everwood or issues since the dosage has been decreased. I'm going to all of my sessions, both with you and the family counseling that Tony and I go to each week." She shrugged and a smile graced her lips. "Things are good—better than good. I want to do it on my own, not with the medicine."

Dr. Brown nodded. "There's nothing wrong with needing medication. Millions of people—"

"Yes, millions of people take anti-psychotic medications. The thing is I understand now what happened to me. I know that my mind couldn't handle the reality that I'd lost my family forever, so I went away. But I didn't lose them. I didn't lose Nichol or Tony. I have them and I'm happy, really happy."

"We're doing tests, monitoring the levels. We've made a significant reduction. These are not medications that you can just stop. It's a process."

Claire nodded. "Can we cut the dosage again?"

"It appears you're in a hurry. Is that true?"

Claire fidgeted with the cuff of her blouse's sleeve. "No, I'm not."

"All right, you're not. Tell me what's been going on. What have you been doing?"

"So much!" Her emerald eyes glistened. "I've learned one thing, well, I've learned a lot of things, but one thing is that every day is a gift. Nichol's a gift. We missed so much time with her. I was afraid that it would never seem like we were truly a family, but it does." She looked away from Dr. Brown's knowing gaze. "I see the way Emily and John look at her sometimes. I know I shouldn't feel jealous, but I do. They shared a part of her life that Tony and I'll never have."

"How does that make you feel to say you're jealous?"

"Like I'm a terrible person. They helped Nichol and us. I should be grateful, not jealous, and now they're having another baby."

"When is your sister's baby due?" Dr. Brown asked.

"In another month. We went shopping for clothes the other day."

"And Emily is having a...?"

87

"A girl," Claire confirmed. "They're having a little girl, and they're naming her after our grandmother Elizabeth."

"How do you feel about Emily and John having a girl?"

"I'm happy. They're excited and I'm excited for them. I can't help but think that in some way she's replacing Nichol. I don't mean that in a bad way. But for over two years they had two children. Soon they will again."

"Is Nichol replaceable?"

Claire's eyes widened. "No! That's not what I mean." She stood and walked about the office, trying to collect her thoughts. "They were a family of four and now they will be again."

"And that makes you feel..?"

Claire spun toward the doctor. "Happy for them, and maybe a little sad for me."

"Help me understand."

A tear teetered on Claire's lid. "They're getting their family back, the one they had with Nichol. Tony and I will never get that time back." She dejectedly sat and let out a sigh. "That's why I think we should cut my medications—not just cut but stop them."

"Help me out. How does your sister's baby relate to your medicines?" Dr. Brown leaned forward. "Before we continue to decrease and maybe even eliminate some of your medications—"

"*Maybe* eliminate?" Claire tried to clarify.

"Listen to me. I'd like you to be honest with yourself and with me. Why do you really want to be off the medication?"

Tears momentarily blurred Claire's vision. "I know why."

Dr. Brown didn't speak; instead, she nodded.

"I want to be me. The medications keep me in the middle. Does that make sense?"

"Explain, Claire. Help me understand."

Claire sat taller. "I feel happy and sad. I become aroused. But it's all in moderation. I want the highs and lows I used to have. I don't want to feel detached. It's gotten a little better since you've made some adjustments. I want it to get all the way better."

"Hmm. Those are valid requests. I know that from what you've told me you and your husband have had an intense past. Do you not feel like it's the same?"

Claire shrugged. "It is and it isn't. We've both been through a lot. We've changed. Our everyday life is everything I'd ever dreamt of. And yes, we're physically compatible."

"Well, *physically compatible*... that sounds sexually pleasing."

Claire stood again, walked toward the side of the room, and pretended to look at the pictures she'd seen a million times.

"What is it, Claire?"

"I think the medicine makes it more difficult for me to..."

"To become aroused?" Dr. Brown suggested.

Claire nodded. "I think there's something wrong with me. When we're alone together, and Tony's all sweet and loving, I'm not as into it as I am when he's more possessive and demanding." Claire turned toward Dr. Brown. "He's not mean. I don't mean that. I just like it when... jeez, I can't believe I'm saying this."

"What you're feeling isn't wrong. The medications you've been prescribed can affect arousal and sexual functioning; however, for you it appears more than that. Go on."

"I like when we're equal partners outside of the bedroom, but in it, I like when he's in charge. I don't want to need him to be that way. I want to be able to like the other times too."

"Tell me about the other times."

Claire sighed and closed her eyes. Sitting back down, thoughts of her husband came to her mind. "He can be romantic and giving.

After all of this time he can take a normal night and make it feel like a date, as if it doesn't matter that he spent his day making multi-million dollar decisions, as if now I'm the only other person in the world." Her heart fluttered. "Honestly, that's the man I fell in love with: the one who would listen to me and talk with me. I didn't have anyone else: he was my world. I knew that he had other people, and I guess I felt special because he chose to spend his time with me." Claire met Dr. Brown's eyes. "Now, we both have other people and he can still do that, still make me feel like it's only the two of us."

Dr. Brown didn't speak.

"Those times make me love him more than ever, and I want to reciprocate his love and gestures. I just feel like sometimes there's a fog, a barrier that I have to push through. And when I hear a more demanding tone or feel a more possessive touch that block goes away." Claire shook her head. "Before the medication I didn't feel like this."

"What happened early on in your relationship when you heard that tone or felt that touch?"

Claire swallowed the lump forming in her throat. "I responded."

"You responded. What if you weren't in the mood?"

"It didn't matter." Tears streamed from the corner of Claire's eyes as she closed her lids. Finally she asked, "Are you saying that that's what's happening? I'm responding now, like a conditioned response?"

"What do you think?"

"I think I love my husband and I want to be with him. I miss experiencing the sweet times and the more erotic times. I want it all."

They sat in silence as more tears formed in Claire's eyes. Her thoughts swirled. This wasn't where she planned on this session going. She loved Tony with all her heart and soul. She adored the man who made her feel as though the sun rose and set because of her, and she craved the man who craved her. As she contemplated the two Tonys, thoughts of Emily's baby infiltrated. Claire knew it wasn't right for her to be jealous of her sister, not after all she'd done for her. However, Emily had experienced all the baby firsts, twice. She'd had them with both Michael and Nichol. Though it was selfish, Claire realized what she truly wanted. It wasn't only to feel everything, no matter how intense. No, she wanted more than that.

Wiping her eyes with a tissue, Claire faced Dr. Brown. "I want another baby. I want to experience the time we missed with Nichol. I don't want to replace her. That's not what I mean. But we missed so much. She was a baby—a tiny baby, three months old. We missed her crawling, walking, talking. When we got her back she was a little person with a mind of her own." Claire wiped the tear from her cheek. "She's the most beautiful, amazing child, but I want what I missed."

Claire's chest suddenly felt lighter with the verbalization of her realization. It was cathartic. Subconsciously, she'd been thinking about another baby for months now. Every time she talked with Emily about Beth, Courtney about Julia, or saw Sue with her two children. But up until this moment, Claire hadn't admitted the truth to anyone, not even herself. Getting off the medication was more than about the way it made her feel. It was about wanting another baby.

"Have you spoken to your husband about any of this?"

Claire shook her head.

"Why?"

"Because, the sex stuff... I don't want him to feel like he needs to behave one way or another for me. I want his true emotions and that's what I want to give him."

"That's fair. What about a baby? Having another baby isn't a unilateral decision."

"I know that, and honestly, I think I just fully realized my desire right here, right now."

Dr. Brown leaned back against her chair. "How do you feel about wanting a baby?"

A smile crept onto Claire's face. "Excited and relieved. It's something that's been lurking for a while, and now, I know that's what I want." Claire didn't want to need these sessions, but maybe she did, maybe the talking did help. "Doctor, I also know my husband. He'll be worried about me. He's already concerned about the decrease in medications. He'll be overly concerned about my getting off of them altogether. And when it comes to a baby, he'll be worried because... because Nichol's delivery was rather difficult."

"Yes, I saw your medical records. The doctor who delivered her sent me his notes."

"But this time... this time will be different. We aren't on some tropical island. I'll be here in Iowa. Things will be better."

"Are you trying to convince me or yourself?"

Claire shrugged. "I'd be lying if I said the idea of giving birth again didn't make me nervous. Tony told me about Nichol's delivery. I don't remember any of it."

Dr. Brown's eyes widened.

"I was unconscious. It's not a matter of selective memory, if that's what you're wondering."

"I have a statement from your husband, one I've had since you were first admitted. I seem to recall the doctor asking him to make a choice."

Claire sat, nodded again, as the lump re-formed in her throat.

"He told me. He said that he told the doctor there was no choice. He had to save us both." A smirk came to her lips. "Anthony Rawlings has a history of getting what he wants."

Dr. Brown's expression hardened. "What if he doesn't want another baby?"

Claire's heartbeat quickened. "He will," she said confidently.

"You know my thoughts. First we need to take our time decreasing the medications, but as we do that, I recommend that you and your husband discuss the expansion of your family. I understand your desire to get off the medicine; however, that isn't the only step to becoming pregnant."

"I know," Claire admitted. "I'm well aware of how it works."

Dr. Brown looked at the clock in the corner of her computer screen. "My only concern is that you thoroughly consider the positive and negative consequences of this train of thought."

"Oh, Dr. Brown, let me assure you, I'm thoroughly aware of consequences."

LATER THAT NIGHT, Claire stood at the window in their master bedroom suite and gazed out over the darkened backyard.

Seven years.

She wasn't sure why the thought hadn't occurred to her until now, late at night on March 19th, but it hadn't. Claire was glad she'd been busy talking to Dr. Brown about her medications, sex, and a baby. The thoughts that she was currently having were not ones she wanted to analyze. Heaven knows they'd been analyzed enough, by her, her doctors, therapists, family, Tony, his therapists, even the whole damn world. Maybe it was that *Rawls-Nichols* card that arrived today. Did the sender remember this date before Claire?

If she did, it didn't narrow the list of suspected senders. The date, March 19, 2010, was well documented in both Meredith's book and in court records.

As Claire looked out to the moonlit trees and beyond she couldn't help but remember the same night seven years ago. The view before her wasn't the same as the one she saw that night from her suite. Reaching for the handle to the glass door leading to their balcony, Claire fought the urge to open it, to assure that it *would* open. Slowly, she pulled her hand away. The door would open, just as the front door did or any other. Hell, she'd been to Cedar Rapids just today. Everything was different than it had been. The whole damn house was different, and yet it was the same. So many things had changed. Claire wished that some of her memories would be forgotten and gone forever.

The man she was currently married to was nothing like the man of seven years ago. She was different too. They'd both been through so much, too much. However, as Claire stared at the woods she knew that there would forever be triggers. She shook her head. Courtney was right. She even processed her own thoughts like her therapists. Dr. Brown called them that—triggers. They couldn't be predicted. Although one would think the date would be a predictable annual trigger.

While she, Tony, and Nichol celebrated St. Patrick's Day with green-frosted cookies and giggled about the way the frosting turned their tongues and teeth green, she had a fleeting thought of a St. Patrick's Day seven years ago. That was it—just a thought.

Now, staring out onto the silver barren trees and feeling the cool glass, the memories were stronger. Maybe it was the fear she harbored about discontinuing her medications. Maybe it was the thought of having another child. Maybe it was her reality. The past would never fully go away.

Lost in those thoughts, Claire momentarily tensed as warm breath skirted her neck. Just as quickly, she relaxed against the solid chest behind her. "Penny for your thoughts," his deep voice murmured near her ear.

Shaking her head, Claire swallowed. For a small sliver of time her thoughts had been dark: of dark eyes that threatened and demanded. It was a rabbit hole she refused to explore. Turning, she bravely looked up into those same eyes; however, the eyes before her were no longer hungry. They were dark with love and compassion, understanding and kinship. They were her drug of choice, the force that kept her grounded while allowing her to fly. Shaking her head, she replied, "I was just thinking. That's all." Her answer was neither a lie nor the truth.

Tony gently reached for her chin. "You've been quiet all night. How did your session with Dr. Brown go today?"

Lifting herself on the tips of her toes, Claire kissed Tony's lips. The connection as they touched was the electricity she needed to jolt her back to her senses. The warmth traveled from her lips to her core confirming that the man who held her close was her other half, what she needed and wanted every day of her life. The two years they'd been apart had been hell. She wouldn't allow that to ever happen again—she couldn't.

Reaching for her shoulders, Tony eased Claire away and stared deep into her eyes. As much as she now loved his dark, penetrating gaze, it also scared her. Not that she feared him. She feared his knowledge of her, his ability to see deep into her soul like no one else. Quickly she diverted her eyes and leaned into his chest.

"We talked about my further decreasing my medications. Dr.

Brown said the process needs to be monitored with blood work, but she said that if I think I'm ready, she'll support me."

His arms wrapped around her petite frame. "There's no rush. Making sure you're all right is most important. Maybe you should wait a while."

Claire looked back up. "It's what *I* want. I'm tired of the way they make me feel. I want to be me—totally me."

"You are you," Tony encouraged. "Listen to your doctor."

"I am." Claire's neck stiffened and her tone dripped with her pent-up angst. "Talk to her if you want. She said it could be done. We just need to monitor everything. I'm not crazy," she added defensively.

His warm embrace pulled her closer. "I didn't say that. No one said that. Well..." He chuckled. "I suppose there are quite a few who've thought we're both crazy for being back together, but for the most part, those people don't really know us. If you have to be crazy to let me back into your life..." He gently kissed her lips. "...then, Mrs. Rawlings, I'm glad you are."

Pulling her hand, Tony led her away from the window toward the sofa. "How about if I start a fire, or are you ready for bed?"

Claire tilted her head to the side. "A fire would be nice. I'd like to talk for a little bit."

"Or," he said with more than a hint of his devilish grin, "we could do something else?"

It was the tone that stirred her, the one she craved. Yet right now she needed to face her fears. Dr. Brown was right. Having a baby wasn't a unilateral decision. Claire needed to be honest with her husband. Feigning a smile, Claire replied, "Let's talk first. You can start the fire, and I'll get ready for bed."

Tony nodded as he turned toward the large fireplace. Though it wasn't as massive as the one in their old estate, it had the similarity that always caused Claire to pause: her portrait hung directly above the mantle. Nichol called it Claire's princess picture. Perhaps she wasn't truly a princess; however, she'd felt like one on that day. Their first wedding was like a fairytale, fast and make-believe. What they shared at that time wasn't like the love they had today. Their paths had taken them on some dark journeys and somehow they found their way back together. Their love today was deeper and more intense than it had been. It had been tested by fire—like the one Tony was building—and came back stronger.

"Claire?"

Her attention shifted to her husband. "Yes?"

"You haven't moved. Didn't you say you were going to get ready for bed?"

She looked down at herself. "Yes, I guess I'm thinking about too much. I'll be right back."

Moments later, she came from their large attached bath, clad in a nightgown and robe. With her face washed and teeth brushed, she gave Tony's cheek a mint-flavored kiss and tugged his hand to move him toward the sofa. Once he sat, she settled in front of him, her back against his chest. Reaching for his large hand, she wrapped herself in his arms.

His voice murmured near her ear. "Now, my dear, what has you so lost in thought? What do you want to talk about?"

With a sigh, Claire relaxed against his chest. "I want to talk about the medication thing. I want you to be honest with me."

"I'm always honest with you. Are you saying that you're not?"

"No. I don't think I was dishonest... not on purpose. But today while I was talking to Dr. Brown I realized something."

Tony let out a long breath. "I'm sorry. I don't know how many ways or how many times I need to say it, but I am."

Claire peered over her shoulder. His dark eyes swirled with remorse. Momentarily, with her concentration on the prospect of having another baby, she'd forgotten the memories she'd been confronting at the window. Suddenly, the sadness in his gaze and tone brought them all back. Reaching up to his cheek, Claire gently palmed the five o'clock shadow. "Tony, that's not what I want to talk about. We've talked it to death. It's funny. I didn't even make the association with the date until a few minutes ago. I think that's a good thing."

"So that wasn't what you and Dr. Brown discussed today?"

"No, believe it or not, it wasn't. Like I said, I hadn't even thought about it until a little while ago."

"Well, I've been thinking about it all day. I've been watching you, waiting for you to bring it up. I thought you were just trying to spare me by not mentioning it."

"Tony..." her voice held more of a plea than she wanted to admit "...I'll talk about it if you want. I'm also fine with not making a big deal about it. Hell, we have anniversaries of many things all the time. Seven years ago..." She felt him tense behind her. "...I woke up on this estate. Today it's our home, one we share with our daughter."

"The thing is," Tony began, "I know it was wrong. The world knows it was wrong. Hell, I spent two years paying the price for it being wrong." His voice softened. "And you've paid more than that, but right now, with the two of us here and Nichol down the hall, I can't say I regret bringing you here. I should, but I don't."

Claire closed her eyes and swallowed. "Maybe we *are* both crazy?"

Tony's arms tightened around her. "What does that mean? You regret it?"

"No, I don't. I regret many things. Being with you right here, right now, isn't one of them."

"I regret the way I treated you, the things that happened... but bringing you into my life..." His lips touched her neck sending chills down her body. "...I'll never regret."

Claire craned her neck allowing her husband better access. As his caresses deepened, she remembered her mission. "I want to talk about the future." He continued kissing. "Please, this is important."

Taking a deep breath, Tony sat straighter. Though his lips were obeying, in the small of Claire's back she could feel another part of him that had other plans. "What, my dear? What about our future? I must say, I like that topic better than our past."

The tips of her fingers traced an imaginary path over the arm that was wrapped about her midsection. "Tony, I realized today while I was talking to Dr. Brown that I have multiple reasons why I want to get off my medications—"

"Wait!" His voice boomed through their suite. "Off? You said *decrease*, not *off*."

Claire turned to face him. "Well, it has to start as a decrease and then it'll eventually be tapered off completely."

"No, not until I hear from the doctor that you can do that. I'm not losing you again."

"Tony," she tried to hide the hurt from her voice. "I'm not going anywhere. Dr. Brown and I discussed it. I went wherever I went—in my head—because I thought you and Nichol were gone. I thought I killed you! I know you're here. I know Nichol's here. This, the real world, is where I want to be. I don't need medicine to keep me here."

Though his dark eyes reflected his unspoken argument, he stopped the words from coming. Finally, he replied, "Next week, I'm going with you to your appointment. I'll have my schedule cleared. I want to hear this from her."

This wasn't going the way she wanted it, but Claire knew if Tony planned to talk to Dr. Brown, she wanted to be the one to mention her desires for a baby. She didn't want it coming up in a group-therapy session. "That's fine. If it'll make you feel better, I don't care, come to my appointment. Before you do, I need to tell you what I realized."

"Shit, that wasn't it? It wasn't about stopping your medicine?"

"No, it wasn't, well not really." Claire eyed him suspiciously. "Forget it. This doesn't feel like the right time."

Tony cupped her chin. "I'm sorry if my concern for your well-being is spoiling your right time. However, I'm not sorry for being concerned. Tell me what you realized."

She took a deep breath. "Once I'm off the medicine and the doctors clear me physically... I want to be off *all* my medicine." She waited for him to understand. The dark eyes before her confirmed he didn't. "Tony, I want to quit my birth control too." Before he could speak or the shock in his gaze registered, she plowed ahead. "I want another baby."

Perhaps the sofa caught on fire. Had a spark jumped from the stone enclosure to their location? There was no other plausible explanation for the speed at which Tony stood, leaving Claire suddenly alone and chilled from the loss of his embrace.

Running his hand through his mane, Tony declared, "No."

Refusing to submit to the tears that stood at the ready, Claire chose instead to fuel her indignation. Her volume rose with each statement. "No? Excuse me. You can't just say no. If you want to talk about it, fine. If you want a doctor's confirmation, fine. But a blanket CEO-tone *no* is unacceptable."

His gaze continued to be one of disbelief. It was as if he were looking at her trying to distinguish which of her three heads was speaking. Finally, he spoke, "That's too bad, because that's all you're getting. I'm in shock that you'd even consider such a thing. What is it? Is it because of Emily? Is it all her baby talk that has you thinking this way? Maybe you should spend your time elsewhere?"

What the hell?

Claire stood. "I'll spend my time wherever I want. And yes, the talk of Baby Beth is part of it. More than that, it's Nichol. Perhaps I shouldn't spend my time with her either?" The last part of Claire's statement dripped with ire and sarcasm.

"You're being ridiculous. Nichol doesn't have you worked up. It's Emily. She—"

"She's my sister and she's having a baby. But it *is* Nichol. I keep thinking about how much we missed with her. Didn't you want to experience all those milestones?"

Tony's chest expanded and contracted with each breath. "I did." His eyes narrowed. "I wasn't the one who kept those milestones away from me."

Claire slapped her hands against her sides. "This isn't about Emily."

Spinning first in place, Tony then paced to the windows and back. "How the fuck did this happen? Ten minutes ago I wanted to make love to my wife. Now we're screaming at one another. There. Is. Nothing. To. Fight. About! We. Are. Not. Having. Another. Baby."

"You're right, Tony, about fighting, but you're not right about a baby. It's my body. If I want to have another baby, I'll have one. I was ready to do it without you the first time. I can do it without you now."

He seized her shoulders. "Stop it. You're not doing anything without me. Don't you get it? Do you have any idea how close to death you were when Nichol was born? I lived through two days of hell on earth thinking you wouldn't survive her birth. There would've been no escape from the pain if you had died. Do you know who would've been responsible for that? Me!" His back stiffened. "I've been in that position more than once. I won't do it again."

Claire saw the man she loved with all of her heart and soul. She saw the pain and anguish and heard the same emotions in his words. Her voice calmed. "Tony, we're not on a deserted island. We're here, in Iowa, in the United States. I'll have the best medical care that money can buy. I'll be all right."

His lips pressed together in a rigid line.

She lifted herself on her tiptoes and gently kissed his scowl. "It can't happen right away, but I want to begin the process. Please..." She kissed him again. "...don't say no and end this discussion. Say you'll think about it. Say you'll talk with the doctors. Say you'll support the idea."

"I so want to end this discussion."

"Think about all we missed. Think about Nichol learning to crawl and walk. Think about her first word. Don't close your mind to having another baby. Please don't say no, say you'll—"

Tony stopped her words with a kiss. "I'll think about it, but know your safety is number one. Will you at least agree with that?"

Claire smiled. "I agree. I also think that since we know it can't happen yet, we should practice. We got lucky with Nichol, but who knows... this baby may take a lot of trying."

Closing his eyes, Tony shook his head. "Yes, Mrs. Rawlings, always the master negotiator."

"Well, you know what they say about practice?"

Tony backed Claire toward the bed. Once her knees buckled, she gazed up at him. "My dear, I'll practice as much as you desire, but I've told you before that I will not survive without you." He ran his fingers through her long, dark hair, fanning it around her face. "You are my everything. All of these plans must meet the doctor's approval. If they don't, the answer is unequivocally no."

Claire tilted her head and reached for his hand. "So you'd cut me off?"

His devilish grin returned as the fire from across the room reflected in his sultry gaze. "I've made our fortune with negotiations. I hope you don't think I'm that easy to manipulate."

Leaning back, Claire untied her robe and allowed it to fall from her shoulders. Scooting back on the bed, she looked up at him through her lashes and pushed out her lower lip. "That's all right. If you don't want to practice..."

Within seconds, Tony was crawling toward her, covering her body with his. "I didn't say that. By all means, Mrs. Rawlings, let's work on our technique."

Chapter 9

April 2017

Tony

———◆———

**Part of the healing process is sharing
with other people who care.**
—Jerry Cantrell

TONY SAT ACROSS the desk from Dr. Brown with Claire's hand in his. It wasn't the first time they'd been in her office together; however, it was the first time they'd jointly had such a personal conversation with the good doctor. Fortunately or unfortunately, Tony had become quite adept at speaking with therapists and doctors. He knew how each one of his words as well as the inflection of his voice was dissected and scrutinized. Maybe scrutinized held too negative of a connotation; perhaps analyzed was a better description.

Nevertheless, as they sat across from the attractive blonde psychiatrist, Tony couldn't help but do the same. He analyzed each word she said as well as her nonverbal responses. This ability didn't begin with his induction into the world of psychoanalysis: it was what he'd done his entire life, how he'd made Rawlings Industries into an international conglomerate. Even with technology and the modernization of video and web conferences, Anthony Rawlings would watch and listen to his associates as well as his business adversaries. Many times it wasn't what was said that was vital to negotiations, it was what wasn't said.

"I understand your concern, Anthony. Over the past few months we've completely eliminated the anti-psychotic medications, and it appears to be without incident. As you're aware, Claire's still on a less potent anti-anxiety medication... two medications," Dr. Brown corrected as she glanced at the computer screen only she was privy to see.

"Without incident?" Tony asked. "What were you expecting?"

"We don't know what to expect. Each patient is unique." Turning her gaze to Claire, she asked, "Claire, we discussed this the other day, but please tell me if anything has changed. Are you noticing any side effects from the medication changes?"

"I'm noticing good side effects. I'm beginning to feel more like myself. I don't feel as stuck in the middle."

"What about your sleeping problems?" Tony asked. "Do you think that can be attributed to the medication changes?"

Dr. Brown looked from Tony to Claire. "What sleeping problems? You didn't mention anything about that."

Claire's green eyes, boring holes through her husband, returned to Dr. Brown. "I'm not having sleeping problems. I wake up sometimes. That's all."

Tony knew Claire didn't approve of his sharing; however, this was her health they were discussing and he wouldn't compromise, not even for her. Steeling his shoulders, he continued, "And she has trouble going back to sleep. Sometimes at night she talks in her sleep. I can't understand it, but whatever it is seems to be upsetting her."

The doctor leaned forward. "Claire, this can't work if you're not honest with me. Are you having nightmares?"

Claire sat taller. "I honestly don't know. I've had a few dreams I remember, but most of the time I don't. I wake knowing that there was something going on, but I can't remember particulars."

"Whatever it is, it's enough to have her awake for hours."

"Tony! Stop," Claire demanded. "I'm fine. Everyone dreams."

Pressing his lips together he looked back across the desk to Dr. Brown.

"Yes, Claire," the doctor began. "Everyone dreams. And to be totally forthright, dreaming is a positive outlet, if you will. Differentiating a dream from reality is the crucial distinction. I don't like that the dreams agitate you. That makes me leery to make any further adjustments on your remaining medications." Before Claire could refute her statement, Dr. Brown went on, "You need to be honest with yourself."

Claire blinked her eyes. "I am being honest. I don't know exactly what the dreams are about. I do know they aren't the exact same. But I'll reiterate: I'm ready to get off all the medicine. I think I'll sleep better without it."

"You never had nightmares before you were on these meds, ever?" the doctor asked.

Tony looked to his right. He knew she did. He remembered the nightmares she had after the Patrick Chester incident, the long nights sitting outside on the patio, looking up at the stars and wishing he could take it all away. He remembered the helplessness as she'd succumb to her tears and melt against his chest. It took months before those fears finally came to rest. His overwhelming desire to help her ease out of this conversation squelched his reasoning to continue it.

"Doctor, can't some of this be normal?" Tony hated using that word. He squeezed Claire's hand, hopeful that she wouldn't assume he was insinuating anything about her was abnormal.

"It is. Dreams are our subconscious way of dealing with stress."

"Isn't it a good thing that Claire's dealing with it?"

Dr. Brown looked back to Claire. "Do you know what the stressor is? Do you know the trigger?"

Claire looked at Tony. He saw the answer in her eyes. The FBI didn't want them mentioning the mailings, yet if he truly thought about it, there seemed to be a correlation. The nightmares would come for a day or two following a new *Rawls-Nichols* mailing.

"The two of you must be straightforward. Is there a problem that I'm unaware exists? Could this be about another child?"

They both turned back to Dr. Brown. "No," Claire answered matter-of-factly. "We've discussed it. As long as you and my other doctors are on board, we're both happy about the prospect of another baby."

Dr. Brown turned her gaze to Tony.

"I've made no secret out of the fact that I'm concerned about my wife; however, the more she and I discuss it, the more I realize I'd love to have another child." He smirked to himself. Damn, that wasn't a sentence he could've predicted uttering five years ago. "But," he added, "Claire's health is the most important. If she can't handle it, then it won't happen. Or..." He looked to Claire. "...we could adopt."

"We could?" Her emerald eyes glistened toward his. It wasn't a subject they'd ever broached. "You're truly on board with this. You want another child that much?"

Seeing the sparkle behind her gaze told him that this was what she wanted. "I am and I do."

Dr. Brown cleared her throat. "I'm glad to hear you've made this decision together. It's not my job to crush my patient's dreams, but I think you should consider your pasts, both of you. Adoption, legal adoption, requires extensive background screenings. I'm not saying that you wouldn't pass. I'm saying that even with the financial means, there's no guarantee."

Claire didn't seem to be hearing Dr. Brown; instead, her eyes were still fixed on Tony's. Finally, she turned to the woman across the desk. "I know what my nightmares were about. I know what triggers them. It isn't anything between Tony and I, not really. We're just not at liberty to discuss it fully."

Before anyone could speak, Claire added, "But in all honesty, I don't think that was the only stimulus. I've been worried that Tony didn't want another child as much as I did. I realize I'm asking a lot." She continued on as if he weren't sitting right next to her, their knees and hands touching. "Tony and I have discussed many different issues that may arise with another child. One obvious issue..." She turned and grinned. "...is age. Sorry." She shrugged her shoulders. "It's not just him. I'm no spring chicken either. I'm thirty-three, but Tony is fifty-two. I've been afraid that if this medication doesn't get out of my system soon, it will be too late."

Claire looked at Dr. Brown as a renegade tear made its way down her cheek. "I'm not saying it's caused me nightmares, but I wake up thinking about it and have difficulty falling back to sleep. I've felt pressured that things must move fast or they never will."

"And now?" Dr. Brown asked.

"Now, I know it doesn't matter. He *is* behind me on this."

"Anthony?"

"Yes, Dr. Brown, I'm supportive of another child. Whether it's our biological child or we're fortunate enough to adopt, I want

Claire to be happy and," he added with emphasis, "I would like another child. I never imagined being a father, never even entertained the idea. Claire's changed my life in ways I'll never be able to articulate. Being a husband and a father has brought me more joy than any business deal or personal quest. Nichol is our world. It seems as though Claire's done well with the medication changes thus far. Whatever you and her other doctors recommend, we'll do."

"Claire, we've determined that some of your dreams make you agitated. Does anything else upset you?"

Claire exhaled. "Yes. Things upset me and things excite me. None of it becomes obsessive or overbearing. It's life. Life has ups and downs. I like them. I like being happy and sad. I like when a book makes me cry or Nichol makes me laugh. I like when my husband's gaze and gentle kiss give me goose bumps with anticipation. Those are all coming back to me and I want it one hundred percent."

Dr. Brown nodded. "I'll authorize it." Her gaze went to Claire. "Thank you for your answer. For all of this to work, I need your continued honesty. You also need to see your gynecologist before ending your birth control. This is the beginning of April. It takes a month, perhaps two, to have all of the anxiety medications out of your system. I recommend alternative forms of birth control in the meantime."

Tony wondered when in his life it had become commonplace for him to have so many people who had a vote in his personal dealings. At one time, he'd never have sat and listened as someone else told him what he was to do and not do. And then, as quickly as that thought occurred, Claire's eyes met his. In her gaze he heard her unspoken soliloquy. It told him everything he needed to hear. His wife was happy, excited, and encouraged.

Though Tony wished he could've been with her in her time of need, here in this very facility, he was relieved he hadn't been. Oh, he would have spent every day with her in hopes of bringing her back to reality sooner; however, the reports Roach had shown him broke his heart. He couldn't imagine seeing those emerald eyes lifeless or without spark. From the first time he'd seen Claire, up close and in person, he was drawn to the life in her beautiful eyes.

Now, the next step was guaranteeing the best doctor in the fuck'n world to assure that if Claire did become pregnant, her delivery would be nothing like what they'd endured in paradise. Obviously they were both entering into this prospect of parenthood with more forethought than they did with Nichol.

Claire

LATER THAT NIGHT, Claire slipped between the soft sheets of their large bed, unable to keep the smile from her face. All she could think about was the fact that Tony really and truly said he'd wanted another child. He didn't say it just in front of her, but in front of Dr. Brown. Claire was more excited than she'd been about anything in a long time. Oh, each day they spent with Nichol was a gift, and their family had become content and stable over the last six months, but excitement and building anticipation had not been part of Claire's day-to-day repertoire for a very long time.

Its presence was like a tiny bud of hope taking root in her being. It was as if she could feel it within her, giving her a promise of more. Its tentacles wrapped around her heart, embraced, and warmed her soul in a way she'd forgotten. The whole world seemed brighter. It wasn't only spring in Iowa, but also in her. The world was being reborn. Small specks of green had formed on the trees outside of her windows. Hues of red sprinkled the landscape as redbud trees came back from their winter dormancy. Even the grass was growing and filled their many yards with color.

For the first time in many springs, Claire was part of it. She was there with Nichol's hand in hers as they walked the paths through the gardens and talked about the flowers peeking up through the earth and ones that together they'd plant. She was with Tony on their balcony or patio in the evenings as the scent of cut grass and sound of maturing insects filled their senses. Most importantly, she was alive, aware, and budding with excitement about their future.

The bed shifted, and Claire turned toward her handsome husband.

"My dear." He kissed her cheek. "Pray tell, what has that beautiful smile on those lips and faraway look in your magnificent eyes?"

His mischievous grin, the scent of his cologne, and his intuitive question all brought Claire back to the present. Her body responded, the way she'd been wanting. Scooting closer, she leaned into his embrace, both of them sitting against the massive headboard with his arm over her shoulder. She loved the way she fit perfectly against him. Suddenly she wished he'd taken off his t-shirt before joining her. Her fingers longed to feel the softness of his chest hair; instead, she settled for nuzzling closer to his warmth.

"I'm happy." Her simplistic answer held so many truths. Some couples may need more: an expansion upon the statement, perhaps clarification: Why was she happy? Did one thing happen to make her happy? Had she been unhappy?

Neither Tony nor Claire needed that confirmation. It was the blessing and the curse of a history and an openness that surpassed all obstacles. His embrace tightened as their lips engaged. With each touch, the desire within her grew. Her nightgown-covered skin sought the sensation of his warmth. Her nipples hardened as her breasts ached for his touch. Words weren't needed as they melted into one another and her petite hands worked their way under his shirt, finding the soft hair covering his broad chest.

Tony slowly reached for the hem of her nightgown, and with his devilish grin, whispered, "Well, perhaps we should do some of that practicing you mentioned, before we have to heed the doctor's alternative recommendations."

Claire nodded, wanting their bodies to become one without barriers. "I like practicing," she murmured as she moved closer to where his intentions were becoming clearer.

"Momma," Nichol said sleepily, as the door to their suite opened.

Both Tony and Claire turned to see their daughter rubbing her eyes and moving toward them.

Stifling their smiles, Claire adjusted her nightgown as Tony groaned and straightened his shirt.

"What is it, honey?" Claire asked as Nichol climbed up onto their bed. Before their daughter answered, she crawled between them and slid under the covers. Once settled, Claire put her arm around her, and Nichol snuggled closer.

"I missed-ed you. I woke up and got scared."

Letting out a deep sigh, Tony wrapped the two of them in his embrace. "Scared? Princess, what were you scared about?"

Nichol shrugged.

"You know that with your momma, me, Shannon, Mr. Phil, Mr.

Eric, and Miss Taylor, you're the safest little princess in the whole world, don't you?"

Nichol nodded. "You're not there."

"Where, honey? Where aren't we?"

"In my room. I'm all by myself. I heard somefing..." Her brown eyes widened. "...under my bed." She leaned into Tony's chest. "I think I should sleeps wif you."

Claire grinned above Nichol's head, her gaze meeting Tony's. "Honey," Claire began, "we've talked about this. You have your own bed. This is Momma and Daddy's bed."

"I don't like my bed. I like yours."

"We like ours too, princess. But it isn't big enough for all of us."

Nichol's dark hair swung over her eyes as her head moved dramatically from side to side. "It is. See, I fits right here."

Though Claire wanted Nichol to feel safe, their child psychologist had been very clear on her opinion of children sleeping in their parents' bed. Giving in, even one time, she'd warned, and a pattern would be set. "How about Daddy and I take you back to your room. Daddy will check under your bed and make sure there isn't anything there making noise. Then we can snuggle with you and read one more story? Will that make you feel better?"

Nichol shrugged again. "Why can't I stay here? I promise I won't wiggle."

Tony laughed as he playfully tickled their daughter. Her pouting lips sprang into a smile as her legs and arms began to flail. "You won't wiggle? You won't wiggle?" he asked jokingly. "You're doing a lot of wiggling right now."

"Stop, Daddy!" Nichol managed through her roars of laughter.

"Tony, she's never going to go back to sleep—"

His grin and wink came as his hands stopped tickling and

Nichol's pleas turned to a sigh. "Miss Rawlings," Tony said as he eased back the covers, stood, and offered Nichol his hand. "It seems as though you have in fact wiggled. That means it's time for your momma and me to escort you back to your own room."

Though she worked hard to pout, her big dark eyes sparkled with adoration. "You'll look under my bed?"

"Yes, I promise."

With that, Nichol stood on the bed and flung herself into Tony's arms. "You have to read me one more story too."

"I do? I thought that was Momma's job."

"Nope," Nichol replied as Claire donned her robe and the three of them made their way out the door. Stepping into the corridor, she continued, "Momma's gonna listen, just like me."

Low lights led the way from the master bedroom suite to Nichol's room, only one door down and across the hall. Turning on the light on her bedside stand, Tony handed Nichol to Claire before bending down and searching beneath the skirt of the canopy bed. Nichol buried her head in the crook of Claire's neck as Tony announced, "Oh my."

"What?" Claire asked with genuine curiosity.

With a huge grin, Tony moved to stand and extended his hand. Within his grasp was a remote control puppy, obviously low on batteries. Every few seconds, one of its legs moved, creating a faint grinding noise.

"Your puppy!" Claire exclaimed. Nichol's head popped up, and she reached for the mechanical dog.

"Bad puppy!" she said with a smile.

"He's not bad," Tony explained. "He just wanted your attention. If he'd have been quiet under there you may have forgotten about him."

Claire set Nichol on her bed and took the puppy. "Let me turn him off. In the morning, we'll find some more batteries so he can play with you."

"Okay," Nichol replied, stifling a yawn and climbing under the covers. "I fought it was a monster."

"A monster? Not in our house. Didn't you know?" Tony asked.

Nichol looked up with wide eyes. "What?"

"No monsters are allowed past the gates. It's a rule," Tony assured.

Lying down next to Nichol, Claire grinned up at Tony. "If you're done with your rules, we're waiting for our story."

Reaching for a book from their daughter's bookshelf, Tony's dark eyes gleamed. "Yes, I'll give you both a story, and then..." His brows rose with his unspoken meaning.

"And then you'll remember to lock the door?" Claire whispered with a smirk, her comment going unnoticed by the beautiful little girl snuggling into her side. Already Nichol's eyes were half closed as she rubbed her cheek against Claire's soft cashmere robe. Looking up to her husband, Claire said, "You'd better hurry, if she's going to hear any of—"

"*Goodnight Moon...*" Tony began his voice low and strong. "In the great green room..."

Closing her eyes, Claire absorbed her daughter's radiating warmth as the baritone words filled the lavender suite. With each page, Nichol's breathing steadied until the rhythmic cadence told them that she was once again sound asleep. Undaunted, Tony continued.

Claire imagined having two children vying for their attention, and with all her heart, she knew that as full of love as she felt at that moment, there would always be room for more. Just like John and

Emily accepted Nichol into their family and how they were not so patiently awaiting the arrival of their daughter. Just as she and Tony adored Nichol, they would have another child and that child too would know this sense of love. Unknowingly, the smile returned to her lips. There was no other cause than the truth: she was truly happy.

Chapter 10

Late April 2017

Taylor

————◆————

If you have to do it, then you're doing the right thing.
—Kathy Valentine

MANY OF THE small towns and counties in Minnesota suffered the same nationwide crisis. Promising young minds weren't content to stay; they wanted the glamor of the bigger cities. In Minnesota, that would be Minneapolis or St. Paul. The small town of Olivia, Minnesota, was no different. Located at the junction of Highway 71 and Highway 212, Olivia's claim to fame was its title: Corn Capital of the World. In reality the friendly people of Olivia were determined to survive despite the odds, and in doing so, they openly welcomed new residents. With a strong sense of camaraderie and a median household income of a little over thirty-five thousand, Olivia was not only a good place to live, but it was also a great place for a person with a large severance package to disappear.

Taylor had never met Patricia, but she'd done her research. She knew all that Phil had told her, and because going above and beyond was the way she worked, she knew a little bit more. The Rawlings security team had questions, wanted answers, and wasn't willing to wait on the FBI to provide them. Was Patricia merely a jaded employee who'd had higher expectations for her relationship with her boss, or was her motive more sinister? Taylor's goal was to learn more about the motivation behind Patricia's mailings by integrating herself into Olivia and essentially Patricia's new life.

Looking for the perfect opportunity, it was decided that Taylor would play the role of the granddaughter of an older couple who resided just outside Olivia. They were relatively new to the area and spent their winters in the warmth of Arizona. Currently, they were still living south of Phoenix. Mr. Townsend, the gentleman whom Taylor claimed was her grandfather, had been dealing with various health issues while away. Since most of the people in town knew the Townsends' background, when Taylor entered the local law firm to discuss the deed to her grandparents' home, no one was suspicious.

Wearing her long brown hair down and wavy with her normal suit replaced by jeans and a t-shirt, Taylor looked at least five years younger, and actually resembled the Townsends' granddaughter. There was a time in small-town America when such a deception wouldn't be feasible. However, even with the sense of community, in today's self-absorbed world, people were willing to accept things at face value. Besides, between Taylor's research and Phil's resources, she was well versed on everything the Townsends' granddaughter should know and had the credentials to prove it.

Since moving to Olivia, Patricia had assumed the alias of Melissa Garrison. Melissa worked in the small law practice of Jefferson Diamond, located in a nondescript storefront on Main Street. Most of Olivia was on Main Street or within a block or two in each direction. Upon entering Diamond's storefront, Taylor deduced that Mr. Diamond's office consisted of a reception area with a large wraparound desk and individual office spaces all accessible through doors off the center room. The paneled walls and vinyl chairs were a flashback to the 1970s and a far cry from Patricia's office at Rawlings corporate headquarters in Iowa City.

After only a few minutes of speaking with the office manager, who'd introduced herself as Ami, Taylor caught her first glance of Patricia. Their suspect barely noticed Taylor as she carried a box of files from one room to the other. Though Patricia didn't look exactly like her photographs, Taylor recognized her immediately. Her body shape and features were the same, but she'd changed her hair. No longer was it long and brown. Now she sported a short, spikey deep-red style.

Not long into her conversation with Ami, the two struck up a kind of friendship. It wasn't until Taylor was about to leave and she mentioned staying alone at her grandparents' home that Ami said, "Oh, you can't be all by yourself way out there all night. Why don't you stay in town and have dinner with us?"

Taylor hid her excitement. It was the perfect opportunity to learn more about Patricia. "Well, I'm not sure..."

"Nonsense, we all hang out on Friday nights at the pub on Main. It has pool tables and darts. There's a dance floor..." Ami scrunched her nose and forehead. "...but no one around here dances. If you want clubs like that you need to drive to Minneapolis."

"Are you sure I won't be intruding?" Taylor asked. "I don't want to get in the way of office talk."

"Mel?" Ami called toward the back room. "Do we talk shop at the bar?"

Patricia shook her head as she emerged from the doorway, wiping her hands on her black slacks. "Nope. It's our time to unwind."

"Do you *all* go? How many of you work here?"

Patricia replied, "There's three of us, four if Jefferson goes, but I don't think Janice thinks too much of that. He's only gone twice since I've been working here."

"Jefferson? Oh, Mr. Diamond," Taylor said, playing her part. Speaking of her boss by his first name and mentioning his wife, Taylor wondered if Patricia had set her sights on her new boss as she had her old. If she had, by the look of the law firm, it was a considerable downgrade from Anthony Rawlings. "Well," Taylor continued, "I need to do a few more things for my grandparents. Can I meet you?"

"Sure," Ami replied. "We usually go home and change into jeans and meet there about 6:30. We'll save you a seat."

Ami's perkiness was contagious. If Taylor truly had been the granddaughter of the Townsends', she would enjoy visiting and spending time with her. As it was, Ami's excessive talking was confirmation of information Taylor already knew—that the law firm closed at 5:00 PM. Since it was nearly 3:00 PM now, Phil had two hours to set up surveillance in Patricia's rented home.

Stepping out onto the quaint street, Taylor looked at the bars on her phone in disgust as she tried to call Phil. It wasn't until she was in her car and driving toward Patricia's rented home that she had enough signal to complete the call. *How could these people stand it?* Taylor wondered. Then remembering the old-fashioned bulky phone she'd seen on Ami's desk, she decided that maybe they didn't use cell phones exclusively—like most of the civilized world.

"It's her," Taylor said as Phil answered.

"We knew it was."

"We assumed it, but I'm one hundred percent certain. You have two hours before she gets off work."

Phil laughed. "I'm done. The equipment is set, both in her house and her car. I'll go back to the law office later and set some up there."

"Did you find anything informative in her house?"

"Nothing I want to discuss."

Taylor didn't like his answer, but time had taught her that Phil would share information when he was ready and not a moment sooner. Trying to ease her own concern, she volunteered, "Ami was kind enough to ask me to join them *all* for dinner."

"You didn't have to invite yourself?"

"No, it couldn't have happened more naturally. I also confirmed that all of the women in the firm go out together on Friday nights to unwind. From what *Melissa*..." She emphasized the alias name. "...said, Jefferson Diamond doesn't usually join them. I'll try to learn his location while at dinner and text you."

"There's a front and back entrance to the law office. Since I'm done setting up the surveillance, you watch the back door and I'll watch the front. Hopefully we'll see everyone leave and I can slip in."

Slowing her car, Taylor steered into a driveway and turned around. "All right, boss."

"Taylor?"

"Hmm?"

"Stay hidden."

"Did you feel the need to say that? I told them I was heading out to my grandparents'. Being seen sitting outside their office would give me away. Don't you think?"

"I just have a feeling about this. I have since the first mailing. There *was* something at her house..." He paused. "...I think there's more to it, and I don't want to blow this opportunity to learn what that is."

Taylor nodded to no one. "What? What's at her house?"

"We'll discuss it later."

Though she knew she wouldn't get anything more at this time, she at least knew her gut feeling had been confirmed. "All right. You tell me when you're ready. I'm heading back."

The line disconnected.

The concern in Phil's voice unnerved her. She knew how he felt about the Rawlingses, and honestly, in the past few months she'd come to feel the same, especially about Nichol. The little girl was both spoiled and adorable—not what Taylor had imagined. Nichol was gracious and polite. Even though she had the world by a string, she was still excited by the simplest of things. For lack of a better assessment, Nichol didn't act entitled. Taylor attributed her behavior more to the Vandersols and Mrs. Rawlings than to Mr. Rawlings. When it came to her father, Taylor doubted there was much of anything that Nichol couldn't get and time would tell how that would play out.

Nichol's interaction with the security team was also a source of enjoyment. From what Taylor had heard and been told, neither Phil nor Eric were used to the presence of children. Mrs. Rawlings joked about the learning curve of the men in Nichol's life. Though Phil would never admit it, when Nichol took his hand and looked up at him with her big brown eyes, Taylor saw that he was putty in her little hands.

Taylor had worked temporary security with other wealthy families. The environment with the Rawlings was refreshingly familial and caring. The lack of pretentiousness, especially from Mrs. Rawlings, endeared Taylor to this family. Claire wanted Nichol to feel as if she was surrounded by family, not employees. Not every household could do that. More than once, Phil slipped and referred to them as his family. With Phil having been with them for years, Taylor understood how he could feel that way.

Taylor made her way to the back alley near the law firm, found a safe, inconspicuous parking space, and waited. Upon her arrival, there were three cars parked near the rear entrance. By 5:15 PM, it was down to one. She sent Phil a text message:

"ONLY THE BLACK CRV REMAINS. PATRICIA AND HEATHER LEFT AT 5:00 PM."

Her phone vibrated less than a minute later.

"AMI AND JEFFERSON LEFT THROUGH THE FRONT. HE LOCKED THE DOOR AS HE LEFT."

Taylor replied.

"WHO OWNS THE CRV? I THOUGHT IT WAS AMI'S."

Phil.

"IT IS. SHE WALKED TO THE STORE. GIVE HER A FEW MORE MINUTES."

It wasn't long until Ami came through the rear entrance carrying two brown bags of groceries. Taylor started to type her text, when her phone rang.

"Get out to the Townsends' farmhouse right away."

"Why?" Taylor asked as she started her car.

"From the bug in Patricia's car, I heard her talking to Ami on the phone. Ami went to the grocery store to get you a few things and she's taking them to you right now."

"Shit! She just got in her car. If I leave now, she'll follow me the whole way."

"I'll delay her," Phil assured. "Just get out there. I've disabled the alarm system. Your key will work fine. Turn on some lights. She won't be too far behind you."

Keeping her head low, Taylor eased her car from the parking spot. Her only choice was to drive behind Ami's CRV. Luckily, Ami was still talking on her phone and didn't seem to notice. Just as Taylor made it to the cross street at the end of the block, she saw Phil, in her rearview mirror, approaching Ami's SUV. Taylor didn't know what he was going to do, but whatever it was, she hoped it gave her more than a minute's head start.

Ten minutes later, Taylor turned the key and opened the back door of the Townsends' farmhouse. Linoleum floor, Formica-topped table with padded vinyl chairs, and more Formica on the counters confirmed that she'd entered their kitchen. Momentarily, she wondered if the interior decorating in Olivia was horribly behind the times or had the whole town had gone retro? Hurriedly, Taylor turned on lights. She tried to turn on the TV; however, it seemed that the cable was off; instead of sound, there was only blue screen. On the kitchen counter, nestled between turquoise blue canisters and an electric can opener, was an old clock radio with numbers that flipped instead of a digital readout. *How long had it been since they made those?* Trying for the homey effect, Taylor flipped a switch and country music filled the air. Just as Taylor settled onto a vinyl chair at the kitchen table, she heard the sound of a car coming up the gravel driveway.

Moments later the knock at the door confirmed her visitor. Taylor grinned at how Ami had come to the same door she'd just entered. It seemed real people in rural towns rarely used the front door. They also didn't have staff to welcome their guests. Taking a deep breath, Taylor peered behind the lacy curtain and through the glass. Feigning surprise, she opened the door. "Ami! What are you doing here?"

With a large smile, the blonde office manager handed Taylor one brown paper sack. "You said you were leaving in the morning. Since your grandparents have been out of town for months, I figured there wasn't much here. I thought you might like some coffee. I got a small creamer too."

"Thank you," Taylor replied. "Um, do you want to come in?"

"Just for a second," Ami said, walking into the kitchen. "I wanted to ask you something before we all got together tonight." Her lips momentarily pressed together. "Well, two somethings."

"Okay," Taylor replied as she took the creamer from the bag and placed it in the refrigerator. Her heart skipped a beat as she realized no light came on within the large appliance. Undoubtedly it'd been turned off for the season. She moved quickly, hoping that Ami wouldn't notice. When she turned back around, Ami was busy looking at the collection of plates hanging on the wall. "What did you want to ask?"

"The first one is selfish, but..." She hesitated. "...I'm just going to ask. Since you're looking into the deed, are your grandparents planning to sell?"

Shit! "Ami, with the way Grandpa's been feeling, they really don't know. They just want to cover their bases."

"Will you remember me, if they do?"

Taylor tilted her head to the side. "Remember you? What do you mean?"

Ami reached in her purse and handed Taylor a card. "I recently got my realtor's license and well, you'll meet Heather. She works with us too. She's been doing realty for a while. So to ask you in front of her..." Taylor tried to listen as Ami shared more information about herself in a period of ten minutes than most people do who've known each other for years. When she got to the part about her little boy, Taylor's listening skills went into hyperdrive.

"...we live with my parents. Working for Jefferson will never get me my own house. I really want that for Brian and I'm tired of living under my parents' roof. I didn't realize how much I wanted a place of my own until Mel moved here."

"Mel? Why? Does she make you feel bad about living with your parents?"

Ami shrugged. "Not intentionally, but with the situation with her daughter, she talks about how much better off she'd be living with her. And it made me think about having my own place with Brian." Ami shook her head. "Mel doesn't like hearing me talk about Brian, unless she's talking about how she's going to win back custody and bring Nicole here to live." Ami's eyes got big. "Oh, that's the other thing I wanted to ask you. Do you have kids? If you do, don't mention them tonight. Mel gets very uncomfortable."

"Um, I don't. I'm not married." Taylor spied a rack of wine bottles. She really hoped they weren't being saved for a special occasion. Ami had just opened a treasure box of information, and if the wine would help retrieve more, Taylor was willing to sacrifice. "Would you like some wine before we go to dinner?"

Ami hung her purse on the back of one of the chairs and unzipped her jacket. "You probably think I'm crazy talking about all of this. But the way I see it, you're practically a neighbor. I don't know your grandparents that well, but they're nice people. Sometimes it's easier talking to people you don't know. This town's so small. You can't say anything that the whole town doesn't find out."

It took two tries, but Taylor finally found the glasses. They weren't wine glasses, but they'd do. The next search was for the corkscrew. She found that in the third drawer she tried. Pouring the wine, Taylor pried, "What happened to Mel? Why's she so sensitive?"

Taking a drink—bigger than a sip—Ami began, "Well, it took me awhile to get the information. Apparently her ex is a piece of work. She won't tell any of us his name. Some court-ordered silence thing. I get the feeling he was abusive."

"And *he* has Mel's daughter? How?"

"Money."

"He's rich?"

Ami nodded. "She hasn't come out and said it. I only learned Nicole's name one time when Mel was drunk. She kept talking about how pretty her daughter is and how much she misses her." Ami leaned forward. "Now that she opened up to me, she talks privately about it from time to time. I'm pretty sure that the prick ex is remarried. Mel's said, more than once, something about getting Nicole away from the bitch playing mommy."

If Taylor's training hadn't kicked into gear, her jaw would have been on the floor. As it was, she was sure her pulse rate was off the charts. "What is she going to do? Is Mr. Diamond going to represent her to win back her daughter?"

Ami emptied her glass and poured another. "You'd think that, wouldn't you? Like if you need to fight a court order and you work for a lawyer..." She shook her head. "I keep expecting Jefferson to tell me to counter something or do something. I want him to. I want to know this dickhead's name, but so far, nothing."

Taylor sipped her wine, using the term loosely. Whatever it was in her glass was too sweet to be considered wine. Not to mention, the insulting aftertaste. Swallowing the liquid, she asked, "So do you all try to keep the conversation away from kids?"

"Yes. Not always. I mean, Jefferson handles a lot of divorces and custody battles. At work we mention them. It's when we're out and she's drinking. Usually she just turns off and leaves. It's only been a few times when it's just been the two of us that she's confided in me. I promised not to say anything." Ami shrugged. "I'm not very good at keeping a secret."

Undoubtedly, a great quality for someone who works for the town's attorney. No wonder small towns get the reputation of gossip mills. "Do you need to go home to Brian before dinner?"

Ami looked at her phone. "Shit, I do. I'd better go. My mom knows I go out on Fridays, but I usually go home and see him first." She continued talking as she put her jacket back on. "My folks bowl on a league on Fridays. Since I go out with the girls, they take Brian with them to the bowling alley. I better hurry before they're gone."

"Okay, thank you for the coffee."

Ami smiled. "Thanks for the wine. I know I sound like a bitch telling secrets, but the thing is, I like Mel." She suddenly looked sad. "Not that she feels the same. I mean, we're friends. I'd like it to be more than that, but I think she's still hung up on that dick of an ex."

Taylor's eyes widened. This was much more information than she'd dreamt of retrieving.

"So the thing is," Ami continued, "I don't want her to get all pissy and leave the bar. I was hoping you'd help me out."

"Sure thing." Taylor pressed her lips together and pretended to twist a key. "Not a word from me. I won't mention kids or dick exes."

Ami laughed. "I don't mind the dick ex conversation. I'm dying to know his name." She reached for her glass and finished off what little remained in there. "This was great wine!"

Taylor nodded, trying to keep a straight face.

"I'll see you in a little bit. Don't forget. Nothing about the realty either, and..." Ami smiled. "...remember me."

"Oh, I will. Thanks, Ami."

Taylor waited until Ami's car backed down the drive to call Phil. As she meticulously put the Townsends' farmhouse back in the order she'd found it, wiped down anything with fingerprints, and headed back to town for dinner, she shared her newfound knowledge.

Early May...

Phil

IT HAD BEEN a long time since Phillip Roach had sat fully on the wrong side of the law. Perhaps all he'd done to help Claire escape the clutches of Catherine London as well as stay off the FBI's radar wasn't legal, but it wasn't this. This was the Phillip Roach of years ago: the one who knew his objective and accomplished it at any cost. This was the man he thought he'd always be but had somehow put to rest. The stark difference between years ago and today was with the issue of the order. In special ops and even in private hire, he received an order and he carried it out.

Today, there was no order.

If there had been, in Phil's current state of employment, it would have come from Claire or Rawlings. Phil refused to allow either of them to be involved. They didn't know his plans or what Taylor had learned from Ami Beech, and they never would.

Somehow, despite the elevated stress the packages and letters instilled, the Rawlingses had come to terms with them. Phil's family had a sense of peace with their security. He had too, until there was too much—too much evidence that moved his calm, experienced mind into a cyclone of terrorizing thoughts. One seemingly innocuous clue was the color of Patricia's hair. Red. People who wanted to stay hidden changed their hair to a neutral color, one that blended into the masses. Patricia's color screamed for attention, or more accurately of arrogance.

Another finding that shouted for recognition was what he saw in her new home. When Phil entered her house to hide the tiny cameras and he walked into a small bedroom, the pink paint and white twin-sized bed made him nauseous. Learning of Patricia's discussion with Ami of *her* daughter turned that feeling into a full-blown sickness. A bead of sweat materialized on Phil's brow at the mere thought. The woman was either delusional or genius. Unfortunately, Phil feared the latter. Patricia was establishing herself in this small community and constructing a believable backstory. If her plans came to fruition, she would arrive back to her house and job with her daughter, the one she claimed was taken by her ex. The members of her inner circle would never question this child and Nichol's life would be forever, irrevocably changed.

With each minute, Phil's blood pressure rose. The thick fluid coursed through his veins, thundered in his ears, until his vision clouded with the red pooling behind his eyes. Patricia's plans would not happen. Phil knew that with all of his heart and soul. He also knew that the Rawlingses would never, could never, know why the mailings stopped. If Phil could have done it without anyone's knowledge, he would have. Unfortunately, he'd already let Eric and Taylor into too much of the operation.

As Phil waited for Patricia's arrival in her living room, Eric waited nearby with the car. Over the years the two men had developed a trust that only comes with time and experience. Eric was a stand-up man who devoted his life to Rawlings, even initially at the sacrifice of Claire. Though Rawlings claimed Eric had nothing to do with Claire's kidnapping, Roach knew in his gut that Eric helped. Rawlings couldn't have gotten her back to Iowa alone. The flip side to their partnership was that Phil himself felt the same way. If push came to shove, and it had come close, Phil would always choose Claire. Knowing that their two main goals were combined gave Eric and Phil the common objective. And with Nichol, there was no doubt: both men would lay down their lives.

Taylor's help had proven invaluable. The pink room was a subtle warning, but Ami's declarations were a full-blown alarm. No one expected the office manager of the Diamond Law Office to be so forthcoming. It was doubtful Eric or Phil would have reaped the same results as easily. Nevertheless, at this juncture, as Phil awaited Patricia's arrival, Taylor was in Iowa with Claire and Nichol: the fewer people who knew the truth about this day, the better. The timing was perfect: with Rawlings out of town, Eric and Phil's absence would appear as though they'd accompanied Rawlings to Chicago.

The sound of a key turning in the lock of the side door brought Phil back to present. Again his heart rate increased, as he heard not only her footsteps on the kitchen floor but the sound of her voice. His surveillance equipment had yielded very little, but it had revealed Patricia's routine. Each night she returned from work, entered through the kitchen, locked the side door, and hung her keys on a nearby hook. Her next stop would be her coffee maker, where she'd set it for her evening cup. On most nights she didn't go out of the house until morning. Never in the time he'd been watching had anyone been with her.

Phil held his breath and listened to Patricia speak and waited for the other voice. The revving of the Keurig echoed, but no other voice came. He sighed with the audible confirmation: Patricia was talking on the phone.

Stepping silently into the shadows of her living room, Phil waited, knowing that her next stop would be her bedroom, where she'd change her clothes. Once her conversation was complete, Phil planned to make his presence known. There was no need to be coy. Patricia would recognize him the moment she saw him. They'd had more than a few conversations in the past.

As she made her way to her bedroom still talking, he remembered hearing about the reason for her firing. A smile graced his lips as he recalled Brent filling him in on the details. Brent was the one to authorize the larger than normal severance package. After all, Patricia Miles had been the assistant to the CEO of a billion-dollar conglomerate. Half a million dollars should have been sufficient to secure her silence and allow her to slip away. Changing her identity was never part of the deal. Brent offered glowing recommendations for Patricia Miles. She could have easily moved to any Fortune 500 company and done well. The situation she now faced was her own doing.

Phil tugged on the fingers of his leather gloves and continued to listen. Patricia was still in her bedroom when she finally said goodbye. It wasn't until she walked down the hallway toward her waiting cup of coffee that he made his presence known. Stepping from the living room, Phil silently moved toward the brightly lit kitchen.

"Ms. Miles," he stated in a cold, even tone.

Patricia's shoulders stiffened as he heard her gasp. Slowly she turned his direction. Confusion and fear swirled in her eyes as anger and determination vied for dominance. Prying her tense lips apart, she finally asked, "Mr. Roach? What are you doing in my home?"

Moving his head slowly back and forth, he said, "Come now. I'm sure you can come up with a better question than that. I have one: what's an MIT and Stanford graduate doing in Olivia, Minnesota, working as a paralegal? Especially someone who received a handsome settlement with the promise of glowing recommendations? Ms. Miles, you could be living the high life in New York or better yet, someplace abroad, perhaps London."

Her ashen pallor intensified as Patricia's gaze slowly moved around her kitchen. "I-I want you to leave."

The spring sky through the window had begun to darken. He couldn't have orchestrated a better cover. Along with removing herself from the radar, Patricia had also chosen an isolated home, at least a half mile from the nearest neighbor. A low chuckle rumbled from somewhere deep within Phil's throat. One that even he thought sounded sinister. "Really, Ms. Miles, your time for making demands has expired. I have demands now."

Her frightened eyes moved to his.

"Ms. Miles, my demands are basic and straightforward. You were given the opportunity to make yourself scarce and go on with your life. Instead you chose to seek revenge. The Rawlingses have had more than enough of that—enough to last a lifetime. I want you gone and out of their lives. I don't want you to attempt to contact them in any way—ever again."

"Who said that I—"

"Don't play dumb. Your intelligence is what's gotten you this far. Try capitalizing on it. It could save your life. Tell me you'll leave them alone."

"Save my life?" she asked. "What does that mean?"

"I gave you the answer. Say it."

"I'll leave them alone."

Phil heard the lie roll off her tongue with ease.

"I don't know what you planned to accomplish with your mailings, but whatever it was, it's over."

"Tell me what you mean, over?" The panic showed in her eyes. "What are you going to do? Does Mr.... Tony know you're here?"

Phil reached into his pocket. "No. No one knows, which is not to your advantage. I'm here to warn you."

"Warn me?"

"Give up your quest, whatever it is. By using the U.S. Postal Service to send your threatening mailings you've committed a federal crime, one that's punishable by up to twenty years in prison."

Her back again straightened defiantly. "I never threatened anyone. And as I recall, you're not in law enforcement."

"I'm not—another disadvantage for you. And you *did* threaten. You also attempted to manipulate and harass, all punishable by law."

"Fine," Patricia said, shuffling her feet to move away from Phil. "No one can prove it was me."

"Wrong again, Ms. Miles. The FBI has your DNA. I guarantee that if they catch you, you'll be spending time behind bars. Perhaps we can arrange a shared cell with Catherine, since you're using her idea."

The color returned to her cheeks. "It was *my* idea to remind them, to remind *her*! No one's taking me into custody. It's her. She's going back to the asylum where she belongs. You don't understand." She shook her head as her hands waved about her sides. "He needs me. I've been there for him. I *was* there for him. She's crazy! She doesn't deserve him..."

Patricia continued to protest as the textured handle of the cool pistol in Phil's jacket pocket fit perfectly into the palm of his hand. The old Phil longed to end her ridiculous reasoning; however, the new Phil recalled Taylor's warning. Never had Phil worried about the consequences of his actions; then again, never before had he had the concerns and relationships he currently enjoyed. The bonds he felt with the Rawlingses were double-edged. While he'd come to enjoy the affiliation and rapport, at this moment he felt that same connection limiting his capabilities. It wasn't that he couldn't kill Patricia. He'd killed before, and doing so again would guarantee her future silence. It was that for the first time that he could recall, Phil didn't want to risk losing the life he lived. He didn't want to disappear. Leaving his current life wasn't an option.

"Enough!" he proclaimed.

The outline of a pistol was easily defined through the fabric of Phil's jacket. Patricia's eyes locked on his pocket. "Are you going to kill me?"

Phil narrowed his gaze. There were no detectable signs of emotion in his expression or tone as he stepped forward. "Give me answers, truthful answers, and we'll discuss it."

Perspiration glistened on her brow. "I-I have a life here," she reasoned. Her body visibly trembled as she stepped back once, then again, inching farther and farther away. Each miniscule movement tried in vain to create an impenetrable gap, as if one more step would be enough to assure her safety. In reality, she could run the length of the house and the bullets in Phil's gun would never miss their target. The two individuals continued to stare as only the sound of their breathing interrupted the looming silence. Finally the squeak of a chair against the worn linoleum announced the end of Patricia's retreat. In an act of desperation, she lifted her chin and quipped, "You can't just expect my death to go unnoticed."

He smirked. "You're living a life that doesn't exist. There's no Melissa Garrison. Once you're gone, and *if* anyone cares enough to investigate, they'll learn the truth: you were a lie. You never existed."

"B-But you said that the FBI is on to me. They'll know."

"They'll know that you willingly disappeared once and you did it again. That's what happens to psychopaths like you. Perhaps you figured out that the bureau was on to you. Once you did, you panicked and moved on."

Though Phil had yet to show her what he held within his pocket, her shoulders slumped in defeat at his reasoning. "What questions do you have?" she asked.

"I want the truth. If you're honest with me, we might be able to work out a deal. If you're not... let's just say that I don't make deals with people I can't trust." His training had kicked into gear. No longer was this emotional—he wouldn't allow it. The outcome was up to her.

Swallowing hard, Patricia looked up. "What do you want to know?"

"What were your plans for Nichol?"

Patricia blinked repeatedly, keeping her gaze toward his ice-cold stare. "I-I didn't have plans—"

Phil released the safety on the pistol. The faint click echoed through the otherwise still kitchen. "Try again."

She took a deep breath. "I didn't have it all worked out, but I've been laying groundwork..." Tears came to her eyes. "She doesn't deserve everything. She took it all from me."

With his free hand he grasped her arm. "What the fuck are you saying? She's a little girl."

"No! Not *her*," Patricia retorted. "Claire! She doesn't deserve to have him as a husband. I'd put years into him." Shaking off Phil's grip, she stared rebelliously. "He used to take me places. Did you know that? Does she? I doubt it. I went with him to business dinners and to meet with associates." She cocked her head to the side. "And it wasn't all business either. We traveled. It all ended when she came around, and I was supposed to plan their wedding? Really? Why would she expect me to do that?"

Phil wanted to shake this woman. When *she* came around? How could Patricia possibly blame Claire for being kidnapped and held prisoner? He also doubted it was Claire who wanted Patricia to plan her wedding.

Patricia went on, "Fine, you're going to kill me anyway. Tell her... tell her that I would've gotten him back too, if she hadn't trapped him by getting pregnant! What a slut! I just figured if I was the one..."

Phil released the gun as he roughly covered her mouth and neck. "My patience is running thin. I asked you about Nichol, *not Claire*."

Her eyes bulged as she gasped for air. When he removed his hand, she answered, "She, Claire, doesn't deserve to have his child. I do. I don't know what I planned to do with her, but I planned to take her."

It was all Phil needed to hear. Taking a step back he nodded. "I asked for honesty. Now we're leaving."

"No!" she yelled, reaching for the edge of the table. "I'm not going anywhere. I was honest. That's the truth."

One swipe of his phone and Phil called Eric. "Plan A. Get us now."

Patricia's eyes filled with tears. "What does that mean?"

"It means we're leaving here. Say goodbye to Melissa Garrison."

Chapter 11

Mid-May 2017

Claire

———◆———

Honesty is more than not lying. It is truth telling, truth speaking, truth living, and truth loving.
—James E. Faust

CLAIRE INHALED THE sweet scents of lotion and powder as she held Baby Beth in her arms. Staring down at her niece, she gently ran the tips of her fingers over the fine blonde hair. "Oh, Em, couldn't you just sit and hold her for hours?"

With emerald eyes that sparkled with both love and exhaustion, Emily replied, "I could. I really could, but I don't believe Michael would approve."

Claire grinned. The thought in her mind shouldn't be voiced, yet Claire couldn't stop herself. "You did this with two, when Michael was born..." She kept her eyes on the beautiful baby, avoiding her sister's tired gaze. "I'm sorry you had to, but you're experienced with two children."

Emily shook her head. "No, Claire, don't be sorry. We love Nichol. You know, I thought I was experienced. I thought this would be like it was when Michael was born, but it's not. It's a whole new world. Nichol was seven months old when Michael came into our lives. It wasn't easy having two babies. That's when we hired Becca." She sighed. "Thank God we hired Becca. Like I said, it wasn't easy, but Nichol wasn't walking or talking or demanding attention... other than what babies do. It wasn't like this. Michael wants to play and go. Nichol was content to be home with Michael and me."

Claire looked up to see her sister's eyes close. "Em, why don't you take a nap? Shannon and Becca have Nichol and Michael outside. I'll take care of Beth for an hour or so. You need your rest."

Emily's eyes opened wide. "No. I can't do that."

"Why not? You just fed her. Look, her little eyes are fighting sleep. She'll be fine."

"I... I just... what if something happens?"

"Don't be silly," Claire scoffed. "Taylor's here. Everything's fine. You should take advantage of the opportunity and get some rest when you can."

Stifling a yawn, Emily stood. "Really, Claire, thank you. I just can't. I'll nap when John gets home. Let me have her, and I'll put her down in her crib. You and I can have some coffee and watch the kids play. We haven't talked in a while, not without the kids or men around." Reaching for her daughter, Emily asked, "Fill me in on what's happening with you?"

Claire felt a cold chill as Beth's tiny warm body was lifted from her lap. Suddenly, sadness filled her chest. She'd wanted a range of emotion and as she contemplated the sudden emptiness, she had it. Fighting the realization of what just went unspoken, Claire feigned a smile. Her sister didn't trust her with her child. Trying to hide her hurt, Claire said, "I'm good, Emily. I'll go make some coffee while you put Beth down. Then I'll meet you on the back patio. It's getting warmer and the children are playing in the backyard."

"That sounds great," Emily replied, heading toward the nursery.

With each step, Claire thought about the disappointment eddying through her. Yes, she'd had mental issues, but never in her life would she have imagined that her own sister wouldn't trust her with her baby. Didn't Emily know how much Claire loved children? With each step she tried to suppress her distress. As she did a new thought occurred to her. Wasn't this a good sign? She wanted the range of emotion that was real life. By decreasing her medications, she asked to once again experience the ups and downs. Claire had just forgotten how painful the downs could be.

As she made the coffee Claire tried to concentrate on the positive. She thought how Beth reminded her of Nichol at that age. Suddenly, her mind went to Madeline. The kind woman's gentle touch, caring words, and wealth of knowledge were Claire's light and encouragement during those first few months of motherhood. Madeline not only taught Claire and Tony about babies, she empowered them to be parents. Thinking about the prospect of another baby, Claire knew what she wanted. She decided that when she and Tony were alone, she'd talk to him about inviting Madeline and Francis to Iowa.

Those thoughts and plans pulled Claire from her feeling of rejection as she settled at the Vandersols' outdoor table and watched the children running furiously about the yard, laughing and kicking. In the past few weeks, Nichol had become obsessed with soccer. Thankfully both children were wearing little shin guards. Heaven knows what type of tragedy could occur without them. Claire shook her head. Although her daughter knew very little about the real game, Claire heard Nichol's voice above the giggles, constantly reminding her cousin of the rules, or more accurately *her* rules. It was at times like this that Claire saw more Tony in their child.

She felt she had a strong argument for nature over nurture. Even without the presence of her father for the first three years of her life, Nichol's words, actions, and even gestures were all miniature copies of her father's. Yet as these thoughts streamed through her mind, Michael fell to the ground, holding his leg. Before Claire could stand, Nichol was on her knees at his side. The injury timeout was short-lived. Soon they were both up and the game was once again in full swing. Claire smiled. Nichol may have Tony's determination, but she also possessed her mother's gentleness and compassion.

"What are you thinking?" Emily asked as she sat and placed the small monitor on the table. The warm afternoon breeze gently blew through their hair.

"I was thinking about how much I enjoy watching Nichol and Michael together." Claire didn't want to address what had happened inside with Beth.

"I do too. They have so much fun together."

Claire nodded as she took a sip of her coffee.

"I especially like how they wear each other out," Emily said. "I hope they welcome Beth into their world."

"I like the wearing out part too, and don't worry, they will," Claire reassured. "Nichol's elated that the girls now outnumber the boys."

"I worry that they'll think of her as a nuisance, being younger than them."

"Did you think I was a nuisance?" Claire asked with a smirk.

Emily grinned over the rim of her coffee mug. "Hmmm. Maybe I shouldn't answer that."

"Well, maybe Beth needs someone closer to her own age?" Claire hadn't broached the baby subject with Emily in a few months. Her sister had no idea of the work she and Tony had been doing to get Claire ready to be pregnant.

Emily narrowed her gaze toward Claire. "If you're talking about me, I think I'm done for a while."

Claire laughed. "Well, since Beth's barely a month old, I'd be shocked if you wanted to jump on that again."

"Then I hope you're suggesting a play group. Claire, you can't be thinking of—"

Claire sat straighter. "Em, don't do that. Don't make everything an argument. You're my sister. You're supposed to be my friend, not my mother."

Emily rubbed her forehead. "I'm sorry, Claire. I'm tired and my filter is sleeping."

"No," Claire replied. "When it comes to me you don't have a filter. Tony and I are planning to try for another child."

Though her head moved back and forth, Emily remained silent.

"We're not jumping into anything," Claire continued. "We've been working with my doctors. I'm off all my medicines." She noticed Emily's eyes widen. "I have been for over a month. We're supposed to wait a little longer, but the doctors are all on board and so is Tony."

"Does that include Dr. Brown?"

"Yes, she was the first one I discussed it with. I still meet with her twice weekly and Tony's been to a few of my sessions with her. We're being careful. I'm doing fine. I feel good, and I mean that in the best of ways. I get happy and sad. It's the way it's supposed to be."

Emily reached out and covered Claire's hand. "I'm not your

mother, but I'm your older sister. I can worry."

"No, Em, you can't. You have enough to concern yourself with John, Michael, and Beth. Worrying about me is not a priority. I have a fantastic family and life with Tony and Nichol. We're ready to try to expand it. Tony even said that if the doctors decide I shouldn't get pregnant, we could adopt."

"Really?" Emily's tired eyes opened wide. "Anthony Rawlings is willing to raise someone else's child?"

It was Claire's turn to narrow her gaze. "What does that mean?"

"Hmm, nothing. I'm just surprised; that's all."

"Don't you think it's possible to love a child even if you weren't the one to give birth to it?"

"You know I know it's possible," Emily replied.

"Then what's the issue?"

Emily momentarily closed her eyes. "Claire, there's no issue. If you're truly doing this with the support of your medical team, I'm happy. I see how excited Nichol is with Beth. She'll be thrilled to be a big sister."

Absorbed in their conversation, neither Claire nor Emily saw the children approaching. "I'm gonna be a sister?" Nichol asked, her cheeks pink from sun and exercise and her eyes wide with questioning.

Claire reached out and rubbed Nichol's back. "You're all hot. Do you want some water?"

"Shannon's getting some. Can we have a baby too?"

"Maybe someday, sweetie," Claire answered. "Maybe someday. Right now you're a big cousin. How do you like that?"

"I like it, a lot!"

Michael ran towards the table as the light on the small monitor flashed and the springtime air filled with the sounds of baby whimpers. "Mommy, baby Bef's cry'n again!" Turning toward Claire he said, "Baby Bef cries a lot."

"Oh, she does?"

Covering his ears, he said, "It's bad. It hurts my ears."

Nichol turned toward her cousin. "No, Michael, Baby Beff's not bad. She wants Aunt Em's tension." She looked back at Claire. "Right, Momma? Just like my puppy. He wasn't *bad*. He just wanted new batteries."

Claire hugged Nichol and winked at Emily. "That's right, sweetie, and listen, Michael. Beth's sleeping again. Sometimes we all make cranky noises and say things we don't mean when we're sleepy."

Emily shook her head. "Okay, Claire. I get it. Let's talk about this later, after I've had a good night's sleep. I know my opinion doesn't matter. I'm sorry."

"Your opinion matters. I just want your support."

"You have it. I'll be more excited after that good night's sleep."

Picking up her coffee, Claire commented, "So in about a year or so?"

"Yes," Emily replied wearily. "Think about that before you do anything rash."

Claire raised her brow.

"Are you willing to give up sleep?"

Nodding, Claire replied, "In a heartbeat to hold a little one again—my little one."

The warm breeze continued to blow as the children ran back to their waiting soccer ball.

Late May

Phil

PHIL LOOKED OVER the FBI report. In a nutshell, it corroborated what he knew: the bureau confirmed that Patricia Miles had been living in a small rented house under an alias, Melissa Garrison, in Olivia, Minnesota. According to the report, she'd been working as a paralegal for Jefferson Diamond, a small-town attorney, doing research for the firm. Mr. Diamond claimed that one day she was at work and the next day she wasn't. Few of her coworkers claimed a private relationship with her. Most people interviewed in town knew her from her job. They all claimed that she was quiet and kept mostly to herself. Ami Beech, Jefferson Diamond's office manager, claimed that Ms. Garrison's skills were impressive in the field of research and admitted to not completing the necessary background check prior to her hiring.

The small home Ms. Garrison rented contained physical evidence to link her to the *Rawls-Nichols* mailings. There were even pre-addressed cards. From her personal items, they were able to test her DNA. It too confirmed that Ms. Garrison, aka Patricia Miles, was the female who sealed the envelopes. For unknown reasons, Ms. Garrison had moved on. The FBI will continue their pursuit. At the end of the report, the bureau asked for continued assistance from all members of the Rawlings security team. They asked to be notified if anything unusual came up or another similar mailing arrived.

Phil handed the report to Eric, leaned back in his chair, and waited for a response.

After a few minutes, Eric's eyes met Phil's and he asked, "Gone. Sounds like no signs of foul play."

"No, apparently not, at least not any mentioned in this report."

Phil wondered if the FBI chose to be unforthcoming with the evidence of foul intentions toward Nichol or if they truly didn't know the information that he and his team had learned. Either way, the report confirmed that the FBI's suspect was missing and the bureau appeared to have no suspects or theories as to her disappearance.

Taylor sat back and waited. "I'd like to read that once you're finished, Eric."

He nodded as he continued to read.

Turning to Phil, she asked, "Do they have any theories as to why she'd disappear after trying to make a life?"

"No," Phil replied. "Not officially. However, I spoke with my contact and the unspoken innuendo I picked up was that they believe Ms. Miles may've become suspicious that the FBI was getting close and decided to move on."

"Is that what you think?"

Phil didn't respond as his mind flashed back to that night in Olivia.

Taylor's voice returned him to present. "Do either of you plan on telling me what happened?"

Eric shrugged. "I don't know what you want to hear. It sounds like she's moved on. I guess we just keep an eye out for her or new mailings. At least we now know for sure who we're looking for."

Taylor crossed her arms over her chest and wrinkled her brow. "I went to Olivia. I haven't said a word to Mr. or Mrs. Rawlings and this is the way I'm treated. If you think I'm naive enough to believe this report at face value, you've seriously underestimated me."

Eric stood and handed her the pages. "Read it, and see if you find something we missed."

As she reached for the report, Eric's gaze met hers and he whispered something Phil couldn't hear. A cold chill filled the room as Taylor turned and met Phil's frigid stare. A moment later the door to the security office closed and Phil and Taylor were alone. Taking the pages, Taylor silently went to the sofa and settled against the soft leather. Her blue eyes scanned each page. Occasionally she'd stop and reread a sentence or a paragraph. Phil wasn't sure. He hadn't heard exactly what Eric had said, but by the way she looked at them, he knew it was about Patricia.

What would she say or think if she knew what went on in Olivia? It wasn't like her record was without blemish. The more Phil got to know Taylor, the more he knew that they were in many ways cut from the same cloth. Maybe that's what bothered him the most. Eric accepted everything as part of his job, part of his responsibility. He rarely questioned. Phil knew that Taylor would want to know more. If the roles were reversed, he'd want more. After three weeks of wondering if he'd made the right decision, Phil still didn't know. That contrary was something new. Never in the past had he second-guessed himself.

Phil turned his chair away from Taylor and watched the monitors. They were on a random feed from all around the estate. Since he'd taken over security, the cameras were more advanced than they had been. The new house also had fewer cameras within the rooms. The first floor was fully accessible to surveillance, even the Rawlingses' office. That had been a point of contention with Rawlings when Phil first took over security, but Phil reminded him that the recorded conversation in his old office was the key to his innocence. They compromised. The office feed was only accessible

with the proper dual code. Only Claire and Rawlings had access-to-
one half of the code. Therefore, the office would only be reviewed if
one of the Rawlingses and a member of the security team were both
in agreement. The lawns, gardens, pool, playground, and all of the
outside grounds were constantly monitored. The capability was
present for the front gate to be either physically or remotely
manned. No one could access the estate without being admitted and
recorded.

Phil closed his eyes and remembered.

Patricia's eyes filled with tears. "What does that mean?"

*"It means we're leaving here. Say goodbye to Melissa
Garrison."*

*Phil pulled the gun from his pocket. Pointing it toward Patricia,
he said, "You have two minutes." In her left hand, she held tightly
to her cell phone. He nodded toward it. "Place that on the table. Go.
Get whatever you'd grab to leave. If you have cash hidden, I
recommend you take it now. You're not coming back."*

"I-I don't have—"

"You do," he said, "in the cupboard in the bathroom. Go now."

*She moved slowly, deliberating each word he'd said. Placing
the phone down, she turned. "How do you know about the money?"*

*"Ms. Miles, I know much more than you'd think. I'll explain it
more once we're gone."*

*Suddenly, she walked briskly toward her bedroom. When Phil
heard the door shut, he shook his head and followed. Though it was
locked, the small key-like object rested predictably above the jamb.
Entering the room, he found Patricia trying unsuccessfully to open
the window. "It's an old house," he said calmly. "The windows have
been painted too many times. Don't be stupid. I'm not alone. Get*

the cash, some shoes, and a jacket." He looked at his watch. "You now have one minute."

"I'm not getting my money. If you're going to kill me anyway, I'm not giving you my cash."

"Fifty seconds, and I assure you, I don't want or need your money. You will. Get it now."

With ten seconds to spare, they stepped from the side door into the night air. "Lock the house," Phil demanded.

She looked at him with the unspoken questions.

"It needs to look as if you've disappeared of your own volition. Locking the door is something you always do."

Nodding, she placed the key in the lock; however, as she started to move toward the carport, Phil reached for her elbow and redirected her toward the driveway. "No, Ms. Miles, we have a ride."

Taylor's hand rested upon Phil's shoulder pulling him from his thoughts and causing him to jump. As he turned he expected to see anger in her blue eyes; instead, it was sadness.

"Tell me. You need to talk."

"Ms. Walters, I assure you—"

Taylor leaned back against the desk. "Don't. I'm not asking you because I feel left out. I'm asking you because I see the anguish. I see you rubbing your neck and rolling your head from side to side. I've seen the way you watch the cameras and front gate. I know you come in here in the middle of the night and review footage."

Phil started to protest. She had no right to spy on him. Yet before he could articulate the proper response, she continued talking.

"I know you take this job and this family personally." Leaning forward, she said, "I get it. I know about your family."

Phil's shoulders snapped back. "I don't have a family."

"You've called the Rawlingses your family more than once. I know about your blood family."

"Don't!" His volume rose as he sprung from his chair. "Forget whatever you think you know. My private life isn't open for discussion."

Taylor stood taller. "We all get into this line of work for different reasons. I understand that you weren't there for them." She reached out and touched his chest. The warmth of her fingers radiated through the material, scorching his skin below. When Phil stepped back, Taylor went on, "You were thousands of miles away on a godforsaken tour."

"Korea," he said, swallowing any emotion. "I was stationed in South Korea. The eighties were a turbulent time. Kim Jong II was in power in North Korea; the tension was building between North Korea and the rest of the world. There were problems with Gorbachev..."

"You were a kid, in your twenties."

Phil nodded. "I was supposed to go home. My father had this gun shop... But I got an offer to re-up. I never went home."

Taylor nodded. "I know, and they died while you were away."

"They didn't *die*. They were murdered in their sleep by a kid who wanted to rob the store. The asshole had tried to rob it once before and only spent one night in jail. He used my father's own gun to shoot them." He shook his head. "My parents lived in an apartment above the shop."

Why had he just said all of that? He hadn't thought about that, not consciously, in years—decades. Taylor reached for his hand. He looked down at the foreign connection, thinking how warm and soft her skin felt against his.

"You weren't there." Her voice was soft yet strong. "But you are here. Whatever happened in Olivia, you're here. That's what matters. The Rawlingses don't live above a gun shop. No one's getting near them. You've done everything to protect them."

He pulled his hand away. The pain in his chest was unbearable. This was shit. He'd done better as the assassin. It was business. This feeling shit was painful. "No! I didn't. I could've done everything, but I didn't."

"What? What do you mean?"

Phil stepped away, pacing about the small office. "I could have. Eric would've supported my decision either way. Don't you get it?"

"No, I don't."

"She was honest. I asked her about Nichol and she was honest. She could've lied. If she had..." He pinched the brow of his nose. "...that's what I told myself, if she lied..."

Taylor moved to her desk and sat. "Help me, Phil. I can't follow what you're saying."

He stopped pacing and turned. "I asked her what her plans were for Nichol. She admitted that she planned to take her."

Taylor's chest moved up and down with deep breaths. "You were doing your job."

"Stop!" He couldn't remember ever feeling so out of control. "I didn't. If I had I wouldn't be watching the damn monitors all night long. But... she was honest. That was the deal."

"Phil?"

The golden flecks in his hazel eyes shimmered with moisture.

"Please tell me."

He took a deep breath and exhaled. "Patricia's out of the country. She has been for over two weeks. I haven't heard from her and obviously, neither has the FBI. I gave her another chance."

Taylor's lips formed a straight line. "So you didn't..."

"I should have."

"Why didn't you?"

He shrugged. "I'd planned to, but she wasn't delusional. She wasn't crazy. She was just hell-bent on revenge. I sound so fucking soft." He fell down onto the sofa. "If anyone in this crazy world deserved revenge, it would be Claire. Yet she's never tried to get it. Hell, she forgave Rawlings. I just thought if Claire talked to Patricia—which I don't want her to do—she'd see that Patricia didn't really want Nichol. She wanted Claire to hurt for hurting her.

"This whole thing is so fucked up. Claire didn't hurt her. Patricia had her sights set on something that would never be. Instead of dwelling on it, and giving up her life and her freedom, I convinced her to leave. I told her to get away before the FBI figured it out. This was her last chance to have a life. We gave her an additional installment on her severance package and provided her with new identification. We explained that she was on her own.

We also warned her. We'd found her once. If she ever came near them or even so much as sent another card, I promised that I'd hunt her down."

Finally, he made himself meet Taylor's blue gaze. She feigned a smile. "Thank you."

"For what?" he asked. "Admitting that I've gone soft and if something happens to anyone in this family it's my fault?"

She shook her head as her smile became real. *Why was she smiling?* "No," she replied. "For showing that you care and that you want to do what's right. From all that I've learned, this family seems to have been consumed with vengeance. You had the chance to continue that, and you didn't."

"She didn't have a plan. If she had... if she'd lied... but she didn't."

"We'll help. You know that, don't you? Eric and I want the same thing you do. I didn't take this job for the money or even the glamorous hours." Her cheeks rose as she found amusement in her own statement.

Despite his mood, Phil grinned too, because though the pay wasn't bad, the hours definitely sucked. "I took this job," she continued, "because I wanted to find a place to make a life. I saw the devotion both you and Eric had. I wanted that. I wanted to feel strongly, and I do. I don't think that making the decision *not* to kill someone is a bad one. It makes me all the more proud to be on your team."

Phil closed his eyes and sighed. He'd always been the one to carry the load. Whether it was the death of his parents or the lives he'd taken, it had always been on him and him alone. He'd never considered sharing. The couch shifted as Taylor sat beside him. He looked her direction. "I'm not sure what made me tell you all of that. I haven't told anyone the stuff about my family. I haven't spoken of it in over twenty years."

Taylor tilted her head. "Sometimes it's healthy to talk. I hope you know that whatever you tell me is safe with me."

Before he could respond, Taylor leaned toward him. Suddenly, his decision seemed right. Phil could live with it, because he wasn't alone. The scent of Taylor's light perfume filled his senses with hope for a future, for not only the Rawlingses, but for everyone. Maybe he was getting soft, but as her lips neared his, it wasn't his decision that consumed his thoughts. It was his desire to feel her softness: her lips, a mere whisper away, her hands, how they warmed his skin. And then it happened. Had he moved forward or was it all her?

It didn't matter. Phil's chest filled with sensations he'd kept buried for too long. He wanted nothing more than to be lost in the sweetness of her kiss.

Chapter 12

Late June 2017

Claire

------◆------

A man travels the world over in search of what
he needs, and returns home to find it.
—George A. Moore

CLAIRE WALKED QUIETLY through the darkened hallways and down the staircase. With Nichol tucked into bed sound asleep, Shannon out for the evening, and Tony not yet back from a business trip, the house was still and peaceful. The serenity gave her strength as she made her way through the living room and outside onto the back patio. Claire smiled as she looked up to the Iowa sky. The black velvet blanket high above glistened with millions of stars shining down like diamonds. As she inhaled the moist, sultry air and listened to the songs of the cicadas, Claire momentarily wondered if Tony could see the same stars from his plane. Did he even notice as he flew home to his family or was he lost in his work?

Despite the late hour, perspiration formed on her skin as she walked toward the pool. Growing up in Indiana, the diversity of Iowa's weather never surprised Claire, but on days such as this, with the temperature high and humidity oppressive, she reminded herself of the barren landscape of winter. Thoughts of the snow that covered their estate six months earlier helped her welcome and accept the heat. Nearing the beckoning cool water, Claire found herself lost in thoughts and memories. She knew it was her hormones wreaking havoc: her ups and downs were more dramatic. One moment she would laugh and the next she felt like crying. Though Tony worried, Dr. Brown assured them it was all normal.

Tony and her doctors were the only ones who knew about her pregnancy. Other than the dramatic mood swings, it seemed to be going well. So far she hadn't experienced the bouts of morning sickness that she'd had with Nichol. However, she was only six weeks along and there was still time. With Nichol, she hadn't even realized that she was pregnant until this time in the pregnancy. With this little one, she knew as soon as she missed her period. Her and Tony's plans to expand their family were a month ahead of schedule. The doctors had told them to wait until this month to try, and they had—well, except for the one night. A smile came to her lips and her cheeks rose. It certainly seemed that when it came to making babies she and Tony didn't require months of practice. The fact that she never became pregnant during their first marriage or before was a testament to the insert she'd had implanted.

Leaving her robe on the lounge chair and her sandals beside it, Claire stepped carefully down the pool's stairs and immersed herself in the tepid water. The goose bumps didn't register as she remembered that night:

She and Tony were in New York alone. They weren't really alone. That rarely occurred. Eric had gone with them while Taylor and Phil stayed in Iowa. It was the first time they'd spent a few *nights away from Nichol since they'd been reunited as a family, and as much as Claire had looked forward to the time away, she missed their daughter.*

Nevertheless, she managed to busy herself with things she used to enjoy: a trip to the spa and time on 5th Avenue. Being the middle of May, the weather was perfect as she walked up and down the New York City streets. It'd been a long time since she'd been to the city, and she enjoyed the contagious energy of its people. The exhilarating vitality rippled through the air, energizing the residents and tourists alike. When thoughts of Rudolf tried to infiltrate her thoughts, Claire would remember that he was still incarcerated and she was safe. Once in a while she'd wonder about the Rawls-Nichols mailings. They hadn't received any in over a month. Tony told her he didn't know why they'd stopped, but he was glad they had. Claire wasn't sure if they'd really stopped or merely taken a break. Either way, the comforting sense of safety added to her euphoria.

Claire had forgotten the invigorating rush of Times Square and the serenity of Central Park. As hours passed, she found herself lost in her own therapeutic and rejuvenating world. Now that she was a mother and their lives involved numerous people and responsibilities, being alone in a crowd seemed like a distant memory. For the life of her, Claire couldn't remember the last time she'd willingly spent the day by herself. Yet with the sun shining down and a gentle breeze, while walking the streets amidst the throngs of people or sitting on the edge of a fountain in Central Park and listening to the street performers, Claire felt revitalized.

Dr. Brown often asked her to evaluate her feelings, to delve deeper into them. Sitting on that concrete ledge with music in the air, Claire came to an important conclusion. She no longer feared being alone. That didn't mean that she wanted to be like that all of the time, but she didn't fear it. There was a time she had. Her life at Everwood and early years with Tony had been a solitary hell. Though it hadn't been a conscious decision, since leaving Everwood and reuniting with Tony and Nichol, Claire had purposely kept herself occupied with everyone else. Whether it was her immediate family, extended family, friends, or employees, she stayed connected. It was no secret that being alone used to bother her. Hell, it was the weapon that Catherine secretly wielded when she encouraged Claire's disappearance. The money Catherine offered was all a ploy to isolate Claire yet again. However, years later, surrounded by strangers, she realized she enjoyed being alone. Perhaps she always had. There was nothing to fear in alone time, as long as she also had her loved ones.

Claire recalled the memories of days spent at her lake. Recently she'd gone there with Tony and Nichol. While they'd had a wonderful afternoon, it wasn't as relaxing and rejuvenating as it used to be. Her lake, the woods, those private times had helped her survive. She realized that it was as necessary in her everyday life as the connections she'd forged. The secret was balance.

During that afternoon, she also realized that if a trip around Manhattan could enlighten her, she didn't need to spend as much time with Dr. Brown. If life were a balancing act and alone time was part of it, then something needed to give. There were only so many hours in a day, week, or year, and Claire had no intentions of decreasing her time with Tony or Nichol. She also didn't want to lose time with Emily, Courtney, Meredith, or Sue.

Claire was ready to take on life again. With the effects of the medications gone, she was ready to experience every day to its fullest. That didn't mean she'd stop all of her counseling. The *family court had mandated a minimum of a year as one of the stipulations of Tony and Claire's regained custody. Everwood had also asked for a year. It wasn't mandated, but just like the medication, a gradual decrease seemed reasonable.*

As Claire walked the paths of the park on her way toward the streets, she recalled the night Tony proposed. A smile materialized as she thought about his words. Though she couldn't remember them verbatim, she did remember her shock at his declaration. As much as her life changed the day he took her, it also changed the evening he asked her to be his wife. That night opened the floodgate for feelings and emotions she'd been fighting. Though they'd had many ups and downs since that night nearly six and a half years ago, Claire knew the love she felt that night was only a seedling to what she felt today.

Lost in her thoughts, it was after 6:30 by the time Claire made it back to their apartment. With the spring sun, longer days, and constant buzz of people, time had been difficult to decipher. When she reached the foyer of their apartment, Claire had a fleeting vision of the man from her past. A bygone aura reverberated through the entry as dark eyes peered down from the top of the stairs and the deep voice demanded answers. "Where have you been?"

Though the scene may have resembled another time, it varied significantly in Claire's response. She didn't fear his question or the consequences of her carelessness. Honestly, she hadn't thought about his reaction at all until she saw him. Rarely was she late; however, when she was, she usually did her best to keep everyone informed. The day and afternoon hadn't been about everyone. It'd been about her: rediscovering herself, by herself.

"I've been all around the city," she replied with a smile

as she began to ascend the steps.

He met her near the middle. "I've called your phone a hundred times."

Claire kissed his cheek. "I guess I didn't hear it. I didn't realize the time until I was in the taxi on the way home."

"And you couldn't call?"

"Tony, I was on my way." Ignoring his darkened gaze, she asked, "Do we have plans?"

Seizing her elbow with his jaws clenched, Tony briskly led her to their suite. Before she could think or register his actions, the door closed and his lips were on hers. This wasn't the sweet and gentle husband who once again instigated a stir deep inside of her.

No, this was a man on a mission. Roughly, his fingers grasped her hair, pulling her head back and exposing her already claimed mouth. His unspoken hunger unleashed in a frenzy as his tongue demanded entrance and her lips willingly parted. The scent of cologne and the taste of whiskey combined to create an intoxicating cocktail as her lips bruised and her insides melted.

As his body thrust against hers, Claire's petite hands found his chest and pushed. She had to know he'd stop if that were what she wanted. She didn't want it, but nevertheless, she needed that grasp at control when he seemed suddenly without any. The temperature of their suite rose and the air stilled as he pulled away and dark eyes bore deep into the emerald green.

"Tony? What's wrong?"

"I couldn't reach you." He gripped her chin. "Do you have any idea what I'd do if I lost you?"

"You're not losing me. Every time I'm out late doesn't mean anything has happened."

He towered above her as each statement came forth louder

than the one before. "Taylor or Roach weren't with you. You didn't have Eric. You were all by yourself. Jan didn't know when you'd be back. I've been here since 4:00. I even called the spa. They said you'd left hours ago. I was fuck'n losing it."

Claire reached for her husband's cheek. "I'm here. You're here. So..." She gazed at him from behind veiled lashes, "...now that you've got me, what do you want to do with me?"

The blackness of his penetrating gaze swirled with suede, a soft light infiltrating the darkness as the heat of his angst morphed into the fire of unrestrained desire.

With another tug of her hair, her head once again went back and Claire closed her eyes as warm whiskey-scented breath bathed her cheeks and neck. Though her swollen lips ached for his, his were busy tormenting her soft skin with kisses that began behind her ear and descended to her neck and below. As he teased and taunted the sensitive skin of her collarbone, her fingers wove through his think mane. Moans and pleas filled the room as with each touch Claire was reminded of the man who claimed her body and soul—the man who at one time starred in her nightmares and now starred in her life. He wasn't her star, but her sun. Just like the real celestial object that controlled the solar system, Tony was the gravitational pull whom she willingly allowed to dictate her orbit and warm her heart.

If they'd had plans for that night, they didn't attend to them. There was no dinner out on the town, no Broadway show nor walk through Time Square, but neither one seemed to mind. Instead, their night was filled with one another. Each one gave and took. Together they reunited as a couple and soul mates. They made love and talked about their uncertainties and discoveries. Claire shared her revelation about being alone, and Tony recognized his distress *of being without her. Even after so many years, they shared and laughed, talked and cried, and when they were done, they made love some more, until sleep overtook them.*

It wasn't until the next morning that either one of them remembered the doctor's recommendation for alternative protection. They reasoned that it was only one night, and the doctors had warned that with Tony's age it might not happen the natural way. So what were the chances?

The water lapped over Claire's body as she floated below the Iowa stars, lost in the memories of that night. It wasn't only their journey that they continued that night; they'd also created the tiny being inside of her. With Claire's eyes closed to the twinkling stars, she imagined her husband's touch and the aroma of chlorine gave way to the intoxicating scent of cologne.

Her body electrified, as it only did in his presence. It was a connection they'd had for as long as she could remember. Words or touch weren't necessary. When they were near one another, the molecules in the air stirred and energy transferred. The scientific result of thermodynamics was heat. Their result was no different. Despite the tepid water, Claire's skin suddenly warmed. She opened her eyes to the sight of her husband: his jacket slung over his shoulder and linen shirt glowing with the colors of the pool's lights. It wasn't his Armani slacks or his shiny black loafers that caught her attention. It was the grin that tightened her stomach as his chocolate eyes sparkled.

"Good evening, Claire." His baritone voice resonated through the country night.

Tony

TIME STOOD STILL as Tony watched his wife, first from the shadows and then from the deck of the pool. Although he had plenty to say, he hadn't spoken a word; instead, he stood and observed as Claire floated near the surface of the colorful water. It was the whole picture that had him mesmerized: the warm, starry night, the way her hair floated around her beautiful face, her peaceful expression, and even the smile that graced her lips—on and off—as if she were remembering something that made her happy. She looked too beautiful to disturb. As the minutes passed and the water ebbed and flowed over her midsection, Tony began to think about their new baby.

He remembered the night, a few weeks ago, when he came home from work and discovered Claire in their suite:

It wasn't like her to be away from Nichol, yet she was, all alone and lost in her thoughts as she stood at the railing of their balcony. His gaze went the direction of her stare, out toward their backyard, where he saw Nichol with Shannon on the play set. It wasn't until he fully stepped beyond the glass doors that Claire turned. When she did, he saw her tearstained cheeks and his heart crumbled.

"Claire." His voice quivered with uncertainty as he reached for her shoulders. "What's the matter?"

She shook her head and melted against his chest. Tony's mind swirled with possibilities, each one worse than the one before.

After a moment, he lifted her chin and stared deeply into her moist eyes. Even with the tears, he knew he could get lost in her emerald gaze. "Whatever it is," he offered reassuringly, "we'll fix it."

Her body tensed. "Tony, you can't fix it. I don't want you to fix it."

"What do you want? What happened?"

She took a deep breath. "Remember we promised the doctors that we wouldn't try to get pregnant until this month?"

He nodded, wondering if maybe she'd changed her mind. If she had, he understood. He'd meant what he'd said about adopting. Hell, maybe they could hire a surrogate? He'd never thought of that before, but now that he had, he liked the idea. It was better than risking Claire's health. Tony thought he'd read somewhere where they can use Claire's egg and his sperm. Yes, that would be best. As the smile came to his lips, with his new idea, Claire's ramblings began to register.

"...I know we didn't mean to. I'm not positive it was that night in New York. I mean condoms aren't one hundred percent effective. I just don't know what they'll say."

The words weren't making sense. "What who will say? It's all right if you don't want to try this month. Maybe it would be better if we waited—"

She took a step back as her eyes grew wide. "Tony, you're not listening to me."

"I'm trying. You said something about New York and condoms." A devilish grin crept onto his lips. "I don't believe we remembered to use..."

It wasn't the same as when she told him she was pregnant with Nichol. That was sheer disbelief. For seconds—that seemed like days—he couldn't wrap his mind around her words. This was *different: the signals were mixed. He remembered that night in New York, their preoccupation with one another. Using protection was the furthest thing from their mind. They'd discussed another child at length. If she were pregnant, wouldn't she be happy? Why was she crying?*

Tony didn't respond appropriately the last time she informed him of her pregnancy. He had no intentions of screwing up the moment again. Summoning his biggest smile and wrapping Claire in his arms, he lifted her off the ground. "Really?" he asked, his dark eyes glistening with excitement. "Already? You're pregnant?"

The sadness or fear he'd seen when their eyes first met dissipated as she gazed upward and her cheeks lifted. "You're not upset?"

Tony put her down, reached for her hand, and led her to the balcony sofa. Though concerns and questions flooded his mind, once he and Claire were seated, Tony reached out and covered her midsection. "You're sure? We have a baby in there?"

Claire nodded and smiled as a tear trickled down her cheek. "We do. I mean the home pregnancy test said we do. I haven't called the doctor. I wanted to tell you first."

"Why didn't you call me?"

"I wanted to tell you in person. I think I was afraid that you'd be upset."

"Upset?" he asked.

"Yes." She looked down at his hand still resting on her tummy and covered it with her own. "We were supposed to wait."

He reached gently for her chin. "Well, I don't think I could be upset. I mean, if this happened that night in New York, we're equally responsible." He sat taller. "And the way I see it, Mrs. Rawlings, we have a new little Rawlings who wants to enter this world. There's nothing in that sentence that could make me upset."

As their lips touched and her petite body moved closer, Tony tasted her salty tears and the rest of the world disappeared. The gleeful noises from the play yard no longer registered, nor did the gentle summer breeze or streaming evening sunshine. Tony's world was only her: his wife, happy and content in his arms when moments earlier she'd been upset. When their connection finally broke, he heard the words that washed over him, filling him like nothing else.

"I love you so much. I imagined your reaction many ways, but this was better than anything I ever envisioned."

"Tomorrow we're going to your doctor. Let me know the time, and I'll be there."

Claire giggled as she wiped her cheek. "It doesn't work that way. I have to call for an appointment. They probably won't be able to get me in for a few days."

He bowed his head until their foreheads touched. "Tomorrow. I want you seen tomorrow." Tony was sure his tone left no room for debate. He'd be happy to use it on some unsuspecting receptionist if necessary. "Do you want me to call?"

Her eyes closed and head moved from side to side. "Oh, no. I don't want that. I'll call."

"And tomorrow..."

"Yes, Tony, tomorrow. I'll call you after I talk to the office and you can meet me there."

"I'll meet both of you there."

Her neck straightened. "I'm capable of driving."

As she spoke, his grin returned. "I wasn't speaking of Roach or Taylor, though you know I prefer that." His hand returned to her midsection. "I meant you and our little one."

The colorful water continued to ebb and flow as Tony imagined the baby growing within his wife. In time it would change her as Nichol had done. He remembered how radiant she looked—well, up until the end of Nichol's pregnancy. Then Claire looked miserable. Since that evening when he learned of their impending arrival, Tony's mood had fluctuated from joy to despair, everything in between, and back to joy. Hell, with as mixed up as he felt, some days he felt as though it could be he who was pregnant. There was no question: if he could, he would. Tony refused—absolutely refused—to allow anything to harm Claire, including their child. Then he'd remember that the doctors had given their clearance. They'd proclaimed Claire healthy enough to have a child. The OB/GYN had even addressed the issue of Nichol's birth. She didn't expect there to be anything like that this time, but if it occurred, they had a state-of-the art hospital and a C-section would be done right away.

When he wasn't thinking about the possible consequences of their decision, Tony concentrated on the new life, the new Rawlings. For a man who'd never expected to have children or be a father, his heart felt like it could literally burst. Never had he imagined the joy of children—the joy of a family. What he and Claire shared was nothing like what he'd known as a child, and at times it was overwhelming. Truthfully, the overabundance of love Tony felt for the tiny being that at this point was only evidenced by a blue plus sign on a white stick and the doctor's confirmation even surprised him.

Tony now understood that he'd wasted too much of his life trying to make the Rawls in him and his past proud, trying to achieve acceptance from a ghost. *Then again, was that true?* If he hadn't had the obsession, if he hadn't spent his first forty-plus years righting unexplained wrongs, then he wouldn't have waited for the woman before him, the one floating with a suddenly mischievous smile. His cheeks rose as he wondered what she was thinking. No, he'd never again regret the years he lost. If he did, he'd regret the life he now had, and that wasn't possible.

Removing his jacket, Tony flung it over his shoulder and moved closer to the pool's edge. With each step, he wondered how to get Claire's attention. With her ears submersed, she probably wouldn't hear him. Should he splash her? The idea of removing his clothes and diving into the water was appealing, but times had changed. For one thing, there was Nichol. As much as Tony doubted that she'd awaken and make her way down to the pool, he didn't want to take the chance. The other difference was the woman who dominated his thoughts and currently his vision. His wife deserved better than to be seen on estate security in a compromising position.

Just as Tony was about to lean down and splash, the most gorgeous emerald eyes in the entire world opened and an even bigger smile blossomed on her face.

"Good evening, Claire."

He walked toward the pool's steps as Claire swam his direction. Soon she was standing and their lips were reunited. Without a word they said so many things. It had been two days since he'd been home. He hated traveling without Claire and Nichol, but he understood. He understood that Claire didn't want Nichol's childhood spent in apartments and airplanes when she had the beauty of an Iowa summer and all the amenities of a five-star resort outside her backdoor. That didn't mean they never traveled, but sometimes separation was necessary. Thankfully with Tim's increased role, it wasn't too often.

"Good evening, Tony. I've missed you," she said with a grin as pool water dripped from her body and puddled near his shoes. "I think you're overdressed for this pool party."

He'd missed her too, every minute. "Party?" he asked, intrigued. Whatever she'd been thinking about had left her in a spirited mood. "I don't believe I was invited."

Pulling his shirt toward the water, she teased, "You're the only expected guest. Didn't you get the invitation?"

Grinning, he stopped her progress toward the water and lifted her chin. "While I like the way that sounds, first tell me how you're feeling."

Her bottom lip playfully protruded as she released his shirt and walked past him to get her robe. Cameras be damned, Tony wanted to touch what was in front of him in the white tankini. He couldn't resist as his hand playfully swatted her wet behind. Though the contact was minimal, the moisture caused the sound to echo as Claire jumped and smiled in his direction.

"Hey, you can't do that!"

"Oh, I can't?" His devilish grin glowed in the darkness. "I thought I made the rules. I asked you a question."

With her lips pressed defiantly together, she donned her robe. As he watched her bathing suit-clad body disappear, Tony wondered how long it would be before her breasts began to grow. As he recalled, that was one of the first things he noticed when he learned she was pregnant with Nichol. Perhaps they had. Maybe he should undo the robe and take a closer look. As those thoughts came and multiplied, Claire reached for his hand and led him toward the chairs.

"If you're not going to swim, sit with me." She patted the cushion beside her.

"You're going to get me wet."

"That's my plan."

Shaking his head, he sat. He didn't give a damn about his clothes as he wrapped his arm around his wife and pulled her close. "Now, answer me. How are you feeling?"

"I'm feeling great!" Her eyes opened wide and sparkled. "I really am. I keep expecting the morning sickness to hit me, and it still may, but so far, I feel good."

"Is that normal?" he asked, obviously concerned. "Aren't you supposed to be sick?"

Claire shrugged. "I don't think there's any right or wrong answer. I was with Nichol, for a while. Some people are sick a lot more than I was. Poor Julia, she's still sick—she's into her second trimester, and she still can't keep food down."

"Yes, Brent told me. He said she's even been to the hospital a couple of times."

Claire scrunched her nose. "I feel awful for her, but I don't want that. The only thing I notice is that I'm more emotional. I was reading a new book to Nichol about a bunny that lost his mitten. Even though I'd just bought it, she told me how much she liked the story. She said it was a story Aunt Em used to read. I started crying. I don't think she knew, but after I left her room I cried for about five minutes for no reason. It's the hormones."

Tony gently rubbed a circle on Claire's back as she leaned into him. The scent of chlorine emanated from her hair, as the cool wetness penetrated his shirt. "Hush, don't cry now. It's probably good that she can talk about it as if it's not a big deal."

Claire nodded.

He wasn't always the most perceptive, but it didn't take long for him to realize she was crying. Hugging her tightly, he lifted her chin again and wiped her tears with his thumb. "You didn't think the pool water was enough for my shirt—you thought it needed tears too?"

Claire grinned and shook her head.

"I love you, Mrs. Rawlings. I love that you're so emotionally bound to a bunny with no mittens that it makes you cry."

"Mr. Bunny had mittens," she corrected. "He'd just lost one."

Tony watched as the gleam returned to her gaze. "How about we take this pool party upstairs to our suite?"

"We don't have a pool upstairs."

Tony stood and reached for her hand. "No, my dear, but we have a shower and a large tub. The advantage of those is the no-bathing-suit rule."

"Oh?"

"Haven't I ever mentioned that?"

Her lips quirked into a knowing grin. "No, Mr. Rawlings. I've heard many of your rules, and I don't recall that one."

"Have you ever worn a bathing suit in the tub?"

Claire shook her head.

"Have you ever worn a bathing suit in the shower?" he asked as they began to walk toward the house.

"No, I can't say that I have."

"Then it sounds as though you've been doing a good job following my rule."

Claire reached up on her tiptoes and kissed his cheek. "I know a few other things I'm good at doing."

He threaded his fingers through hers. "I think I may have an idea, but we'd better get upstairs and check out each one."

"Oh, we will. There's no stopping mid-list. That's *my* new rule," Claire added with a grin.

Chapter 13

December 2017

Phil

———◆◆◆———

Love is friendship that has caught fire.
It is quiet understanding, mutual confidence,
sharing, and forgiving. It is loyalty through good
and bad times. It settles for less than perfection and
makes allowances for human weakness.
—Ann Landers

IN MANY WAYS the Rawlings estate was like a small town: the people were close and not much went unnoticed. Though none of the staff except Shannon was required to live on the grounds, Phil had no desire to live anywhere else. His sentiments were shared by most of the other employees. At the old estate, each person had housing in the main house, now each person had his or her own apartment and all of the apartments were located in the same building. Needless to say, with the closeness of their working and living, private lives weren't very private.

The clock read after eleven when Phil heard the knock on his apartment door. With a grin, he threw on a pair of sweat pants and went to answer it. As he reached for the handle, he fully expected to find Taylor on the other side. Though they didn't always spend the night at each other's place, it did happen. In a modest attempt to keep their relationship under the radar, they would often wait until later at night to visit one another.

Phil and Taylor's relationship had been building since she first started working for the Rawlings family. At first Phil wondered if he was the only one who had feelings beyond that of security professional and coworker. He fought those thoughts as long as he could. Then as time passed, things became more personal. The first sign wasn't truly sexual: it was a kinship. Phil could talk to Taylor, really talk about things that he'd never uttered to anyone else. It started the day he told her about his family and continued to grow. The night he confessed his failure to protect Claire from Patrick Chester was the night he knew that Taylor was more than a friend.

Their conversations weren't one-sided. Although he thought he'd learned all there was to know about Taylor Walters before he authorized her hiring, he hadn't. Her backstory was as messed up as his. Getting shot was a pivotal point in her life. The rehab was hell and she hated working behind the scenes. Neither one of them had been married or even in a relationship in recent history. Neither one believed another person could be trusted enough to be let in, especially let in on secrets. In some way, it was when Phil realized that he fully accepted and trusted Taylor to protect the Rawlingses that he could also trust her with his own story.

Perhaps that's how it was meant to be, just like the saying goes: *birds of a feather.*

Romantically, Taylor had been the first one to make a move. Truthfully, if it had been left up to Phil, they'd probably never have made it out of the friend/coworker stage. Thinking about last night, the blood returned to his cheeks and a smile floated across his lips. They'd definitely moved beyond.

Reaching for the handle, Phil opened the door. His smile quickly disappeared at the sight of Eric. His friend's somber expression spoke volumes of unuttered concerns. Finally Phil broke the silence. "Hey man, what's happening?"

Eric's worried eyes met Phil's. "Can I come in?" He paused. "I mean, you're alone, aren't you?"

"Yes," Phil said, stepping backward, and opening the door farther. "Come in. What's happening? You look like someone just killed your dog, and I know for a fact you don't have one."

Eric closed the door behind him. "I just pulled up your surveillance on Patricia."

Phil had a program that continually monitored her virtual presence in her new identity. From her work presence, to her personal interaction, any time Patricia Miles logged into the world of cyberspace, it was duly recorded and catalogued. Though the program ran continually, Phil didn't check it every day. He'd had his eyes on it more frequently at first, but lately it had been about once a week.

"You did. Why?"

Eric shrugged. "I know you check it regularly. I guess, with Nichol's birthday and the anniversary of Mr. and Mrs. Rawlings' first marriage all coming up, I had a feeling."

"A feeling?" Phil didn't like the vibe he was sensing. "What did you find?"

"Nothing."

Phil waited for more as he contemplated Eric's answer. Finally, reaching for his tablet, he said, "Fuck. What do you mean *nothing*?"

"I mean nothing. There's no record of her doing anything for the last four days."

Since Phil's last check had been less than a week ago, four days would make sense. Bringing the program to life, Phil asked, "Have you mentioned this to anyone else?"

"No. I found it earlier today. I ran some tests to see if maybe it was the program. When I couldn't get anything definitive, I waited until you were alone to see if you could learn more. I'm hoping it's some kind of glitch or malfunction with the surveillance."

"Have you mentioned anything about Patricia—at all—to Rawlings?"

"No. With the new baby coming, he'd lose it. And I sure as hell wouldn't say something to Mrs. Rawlings without telling him first. It's just us. I wanted to run this by you. I wasn't even sure how you felt about Taylor knowing."

The two men sat across the table from one another as Phil searched his tablet, typing furiously. "Stupid bitch." He pinched the bridge of his nose. "She couldn't let it go."

Eric nodded toward the tablet. "Can you verify her location?"

After a moment, Phil nodded. "The last time I checked, her virtual presence was still in London. Her login information was active from her place of employment and her home." He continued to type. "I see here where she applied for a new credit card." The blood drained from his face as his heartbeat intensified. "Shit. You're right. She hasn't logged in from work in the four days. The new credit card isn't under the same name we gave her, but it's here. She was dumb enough to use her work computer to complete the application." The two men sat in silence as Phil read his screen. "Shit. Here's an airplane ticket. She probably thought that if she bought it at the airport using the new credit card we wouldn't know."

Eric's head moved slowly from side to side as he watched Phil.

When Phil looked up, his hazel eyes narrowed. "She's fuck'n stupid. By tracing the card I can even see the hotel where she's staying."

Eric leaned forward. "In the States?"

"In Cedar Rapids."

The air in the room dissipated as the sound of their breathing echoed. Finally, Eric asked, "Can you tell the room number?"

Phil swallowed as their eyes met. "Yes."

"We gave her a chance—two really."

Ignoring the exorbitant pressure, Phil clenched his teeth harder. "That was two too many. Don't say a word to anyone—anyone. I'll be back by morning."

"I'm going with you," Eric declared.

"No, you're not. You're staying here." Phil didn't wait for Eric's response. He was in order mode. "Watch the gate, watch the monitors. There's no guarantee she's sitting in that hotel room. Fuck!" Phil's voice rose. "She's been here for three days. What if she'd—?"

"Like you said, she's stupid. She doesn't know we're on to her."

"She's arrogant. She thought by using a new name on the airline and hotel reservations we wouldn't be able to find her." Phil leaned over his tablet and typed again. Only the sound of the clicking keys filled the air until he stood and said, "She has two tickets for her return flight to London, the day after tomorrow."

"Two?"

"Yes, the second ticket is for a child."

Eric nodded. "I'll go to the security office right now and watch. If you need me, call. I'll be there."

"If anything happens, you don't know a damned thing about this."

"Are you kidding me? Nothing's going to happen. I've done my homework too. You've got this."

"I do," Phil confirmed.

THE SKY WAS still dark as Phil drove back to the estate. Though perhaps he should feel remorse, he didn't. Patricia planned to take Nichol back to Europe. He saw the evidence in her hotel room: the drugs to subdue her and the hair bleach to change her appearance. When it came down to his family or Patricia, the subject wasn't open for discussion. This time he didn't give her a chance to explain.

As soon as Phil found the airplane reservations he knew Patricia's plans. Not only had she used a new alias for her trip, she also had an alias for Nichol. He found their fake passports when he cleaned out the hotel room. In his opinion, Patricia's plan was confirmation of her ingenuity as well as her stupidity. The identification she had would lead the police to no one because *Charlotte Peterson* didn't exist. Besides, it was winter in Iowa. The fields were frozen and covered with snow. Digging even a shallow grave was like digging through rock, but Phil did it. Unless her body was eaten by animals, which was a possibility, the insects would begin to feast in the spring. Soon after, the farmers would be out tilling their fields. Spring and autumn were the times of year when bodies were often discovered in rural America: planting and harvest season. After all, long desolate stretches of highway with nothing more than corn and soybean fields for miles and miles made the perfect dumping grounds. It happened all the time. In an attempt to further thwart police efforts at identification, Phil was kind enough to leave her identification—or her false ID. Without it, DNA tests would be done. Phil's plan was that with the identification, evidence would be taken at face value: a woman named Charlotte Peterson was robbed, killed, and dumped. With a number of similar cases happening all the time, it was unlikely any further research would be performed. The case would be closed and another unclaimed body would be disposed of by the state.

At a little after 5:00 AM Phil quietly made his way to his apartment. The cooks would be up and moving about soon, and he hoped to avoid their prying eyes. It wasn't until he closed his apartment door and turned around that he saw Taylor. She was sitting up from where she'd fallen asleep on his sofa.

"What the hell are you doing in here?"

Her blue eyes scanned him up and down, obviously taking in the caked mud on his boots and jeans. When she didn't answer, he silently walked past her into his bedroom. Looking in the mirror he tried to imagine what she saw. Not only were his jeans and boots dirty, so was his jacket. Taking it off, he looked at his shirt beneath. The wrinkled cotton stuck to his skin, wet with perspiration. Thankfully there wasn't any blood. Pulling his shirt over his head, he threw it toward a pile of laundry. As he did, he saw Taylor leaning against the doorjamb.

"I never thought of you as the four-wheeling type."

"Taylor—"

She shook her head. "Please don't."

Sighing, he sat on the end of his bed and began unlacing his boots. He didn't want her to know what he'd done. It wasn't because of some false sense of pride. Phil wasn't worried about what she'd think of him. He'd told her things he'd done in his past and she'd shared things she'd done.

No, he didn't want her to know because he wanted to protect her. Protect her, the Rawlingses, everyone. The fewer people who knew what happened, the better. Phil hadn't seen her move, but now the bed shifted and she was sitting beside him with her hand on his back.

"I don't want you to lie to me," she said.

"I don't want to, but you have to understand..." He continued to look down at his now loosened boots.

Taylor reached for his face and turned it toward hers. "I do." She gently kissed him. "I'm taking Mrs. Rawlings and Nichol to the Simmonses' house today for her baby shower. Shannon's coming with us. Eric will take Mr. Rawlings to the office. I don't think he'll be there all day, but either way, Eric will take care of it. Get some sleep..."

"No, I can't sleep." He still couldn't look her in the eye.

She rubbed his bare shoulders. "You can. The adrenaline will ebb and you'll crash." She kissed his cheek. "I've been there."

Phil nodded. "I can't tell you."

She continued to rub his shoulders. "I'm not asking. Someday if you're ready, I'm here."

He turned to meet her light blue gaze. Phil didn't know what he expected to see: condemnation, suspicion, or maybe judgment. Whatever he expected was not what he saw; instead, it was understanding and acceptance. Kissing her gently, he nodded. "Why were you here? How did you—"

"I was on my way over to see you when I saw Eric. He didn't see me but I waited for him to leave. He did, but you left at the same time. When you didn't return, I went back to the main house to the security office and found him."

"Did he...?" Phil stopped, afraid of the answer he'd receive.

"No. I didn't pry. I could tell he was agitated. I don't know what went down." She glanced at Phil's muddy boots and jeans. "And I don't need to know, but I think you should try to sleep."

Phil's arms suddenly became heavy and his shoulders ached. Stretching his fingers in and out he groaned. He wasn't accustomed to manual labor and the shovel work had been incredibly difficult with the frozen ground. Phil nodded. "I think a hot shower first."

Taylor kissed him again. "I'd join you, but I'm guessing you're not in the mood."

One corner of his mouth rose as he scanned her from head to toe. Though most of her long hair was secured behind her neck in a loose ponytail, sleeping had caused a few renegade strands to dangle near her pretty face. Her soft pants were tight in all the right places, and her big t-shirt was wide at the neck and exposed one of her bare shoulders. Her deep red, shiny toenails peeked out from the wide cuffs of her pants. Phil liked that no one but he ever saw those polished toes. Reaching out he tucked a strand of hair behind her ear. As he looked into her blue eyes and loving smile he mused how much he liked Taylor's relaxed side. The softness was a stark difference from her professional demeanor.

Tipping his forehead toward hers, he said, "I know I'm an idiot for turning that down, but you're right. I think I'm coming down, and I should try to get some sleep."

"Don't worry," she whispered as she palmed his cheeks and kissed his lips. "Eric and I have today covered."

Phil nodded.

"Besides, I'm guessing our threat level has decreased."

Phil closed his eyes. Damn, even his eyelids were heavy. "Taylor..."

She stood and looked at the clock on Phil's bedside stand. "Shit, half the staff will be up and moving about, and here I go: the walk of shame."

He reached for her hand. "Sorry."

"I'm not. I'm glad you're back, and I trust this won't come back to anyone here?"

"I did my best to assure that."

"Nothing more we can do."

She bent down and kissed him again. "I'll tell Eric you're back."

"I called him, but thanks."

With a faint smile, Taylor stepped back into the living room. As Phil took off his boots, he heard, "Walk of shame, here I come." Carrying the mud-covered boots to the bathroom, he decided they needed to be thoroughly cleaned and his clothes would go in the washer before he put his tired body in that shower.

Hours later the incessant ringing of his cell phone brought Phil back to life. His entire body ached as he rolled toward the sound. *What time was it?* He wrestled with his orientation as the name on his screen came into view: *Rawlings.*

"Hello?" Phil managed, trying not to sound like he was asleep in the early afternoon.

"Roach, we need to talk."

Phil's mind suddenly cleared. *Had someone tipped off Rawlings?* He sat up in bed, convincing himself that neither Eric nor Taylor would do that. *Could Patricia's body have been found?* So many thoughts flew through his head as Phil replied, "Now?"

"Yes, now. Come to the house. I'm in the office."

Phil closed his eyes as the line went dead.

Claire

"THIS PARTY'S FOR my baby brover. My party's gonna be bigger!" Nichol exclaimed.

Claire shook her head. "Well, I'm not sure about bigger, but it will be for you."

"Yep," Nichol reached out and spoke to Claire's enlarged midsection. "Today's for you, baby. Maybe you could decide to be a sister?"

"Honey, we've talked about that. The doctors can see your brother with a special camera and they know he's a boy."

"How do they know?"

Claire looked from Nichol to Shannon who was shaking her head with a grin. "Oh my goodness, I'm not ready to have that talk with my three-year-old daughter."

The other ladies at the shower all laughed.

Nichol's forehead wrinkled. "I'm four."

"Well, not quite yet," Emily corrected.

"Aunt Em, did the doctors see Beff and know she's a girl?"

"They did."

"Momma, did you know about me too?"

"We didn't. Remember, Daddy and I were on the island when you were born. When we tried to find out, you didn't want to tell—you were teasing us."

"Maybe my sister's teasing you, too." She leaned her mouth toward Claire's stomach. "Are you teasing in there?"

"Mrs. Rawlings, I'd be happy to take Nichol to the other room. I brought some books and games," Shannon offered.

"Nichol, why don't you go with Shannon and when we open your brother's presents you can come help me."

Nichol got down from her chair. "Okay." She took Shannon's hand and Claire mouthed "Thank you" to her nanny.

"Wow, Claire, I can't wait to see you with two," Meredith said with a smile.

Claire leaned back and stretched her back. "I'm ready."

"I know that feeling," Emily and Julia said in unison and laughed.

"Now, Claire," Sue began. "I think it's time to spill the beans. This shower's the perfect opportunity to share with all of us, your closest friends, the name you and Tony have chosen for your son."

Claire pressed her lips together and smiled. "We've talked a lot about his name, and we think we have the perfect one. I mean, it's not easy to be Anthony Rawlings' son. His name has to be special, like Nichol's is for us. When he joins us, we'll let you all know."

Whispers of understanding filled the room. Finally, Courtney asked, "Would anyone like anything else to eat or more coffee or tea?"

As everyone chatted, Claire looked around Courtney's living room and sighed contently. She was surrounded by her family and friends. There was something about having everyone's support that made this pregnancy easier than her first.

Just as they were about to open presents, Courtney stood. "Before we begin, I promised Tony I'd help him with his gift. You all know how persuasive he thinks he is. Well..." She smiled at Claire. "First, I convinced him that he wouldn't enjoy the shower, but that didn't stop his plan. He wanted to get Claire a gift she wouldn't forget."

The whole room inhaled with anticipation as Claire

contemplated what Tony would consider an unforgettable gift. They had the nursery complete. It was much larger than Nichol's had been on the island, but like Nichol's it was attached to their suite. Claire remembered listening to Tony rock and talk to their daughter in the middle of the night. After she'd feed Nichol, she'd lay awake and listen as he promised her the moon and stars and his unending love. As the contractors drew up plans for the nursery, Claire knew she wanted that again.

"A diamond-studded car seat?" Emily suggested.

"Maybe a golden cradle?" Sue replied.

"I think you could guess all day and you wouldn't come up with the right answer," Courtney said. "Personally, I think I've kept your gift hidden for too long. And you know how hard secrets are for me." She shrugged and with a grin, added "Although... Brent and I have enjoyed having these gifts here with us for the last two days."

"Two days?" Claire said as she turned toward the archway. She could hardly believe her eyes as she saw Francis and Madeline and a lump formed in her throat. "Oh!" she exclaimed as Courtney helped her from her chair; she rushed to the couple and was swallowed in their embrace.

When the tears and hugs finally calmed, Madeline said, "Madame el, the next time you have a bébé, could it be when the weather is warmer? This is the first time we've seen snow. It is very cold."

The room erupted in laughter.

"Oh, Madeline and Francis, I don't know if there'll be a next time." She pulled them by their hands to sit beside her. "How long can you stay?"

"How long do you want us?" Madeline asked.

"We will stay that long," Francis added with his large, loving smile.

"We are so pleased to be here, but..." Madeline's big dark eyes narrowed. "...this bébé, I not deliver him."

"No, Madeline. This little guy will be born at the hospital."

Claire made all the introductions or re-introductions. Many of the ladies had met Francis and Madeline a year ago when they all visited the island. Her heart swelled with love as she took in the kind couple and their genuine smiles. When she'd called and asked them to come to Iowa, they acted apprehensive about leaving the island. Though she was disappointed, Claire understood. It was a long trip and neither of them had ever been to the United States.

As the room erupted in chatter, Brent entered. "Francis, now that Claire knows you're here, would you like to go downstairs with me? There's a lot of estrogen in this room."

Francis nodded. "I'm not sure of estro-gen, but if there be less laughing ladies, I say yes." He reached for Claire's hand. "Madame el, we are so happy to be here. Thank you."

Claire squeezed his large hand. "Thank you. I feel better having you two here."

It wasn't until near the end of the baby shower that Courtney's doorbell rang. Claire didn't need to look: she knew who couldn't stay away. When she did glance toward the door, despite the crowded room, her eyes met his and her heart melted. She saw the satisfaction in his devilish grin—he'd successfully surprised her.

Tony wasn't alone. Phil, who looked tired, was with him. After a moment, Phil excused himself to join the men downstairs, and Tony walked toward Claire. The floor and table around her were cluttered with gifts. "Well, my dear, it looks like our little man made out like a bandit. Are you pleased with all your gifts?"

"They're not for Momma. They're for my brover," Nichol corrected.

With her eyes still on her husband, Claire replied, "I love *all* my gifts, and I can't believe you surprised me like this. How could they be here for two days and you not tell me?"

Tony chuckled. "It was difficult. I didn't even let Roach know until this afternoon. I wasn't sure he'd be able to keep it from you. As soon as I told him, he insisted that he come over here with me to see them." Tony turned toward Madeline. Bowing slightly at the waist, he said, "Hello, Madeline. Welcome."

"Monsieur."

"Claire," Courtney asked, "do you remember yesterday when you wanted to come over and help me get ready for the shower?"

Claire nodded.

"Now do you understand why I said you couldn't? Madeline and I were cooking."

Claire reached for Madeline's hand. "Oh, cooking with you! I love cooking with you."

"You still cook?" Emily asked jokingly.

"Well, not really, but I did on the island. Madeline taught me some of the most amazing dishes."

"Oui, Madame el, we may cook." Madeline looked out the window. "I think the seafood here may not be as fresh."

"You make a list, Madeline," Tony said. "For your fantastic meals, I'll get you whatever you need and as fresh as possible."

Her cheeks lifted as her eyes went to her lap. "Monsieur, you're always too kind."

THAT EVENING CLAIRE, Tony, Shannon, Phil, Taylor, Madeline, and Francis all sat around the living room of the Rawlings estate and chatted. Each time Madeline would try to do something for Claire, Claire would remind her that she was a guest in their home.

"No. We come to help you, not to be waited upon."

"You've already helped me. I know everything will go well now that you two are here."

Francis's smile lit up the room. "We have been praying for you and this little boy since Monsieur called. Everything will be well with you and with him; we know that."

Claire wasn't sure how a proclamation like that could ease her anxiety, but it did. A peace settled over them like a blanket that warmed and comforted not only the room or the estate but also her. At first Claire thought it was only she who felt it, but as the weeks progressed she knew that it affected everyone. Nichol was head over heels in love with Francis and Madeline, and the feeling was mutual. They doted over her like grandparents. Nichol would sit for hours and listen to Francis' stories of the island and paradise, just as Claire remembered doing when she lived with them.

Whether it was Shannon or the cooks, no one seemed to mind having Madeline's assistance. She was everyone's friend. It wasn't until after the first of the year that Madeline told Claire the secret that apparently only she hadn't fully recognized.

"Madame el, you have a blessed house." She and Claire were folding small blue and green sleepers and other tiny clothes.

"Thank you, Madeline. I agree."

Suddenly a large dark hand covered hers. "We prayed for love and guidance in your lives. You have so many people who care."

"I do. Thank you for reminding me."

"And Monsieur Phil, it makes Francis and me happy to see him with someone who truly loves him, too."

Claire's eyes opened wide. "Monsieur Phil? We all love him. I don't know what we'd do without him."

"Oui, but not that kind of love: the kind like exists between you and Monsieur Rawlings—it's written all over their faces."

"Do you mean Taylor?" Claire asked as she stopped what she was doing and tried to remember. Had she been so caught up in everything to do with herself that she hadn't seen it? Perhaps she had. She mentioned it once to Tony, but that was a long time ago. Claire contemplated Madeline's information. She knew better than to question Madeline. The sweet woman undoubtedly had a sixth sense about everything and everyone. "I don't think I realized." Her emerald eyes sparkled. "I'm happy for them... but they haven't mentioned it, so we'd better pretend like we don't know."

Madeline continued to fold and put clothes into the cherry dresser. "Words are not the only way we communicate. You can give your blessing through your actions. I believe he's afraid to tell you."

"Why? Did he tell you that?"

"No, Madame el. He did not need to."

Claire didn't reply as Madeline's words registered. She and Phil were friends. He'd protected her and Nichol when they needed it most. He'd stayed true to her family when the world was in chaos. She wanted him happy, and if Taylor did that, she wouldn't be the one to spoil it. After all, he'd been the one to support her and Tony. Had he not traveled back to Europe and brought Tony to the island, Claire's life, as well as Nichol's would be totally different.

A few days later, Claire asked Phil to her office alone. As they sat and talked, their years of friendship were evident. As with many of the relationships in Claire's life, it had begun rather unconventionally—Phil was sent to California to spy on her—yet with time things change. When he stood to leave, Claire reached up and hugged him. "You know I only want what's best for you."

Phil nodded. "The feeling's mutual."

"I like Taylor. She's been around for a year and feels like one of the family."

His cheeks rose and the flakes of gold sparkled in his eyes. "We weren't hiding. We're trying to be professional."

Claire rubbed his shoulder. "As long as you know that we know, we're good. I don't want to ever make you feel uncomfortable. Honesty has always been our strong suit."

"All of you are our responsibility," Phil said. "Neither Taylor nor I nor Eric would allow anything to happen. I don't want you to think our loyalty is divided."

"It better be," Claire proclaimed.

Phil took a step back. "What do you mean?"

"When you first started working for me, it was just me. Then you brought Tony back, and then Nichol came. Now our little man is on his way." Claire smiled. "I've never felt less protected because you had more than me to babysit."

Phil's smile broadened at the term. "Babysit..." He said shaking his head.

"Taylor can be on that list too. I know you, and I know you won't let any of us down."

"Thank you. Just so you know," Phil said as he opened the door, "there's only one Mrs. Alexander."

Chapter 14

Early February 2018

Tony

———◆———

Until we have seen someone's darkness,
we don't really know who that person is.
Until we have forgiven someone's darkness,
we don't really know what love is.
—Marianne Williamson

TONY WOKE WITH a start from the sensation of falling—from where he didn't know—down to an unknown chasm. The downward sensation could either end in a crash, the ramifications undetermined, or by sheer will. That wasn't even a conceivable choice. Anthony Rawlings couldn't plummet into the unidentified abyss; he chose will. The subconscious decision was evidenced by his increased heart rate as well as elevated temperature. Tony's brow glistened in the moonlit room. Taking a deep breath, he reached for his anchor, his rock, his life, but the bed beside him was empty. The more he groped toward Claire's side of the bed, the more he found only cooled, lonely sheets. Looking to the clock near the side of the bed, he saw that it was a little after 2:00.

Sighing, he threw back the covers, sat, and allowed his eyes to adjust to the darkness. "Claire?" he called, quietly, so as to not wake her if she were asleep somewhere else. Evenings past, he'd found her that way, sleeping on the sofa before the large fireplace. Her back had been giving her bouts of pain, and Tony knew that some nights she was having increasing difficulty staying comfortable and asleep. Not finding her on the sofa, he smirked. The best chance of her location was behind the door to their private bathroom. Nichol had done the same thing to her, especially late in the pregnancy. Two or three trips in one night were not uncommon.

Opening the door, he stepped onto the cool tile floor. The room was empty. As he returned to the suite, he heard her voice coming from the darkened nursery. "Tony, why are you awake?"

The smile that came to his lips did little to hide his relief. He knew his anxiety at ever losing her again was both unfounded and obsessive. It was his most discussed topic with his therapist. Over time he'd come to realize that of the few people who'd occupied a place in his heart, Claire was the only one who remained. The others had either died or disappointed him beyond repair. Her steadfastness gave him something he'd never before had, and there was a part of him that feared losing it. That wasn't Claire's issue; it was his.

If asked, Tony would tell the world he didn't need the psychobabble shit. He'd tell them he was done and it was all a farce. However, he knew that answer wouldn't be the truth. Like Jim at Yankton, his current therapist expected honesty, and somewhere in the last three years, Tony had found an acceptable outlet in the weekly sessions. Claire didn't need to be bothered with his irrational thoughts; truly, she'd dealt with enough of them from both him and herself. Tony would never speak to Brent or Tim of anything so personal. Perhaps that was the difference between most women and men. Claire had cut back her therapy to once a week, claiming that speaking to her friends, especially Courtney and Meredith, was as helpful as speaking to Dr. Brown.

Tony's personal relationships with his friends had changed over the years, since Claire. Everything in his life could be divided into BC or AC: Before Claire or After Claire. It was hard not to think that way: the difference was too extreme. From his cold detached way of conducting business, to his peripheral personal relationships, and his private life, what Tony lived now in the AC was almost a dream in comparison to the way he had lived.

Long ago he'd stopped wondering how someone so lovely and loving could love him. He had to. The obsession almost cost him everything. At Yankton he'd come to the conclusion that it wasn't truly possible. Claire's love couldn't be real, not for someone like him. Subsequently, the reality he finally reached was that he couldn't accept her love and forgiveness until he loved and forgave himself. It was a breakthrough realization. No one in his life had ever forgiven his indiscretions. No one in his life forgave; instead, they sought justice and vengeance. It was all he'd ever known, until her: the one woman who had every right to hate and seek revenge didn't. The one person he'd wronged more than any other, and instead of cementing his tomb of hatred, she shattered it into a million pieces, giving him light where there had only been dark.

That realization changed everything. Tony no longer conducted his business affairs as he had, and yet he was still successful. He no longer treated his friends as he had, and they were closer for it. The difficult side of this new way of living was the dependence he now felt toward Claire. Before Claire, he was an island. Tony needed no one, nor did he depend on anyone. At the time, the isolation was comforting. If no one knew the real him, he would never be hurt. If he looked at spreadsheets and saw only numbers, not lives or livelihoods, decisions were easier. The world of black and white may be a solitary place to live, but it's an easier one to navigate. The colorful explosion that occurred AC was blinding and exhilarating. Everything in every aspect of his life was now different.

Anthony Rawlings knelt beside the woman who'd changed him in more ways than he ever thought he wanted to change her. As he did, he knew he wouldn't go back to black and white, to BC. He didn't want to. She was one of his anchors, keeping him from slipping back into that abyss. In a short time he'd have another—another child, another anchor. Tony's life was about more than himself. It was about Claire, Nichol, and soon Nathaniel. Tony looked up into the color that changed it all, the one shade that began the cascade of pigments that transformed his world forever. Tony gazed into the depth of emerald green.

Claire's chair moved back and forth as he placed his hands on her midsection and asked, "Is it your back?"

She nodded. "It was, but now I'm just thinking."

He waited for more. When none was given, he asked, "About?"

Her petite hands framed his scruffy cheeks. "Tony, will you promise me something?"

Feeling the movement within her, he knew there was nothing within his power he wouldn't do. She truly didn't need to ask. "Anything."

"*If*, and I'm not saying it will happen, but *if* you're faced with the same question you were when Nichol was born, and *both* isn't an option..." She took a deep breath. "...choose Nate."

Tony sat back on his heels and stared. "No."

Tears descended her cheeks and her nostrils flared, yet her voice held no sign of emotion. "I've been thinking about it. I know the chances are slim. All the doctors have been satisfied with the way this pregnancy has progressed. Even Madeline keeps reassuring me. But Tony..." She reached for his hand. "...you always get your way."

"That's not always true, but if it were, my way is you."

"No, listen," Claire implored. "You always get your way. If you demand they save Nate, they will. And..." she began before Tony could speak. "...I want you to know, I'm all right with that decision. I never want you to question yourself. I've lived the most amazing life. I've known every emotion, experienced the lowest lows and the highest highs. I know both love and hatred. I've seen places in this world that I never as a little girl even knew existed. Though I've lived through nightmares, you've fulfilled every dream. Tony, that's more than most people experience in a lifetime."

He couldn't stop the emotion building in his chest. "Claire, this conversation isn't necessary."

She nodded. "I hope you're right. I want more. I want to hold Nate in my arms and shower him with kisses. I want to look into Nichol's beautiful brown eyes and tell her I love her as she goes to college or walks down the aisle. I want to sit beside you and watch our grandchildren play." Her quiet tears turned to sobs. "But if I don't, if all that I've done is all that I do, being loved by you and giving life to two amazing children are the greatest accomplishments I could ask for." She gasped for breath. "Please, Tony, please promise me that you'll choose Nate."

He couldn't go another second without the woman before him in his arms. Tony stood and gently tugged Claire from the chair. When she stood, he wrapped her in his arms, and they stood in the stillness of the nursery. As her shoulders shuddered and she buried her face against his chest, tears coated his cheeks. Facing their previously unspoken fears allowed a peace to settle. Finally, Tony leaned away and wiped her tears with his thumb. "My dear, there is nothing I will ever deny you and you know that. As soon as Nathaniel Sherman Rawlings is ready to enter this world he will, and when that happens, he'll be laid in your waiting arms, awaiting the shower of kisses. That is not debatable."

Claire

SHE NEEDED TO hear her husband's words and tone. Her anxiety had been building stronger with each day as Nathaniel's due date approached. Claire didn't want to leave her family, but she unselfishly loved them more than herself. Though Madeline's reassurances had helped, hearing Tony's proclamation made it better. The tone he used as he uttered the words: *That is not debatable*, was a melody to her ears and a shot of reassurance to her heart.

Claire nodded. "I love you so much."

Tony took her hand and walked them back into the suite and toward their bed. "Mrs. Rawlings, I've said it before and I'll repeat it until the day I die. I love you. You're my life, my drug, my anchor. You've made me into a man who deserves to have you in his life."

Claire shook her head and put her finger to his lips. "No, Tony. I didn't *make* you into anyone. You've always been this man. People don't change: they hide. The man you were was a shell hiding the man you are today. The woman I was, when you first took me, was a shell hiding the woman I was afraid to be. I didn't make you. You didn't change me. And I thank God that once our shells were broken that the two people we really were fit together so well."

"Oh, and we do," he reassured with a grin. "I think we fit together very well."

Claire sighed. "I don't fit very well right now."

Lying down, Tony pulled her close against his side. It was true that as their son grew, they fit together differently than they had a day or week before. With Claire's belly resting against Tony's side, Nathaniel made his presence known.

Feeling their son move, she asked, "Did you feel that?"

"I did," Tony replied with a lighter tone. He reached for her midsection, his large palm covering their son. "I love this. I'm sorry your back is hurting, but I love the sensation of him moving within you. I remember sitting for hours on the island's lanai and feeling Nichol. It's truly an amazing thing."

Claire swallowed. "I love it too, and I'm ready to be done."

"I know now isn't the time to ask, but do you think you'd ever be ready to have another?"

Claire awkwardly moved to a sitting position. "I know you're smarter than that," she said with a smirk. "I mean, if you're asking if I want to have sex, I'm game. If you're asking if at almost forty weeks of pregnancy I'm ready to try again, well, my answer is not right now."

Tony gently pushed her shoulders against the pillow and towered over her, his dark eyes penetrating into her soul. In mere seconds, she found herself lost in the sparkling gleam in front of her. "Oh?" he asked, "You're game? After that emotional outburst in the nursery, you're game?"

Giggling, Claire nodded. "It's the hormones. I'm all over the map."

"I think you said the other night that you read that sex can induce labor. Should I feel used?"

"Hmm, Mr. Rawlings, forgive me if you feel used. I just want to be with my husband before we can't."

He kissed her lips. "Damn, how could I forget about the *can't* part? Then by all means..." His lips teased her neck while his skillful fingers removed the straps of her nightgown. "...I'm all yours. Use me to your heart's content."

"That's a pretty big order. As you may have noticed, food isn't the only thing I crave while pregnant."

"Why do you think I'm asking about number three?"

Claire smiled. "Ulterior motives. No wonder you're so successful at business. I didn't see that one coming."

"No rush. I'm all for waiting a month or two until after Nate's born."

Claire reached for his cheeks and brought his lips to hers. "New rule: no talking about future pregnancies while I'm pregnant. For now, let's concentrate on the task at hand."

"At hand?" His brows quirked upward. Sliding her satin gown over her head, Tony's lips found her sensitive breasts as his fingers wandered lower.

"Yes, Mr. Rawlings, *at hand* is a good place to start."

A FEW DAYS later, Claire walked about the kitchen retrieving the ingredients Madeline requested for their dinner. "Madame el... Claire," she corrected, bringing a smile to Claire's face. "I can do this alone or with your cook's help. She's very nice to allow me access to her kitchen. You should be resting."

Claire shook her head. "Honestly, I don't know what it is. I feel great, like I could hike to the lake and back. Well, if it weren't snow covered and frozen."

Madeline grinned. "I'd love to see this lake, when warmth returns to your home."

"Oh, Madeline, I'd love for you to stay long enough to see spring. I know this all looks desolate right now, but once the green returns... it's not as lush as our island, but it's a renewal, a time of new birth. I've always loved the springtime."

"Time will tell of our departure. Now we're happy to be here with you and Monsieur and of course your bébés."

Claire rubbed her belly. "Babies! Soon." Her bright eyes looked up to find Madeline's caring gaze. "Can you believe it? I can't believe he's almost here."

"Why do you not tell his name?"

Claire made her way to a tall stool and sat. "I guess we're afraid people will try to talk us out of it."

"Come now, do you believe that anyone could talk you or Monsieur out of something? I do not."

Claire smiled. "I guess we don't want them to try."

"Though I don't understand, I'm glad this time you have a name. Last time..." She looked up and shook her head. "...my heart nearly stop when Monsieur say he wait to name your daughter."

"Well, we don't have those traditions here, and I guess it doesn't matter. We know his name." Claire and Tony had chosen Nathaniel's name after hours, days, and weeks of deliberating. They both knew their reasons and were happy with their decision. Though they'd kept the name between just the two of them, there was something about Madeline that made Claire want to share. She took a deep breath and peered around the kitchen. "I'm dying to tell. If I tell you—"

Madeline's hand went into the air. "Madame el, I do not keep secrets from Francis."

Claire didn't care. Honestly, if Francis were with them now, she'd still feel confident in their combined confidentiality. "Not Francis, but everyone else, not until he's born."

Madeline nodded. "Very well, I'd love to know."

"Our son's name is Nathaniel Sherman Rawlings."

"A handsome name. Why do you not want to tell?"

Claire took a deep breath. "It's a long story, one that you and I've never discussed."

"If you speak of that book, we do not read it." Madeline looked up from the vegetables she was cutting. "This world is full with people who make things big, sensationalize. I will say, when your friend Meredith come to the island, we are surprised. She has the same name—"

Claire nodded. "She has the same name as the author of the book because she is. And yes, her publishers sensationalized some of it—I've read it. However, most of it is true."

Madeline's cutting stopped mid-slice. "No, Madame el. I know things. From the moment Monsieur Rawlings arrive on the island, I feel nothing but love. Those things that people said—"

"I can't explain all of it. However, you're right. We love one another—now and then. It's almost as if the people in Meredith's book were two different people than who we became. In some ways they were. The thing is that in this long, complicated story, our paths would never have crossed, we'd never have the love and the family we do now if it weren't for our grandfathers. They met one another when I was about Nichol's age: Tony's grandfather, Nathaniel, and my grandfather, Sherman. Had it not been for them, we wouldn't be here. I loved my grandfather very much."

She sighed. "I didn't know the professional man whom Tony met as a young man. I knew the kind, loving grandpa who told me stories, took me fishing, and listened to everything I had to say. I knew he had an important job, but that never mattered. He always made me feel special." Her green eyes brimmed with tears. "I lost my grandparents and parents too young, but in the short time they were in my life, they gave me unconditional love and I'll always be thankful for that."

"And Monsieur's grandfather?"

"I never knew him, but I feel as though I did." Claire recalled the Anthony Rawlings of her past and the pictures and stories she'd heard of Nathaniel. "You see, I've seen pictures, and Tony looks a lot like him. The man Tony respected and loved was hard, yet like my husband, I believe it was a facade that he showed the world. Nathaniel made mistakes in his life and poor decisions, but that doesn't take away from the fact that he was the man my husband loved as a child. Tony chose to end the history of revenge when he named our daughter. She carries my surname: Nichols. We choose to further that mend and unite our two families with our son's name. Nathaniel Sherman will carry both names of our grandfathers. Someday I want him to know that even though there are forces in the world that want to destroy what we hold dear, love and acceptance can overcome. If it didn't, our Nate wouldn't be coming into this world."

"That is beautiful," Madeline said with her hand to her chest. "Your Nathaniel will be blessed with the strength and love of both of his families."

Claire smiled past the tears teetering on her lids. "Oh," she said as her midsection painfully hardened.

"Madame Claire, are you all right?"

"I-I think." The hardness persisted. "I've been having the Braxton Hicks contractions for some time." She inhaled again. "This seems different."

"Where is your phone?"

"No, Madeline, let me just rest. I don't want to alarm anyone."

"No." Her voice was uncharacteristically hard. "I listen to you last time. Not today. Tell me how to reach Monsieur Rawlings, and we will have Monsieur Phil to take you to the hospital right now."

The tightness only intensified. "All right." Claire pointed toward the counter. "There's my phone. Tony and Phil's numbers are in there. Can you please call?" Claire eased herself from the stool and squatted near the floor. "Please, this isn't letting up."

DESPITE THE ERUPTING chaos around her, Claire tried to maintain her calm. Phil was almost as nervous as an expectant father as he drove toward the university hospital. "Did you call your doctor? Does she know we're coming?"

"Yes," Claire reassured. The tightening had subsided. Though her back was still hurting, she wondered if this was all a false alarm. "Maybe we should go back home. I'm not feeling it anymore."

"Claire, we're on the way. Rawlings is meeting us. Let's just let them check you out."

She began to puff her cheeks and blow in short bursts as the tightness returned. "Phil, Eric's with Tony, isn't he?" Claire knew her husband would think nothing of risking his own life to get to her. She didn't want him driving on the snow-covered roads.

"Yes, Eric's got him. Madeline, Francis, and Shannon are with Nichol. Everything's fine. You worry about you."

"I wish Taylor were there."

"She's due back tomorrow. You're a few days early. Besides the estate is secure. Everyone there is safe."

Claire nodded. She knew he was right. There hadn't been any mailings for a long time. When Taylor had asked for the time off to go to a wedding, Claire didn't hesitate. Her staff deserved personal time as much as she and Tony. Although, if Claire said she wasn't relieved when Phil said he wasn't going with Taylor, she'd be lying. Even though Claire tried to assure Phil it would be all right, he refused to go. Now watching his leather gloves stretch as he gripped the steering wheel, she knew she was glad he'd stayed.

The tightness subsided as they pulled up to the emergency room. Perhaps that wasn't the only thing that gave Claire the strength to move from the SUV to the waiting wheel chair: it was the dark eyes that immediately met hers.

The next few hours ebbed and flowed in tempo. Some sped by in a blur, while others moved at a snail's pace. People came and went. Phil brought Shannon and Nichol to the hospital to assure Nichol that her momma was all right. Nichol wanted to stay to meet her baby brother, but as evening came, Tony and Claire promised her she could return in the morning. Emily and Courtney stayed in the delivery room as things progressed. There were others waiting outside of her room. John and Brent came in from time to time to squeeze her hand and give their support. The epidural dulled the pain, but more importantly, it didn't reduce her understanding. Unlike with Nichol, Claire was conscious of everything around her. It wasn't until the doctor announced that it was time to have only two people in the room that Claire sighed with relief. For the first time in her life, she was about to experience the joy of childbirth.

"Honey," Emily said as she hugged her sister, "Courtney and I have talked about this. We're both leaving."

Claire's eyes widened. "One of you can stay."

Emily shook her head. "We love you and we're right outside." She looked past Claire to Tony. "This is something the two of you should share. Just please, let us know as soon as you can."

Tony nodded to Emily and hugged Courtney. "I will," he said. "I'll be out as soon as I can."

As Tony moved to his place by Claire's shoulder and held tightly to her hand, she watched the mirror near the end of the bed. Each time the nurse told her to push, she did. Each time the doctor said to breathe, she did. Following instructions had never been a problem, especially when the payoff was on the horizon.

How long did labor last? Claire couldn't recall. Later she'd remember pressure and some commotion. She'd recall reassuring touches from the dark-eyed man at her side and words from her doctor. She'd also remember that Tony was never asked to decide who would survive. There was never a need. Early in the morning on February seventh, Nathaniel Sherman Rawlings officially entered their lives.

Claire didn't know if Nichol had entered with as loud of a cry, but the one she heard from her son warmed her heart and soul.

"Yes, Claire and Anthony, your son is announcing his presence," the doctor proclaimed, lifting their son in the air.

As Claire looked up at her husband, she saw the moisture on his cheeks that she felt in her own eyes. He leaned down and whispered, "I love you."

She couldn't form words until the nurse laid Nathaniel on her chest and covered them both with a blanket. "Hi, Nathaniel," she cooed. "I'm your momma."

Tony stroked the small head covered in dark hair. "Hello, son, I'm your daddy."

It was then their son's eyes opened and Claire and Tony were lost in the sea of emerald. Warmth enveloped their bubble as Tony embraced his family. "He has your eyes."

They stayed like that for a while, not ready to share the moment with those outside the door. It was one of those rare occasions that can be looked back upon as lasting both a second and forever, a life-changing eternity that cemented the past with the future.

Chapter 15

Mid-February 2018

Claire

———◆———

To the world you may be just one person,
but to the one person you may be the world.
—Mother Theresa

CLOSING HER EYES Claire listened to the sound of her husband's voice. The cadence reminded her of a lullaby, yet his words were not that of a song or a fairytale. His words were those of a father talking to his son: words of love and encouragement, as well as promises that only time could substantiate. Just as it had been when Nichol was a baby, the middle of the night feeding was among Claire's most cherished time of day. Tony would wake to their son's cries and change Nate's diaper, bringing a fresh, sweetly scented baby to Claire's arms. For a two-week-old baby, Nate was a fervent eater. Undoubtedly eating was his favorite activity. Once he started, he'd use all of his energy to devour everything that Claire had to offer. When he was satisfied, his little eyes would blink until the emerald disappeared and long lashes rested peacefully upon his growing cheeks.

It was then that Tony would take him into the nursery, sit with him, and rock him. Claire didn't always know how long they spent together. Most nights she'd fall back asleep listening to the deep baritone voice waft through the quiet night air. This was Tony and Nate's special time, and she didn't want to interrupt. When she and Tony talked about another child, Tony confessed that those hours spent with Nichol in paradise, in the middle of the night, were instrumental in keeping his sanity while at Yankton. He said that he'd lie in his bunk, night after night, and relive those hours in his head. The softness of her tiny hands and the scent of baby powder would tease his senses until he fell asleep. He knew it wasn't real, but the illusion was better than what his real life offered at the time. He couldn't stop his mind from going to that small nursery when his eyes closed.

The difference between their bubble on the island and the one they now enjoyed was the addition of the sleeping child beside Claire. Despite the child psychologist's recommendations, after the birth of her brother, Nichol found her way into Tony and Claire's bed. It didn't happen every night, but it did happen. Surprisingly, the peace and security their daughter found snuggled between her parents allowed her to sleep peacefully even through Nate's waking and feeding.

It was Madeline who attested that Nichol's behavior was acceptable. After all, Nate's room was attached to Tony and Claire's; how could Nichol not feel left out across the hall in her separate bedroom? Madeline also reassured Claire that in time their daughter would once again be content in her own space. For now, Nichol needed to know that she was a part of what her brother shared. When Claire confessed Nichol's new sleeping arrangement to others, she was shocked and surprised to learn that they too had similar stories. Michael spent much of Beth's first few months in John and Emily's bed, as had Caleb, many years ago, when his sister Maryn was born. Even Meredith had similar tales with her two children. Though Claire was confident in their decision to allow Nichol this luxury, hearing that others had done the same helped reassure her.

Snuggling close to Nichol, Claire sighed. She could no longer differentiate Tony's words, but the rhythm comforted her as she drifted between wake and sleep. It wasn't until she heard her son's whimpers that Claire realized morning had arrived. Looking to the other side of the bed she saw only Nichol. By the numbers on the clock and the sound of water from the attached bathroom, Claire knew Tony was awake and getting ready for work.

A cloud of steam welcomed Claire as she opened the bathroom door. Once inside it was the magnificent sight of her husband stepping from the shower that fully woke her senses. As he reached for his towel, their eyes met. Droplets of water sparkled on his warmed skin as they descended from his broad shoulders down to his toned legs. Claire made no secret of her scan as she took in the nude man before her.

"Good morning, Mrs. Rawlings," he said with a grin as he wrapped the towel around his waist.

Closing the gap between them, her emerald eyes sparkled. "Good morning. Were you up a long time with Nate last night?"

"No, not too long. Is he awake?"

Rubbing her petite hands over his shoulders, Claire replied, "Yes, I just came in here first so I could feed him again."

Reaching for her hand, Tony kissed her fingers. "Again? I think our son has an insatiable appetite."

Claire's breasts ached as she thought not about Nate's appetite, but the one of the man before her. Closing her eyes, she imagined Tony's lips not on her fingers, but on other parts of her body. Though the doctors had told them to wait six weeks before resuming relations, Claire knew that she didn't want to wait. Nate's birth had been much kinder to her body than Nichol's. Reaching with her other hand to Tony's shoulder for support, she felt his muscles tense as she moved her fingers down his arm. Inch by inch, Claire's own appetite began to grow.

Remembering Tony's comment about Nate, Claire finally replied, "Hmmm. Yes, he does."

As Tony continued his gentle kisses of her fingers, she felt the release. Looking down, she saw the evidence on the bodice of her nightgown. "Tony..."

His dark eyes followed hers, and his devilish grin made her smile. "I'm glad to know that Nate isn't the only man who can do that to you."

Playfully she pulled her hand away and swatted his bare shoulder. "You're awful."

"I am?" he asked with his most innocent tone. "I thought I was pretty good. I mean if I were awful why would you..."

Claire shook her head as she disappeared behind the next door. Minutes later, she was in the nursery with Nate: his little lips latched and lower jaw began moving with vigor. The relief was instantaneous as he suckled and her body relaxed. Once she'd moved Nate to the other side, Tony stepped into the nursery. Though he was now fully dressed, Claire still enjoyed the view. His customary Armani suit and shiny black loafers reminded her that he wasn't only a daddy who would rock his child in the middle of the night, but also a businessman who spent his days making decisions that affected multitudes of people. Though the silk spoke of importance, the way the jacket stretched over his broad shoulders and tapered to his waist, reminded her of the man she'd watched step from the shower. Though her mind was there, Tony had obviously moved on.

Leaning down, he kissed her cheek and said, "Nichol's still sound asleep. Do you want me to wake her?"

"No, let her sleep. I'm sure Shannon's awake, but Nichol's been fighting naps. The longer she sleeps in the morning, the better it is for all of us this evening."

Tony laughed. "Then, by all means, let her sleep." His brows peaked. "I'm on my way to the kitchen for breakfast. Would you like me to have something sent up?"

Claire looked down at Nate, his suckling now slowed. "No. If you're going to eat here, I can come down in a few minutes."

Tony glanced down at her nightgown and lifted his brows.

"Yes, I'll be sure to change or wear a robe. I know I'm comparatively underdressed."

He teased the strap of her nightgown. "I like the way you're dressed."

Claire shook her head. Maybe he hadn't moved on.

"I'll be sure they have your tea ready."

"Ugh," Claire replied. "I'd give anything for a nice cup of caffeinated coffee."

Tony smirked. "Sacrifices, my dear."

"Sure, that's easy for you to say."

He reached for Nate's head. As he stroked the fine hair, the tips of his fingers purposely caressed Claire's breast. "I believe I'm sacrificing too."

"Yes, but your sacrifice is a sacrifice for me, too."

He lowered his lips near her neck, purposely bathing her

sensitive skin in his warm breath. "Would I be *awful*," he emphasized the word, "if I were glad to hear that?"

Inhaling deeply, Claire sighed. "No. No more awful than you already are."

As she did the mental math, Tony turned to leave. Just before entering back into their suite, he muttered, "Three and a half more weeks."

A smile came to her lips and her cheeks rose. That was exactly what she'd been thinking.

THE SOUND OF Madeline's deep laugh echoed through the foyer as Claire approached the dining room. Turning the corner her heart leapt. Madeline and Francis truly were like family as they sat conversing with Tony over their breakfast. On the island, they used to eat their midday meals together, all four of them. In Iowa, Tony was rarely home for lunch and dinner was an off and on occasion for them all to be together. Though Claire always asked the older couple, Madeline insisted that the evening meal was an important time for the family.

Family was what Claire saw as she stood in the doorway and watched the three casually discussing daily events. Madeline and Francis were as close to parents as Tony or Claire would ever have. Their knowledge and wisdom affected both Tony and Claire in different ways. Claire welcomed Madeline's advice to the point of seeking it on many occasions. Tony was less forward, yet Francis had found a way to interject his beliefs and wisdom into Tony's life. Perhaps they were continuing their parent lessons without either Tony or Claire realizing what was happening.

"Oh, Madame Claire, let me hold Nate while you eat," Madeline said when she turned to see Claire.

As Claire placed Nate in Madeline's arms, she smiled at the way he nuzzled against the large woman. "I think we're spoiling him. He could be in his chair."

Madeline's dark eyes beamed. "Oh, no. Loving a bébé is not spoiling them. It is making him feel safe so that one day he can be in his chair and know he is still loved."

Sitting next to Tony, Claire smiled. "Well, he's definitely loved."

"And Nichol?" Francis asked.

"She's loved too," Claire answered quickly.

"No, Madame el, Nichol? Where is she?"

"Oh," Claire giggled. "She's still asleep." Before they asked, she volunteered, "She slept in our bed again last night."

"Was she upset?" Madeline asked.

"No," Tony answered. "When we started to tuck her in, she ran to our room and said she wanted to be close to her brother." With a scoff, he added, "That sounds all well and good, but so far she's yet to be any help with the middle of the night feeding."

"Oui," Madeline laughed. "She's a smart one, your daughter. She is very good at reasoning."

Claire nodded as she sipped her warm, decaffeinated tea. "Too good, but the night before, she slept fine in her bed. I hope..."

Madeline's knowing eyes peered toward Claire. "Do not worry. She will sleep in her own bed before she goes to university."

Tony's cough and laugh filled the dining room. "Well, let's hope it's way before that."

The four continued to chat until they heard the sound of little feet coming through the foyer. They all turned as Nichol made her way into the dining room and walked toward Claire.

"I woked up," she said sleepily.

"Yes, you did. Did you sleep okay in our big bed?"

Nichol nodded, and then with a grin she said, "Eccept Daddy snores."

The room erupted with everyone's laughter, followed by a dark-eyed stare coming from the head of the table. Playfully, Tony replied, "Well then, I guess you'll need to sleep in your own room from now on."

Nichol giggled. "I like your snoring, Daddy. It sounds funny." She looked up at Claire. "Doesn't it, Momma?"

Stifling her laughter, Claire's eyes met Tony's. Truthfully, she'd never noticed. Well, maybe when they first began to sleep together, but Claire always considered it rhythmic breathing more than snoring. Then after they had been separated, once they were reunited, she welcomed the sound of her husband sleeping beside her. "I think it sounds nice. That's how I know your daddy's there."

"Good answer," Tony declared. "You may have been sharing a bed with Nichol, in her room."

Claire's emerald eyes sparkled. "I don't think I need to be too concerned."

Tony stood, leaned down and gave Claire a kiss and Nichol a peck on her hair. "That's it. I'm leaving before you start discussing any more of my bad habits."

"We can save that for another time," Claire offered. Peering toward Madeline and Francis, she joked, "I'm sure you don't want to spend all morning sitting here. The list is rather lengthy."

Tony shook his head with a grin as he whispered near Claire's ear, "There's that smart mouth I love."

When he turned to leave, Claire asked, "Nichol, are you ready for some breakfast?"

As she spoke, the cook came from the kitchen with a tray, and Nichol climbed onto the chair beside her mother. "I do fhink it sounds funny," she whispered as she watched her breakfast being served.

Early May 2018
Phil

THE TIRES OF the rental car bounced as Phil turned onto the private lane. Was the loose gravel the cause of his trembling hands or was it something else? As the silence within the car loomed, Phil's grip upon the helpless steering wheel tightened, blanching his knuckles and straining his wrists. Outside the windows large trees lined the lane while manicured lawns filled the landscape. The large, strategically placed trees created a canopy over the lane, allowing minimal illumination from the evening sun. The resulting strobe of the sunshine reminded Phil of the lane on the Rawlings estate, except these trees weren't oak. These trees were cypress and draped with beautiful Spanish moss that veiled the full beauty of the resort. As the trees parted, the main lodge came into view. Above the plantation-style mansion, the sky filled with a kaleidoscope of color. Reds swirled with pinks as shadows took on a purple hue.

"This is beautiful." Taylor's statement shattered the silence, relieving a fraction of the tension from Phil's grip.

He turned to his right. "It is. Have you ever stayed here before?"

"No," Taylor answered. "Not here. I mean, I grew up about fifty miles away, near Sebring. I'd heard of this place, but..." She shrugged. "...I guess I thought I was done with this area of the country."

Phil slowed the car as he eased in front of the main building. Putting the gear in park, he reached for Taylor's hand. "We don't have to do this, you know. We can drive back to the airport right now. The Rawlings Industries plane is there and the pilot is on standby. You say the word and we can fly back to Iowa."

Inhaling deeply, Taylor shook her head and turned her gaze toward the side window. "No, Phil, I have to do this. If I don't, I'll always wonder if..."

Phil waited as Taylor collected her thoughts and silence once again filled the car. There was so much he wanted to know: so many questions. Only knowing bits and pieces about someone's past was the penance for not meeting one another until later in life. Those lives and stories, the ones that created a foundation of the present and future, remain hidden, until access was granted. He understood the need to keep the past from crashing with the present. Hell, his walls were tall enough to keep a fuck'n ninja from scaling them, and for that reason, he didn't pry. That's not to say he hadn't done his research before Taylor was hired; however, that was business. This no longer was.

It wasn't until they landed in Fort Lauderdale and began the drive away from the crystal blue ocean that Phil got a rare glimpse of the private woman beside him. Through the past two years he'd seen many sides of her—sides he enjoyed—but this was different. There was a cyclone of emotion he'd never witnessed. He didn't know the particulars of what was happening behind her beautiful blue eyes, yet he knew enough to know it was causing her pain. That alone was more than enough reason to make him want to turn the car around and take them both back to the cooler world of Iowa.

As the warm Florida air stirred, the clouds above the columned mansion continued to swirl, brightening and darkening the landscape as shadows collided with light. Everything around him was happening in slow motion. Only Phil's thoughts were occurring at a normal speed. He felt his blood pump and echo in his ears. Each beat of his heart intensified the silence. He was a man of action, a person who fixed things. He made them right. Sitting and watching the woman in his life, the woman who was usually a rock, crumble in the seat beside him was pure, unadulterated torture.

If he could, he'd take away her memories as well as her thoughts. If he could, he'd eliminate the current cause. He'd eliminated threats before. But alas, this was beyond his realm of expertise. Only current dangers could be eradicated. Purging the past was not something he could do. It was up to her. For that reason and possibility at liberation, Phil supported her.

After what seemed like hours, but according to the dashboard had only been a few minutes, Phil rubbed Taylor's shoulder. The quaking beneath his fingertips told him what she'd been trying to hide. Throughout the two years they'd known one another, never before had he seen her cry. She wasn't like Claire: that woman could cry at the drop of a hat. No, Taylor's emotions were usually concealed, the perfect attribute of a bodyguard or an agent: slow to anger and quick to react, conscious of everything at all times. Yet, the emotions Phil now witnessed were not a quick reaction. No, they'd been building over time: long before he knew Taylor Walters.

"I'll go get us checked in, and we can get some rest before your appointment with the attorney tomorrow."

Taylor nodded as she continued to look away.

A few minutes later, Phil apprehensively returned to the car. He could handle a confrontation with an adversary, chest to chest and guns blazing; however, confronting emotions that bubbled like a tar pit—thick, dense, and capable of suffocation—was out of Phil's element. With each step he contemplated his next move. Opening the door, he sighed with relief. Staring up toward him was one of the most beautiful smiles he'd ever seen. Somewhere in the time since he'd left and returned, Taylor had taken hold of her grief and returned it to the place that not only concealed it from the world, but from her heart. Though her eyes glistened with the remnants of tears, her gaze was clear and precise. Seeing the obvious change, Phil couldn't stop the relief suddenly surging through him as the smile returned to his lips.

"We have a private cottage near the back of the estate. I thought you might like the privacy."

Her brows rose in question.

Phil's smile quirked to the side. "That's not what I meant."

Taylor's hand covered his as he started the car. "I know. Thank you."

He didn't respond as he turned toward her. There was nothing he could think to say. Taylor shouldn't thank him. It was her. He should be the one to thank her for applying for the job with the Rawlings family, for bringing a part of him back to life. Hell, not back to life, but to life. She'd shown him that he could do his job, protect those he cared about and still have more.

"Taylor, don't thank me. I'm totally inept when it comes to what to do here."

She shook her head. "No, you're not. You're giving me exactly what I need. Sometimes more can be said with silent understanding than all the words in the world. If it weren't for you, I'd be facing this alone." She leaned near and kissed his cheek. "When it all happened, I never imagined ever again having someone

I trusted enough to be there for me."

He squeezed her hand and put the car into reverse. "Let's go see this cottage. They promised me it was the best one on the property."

In no time, Phil was swiping the plastic card against the reader on the door of the quaint Florida styled cottage. The manager at the desk had been right about its isolation. After passing many smaller dwellings, the road narrowed and disappeared into the jungle of cypress. The manicured lawns disappeared as only underbrush could survive the denseness of the vegetation. Then, like lifting of a blanket, the trees parted and a cottage the size of many homes came into view. By the description and map that Phil had been shown, he knew that there was a rear screened-in patio that looked out to a small pond. There were also trails that could take them around the grounds, and back near the main mansion was a stable with horses available for the guests. Not knowing how tomorrow would go, Phil had gone ahead and booked the cottage for multiple nights.

"Oh, my!" Taylor gasped as she stepped into the living room. "This isn't a cottage; it's a house."

Setting down her purse, she roamed from door to door. Everything was open and bright with white tile floors, yellow walls, and colorful cushions gracing the furniture. Each room had large windows offering natural light in the heat of the day. In the kitchen, with a counter that arched toward the living room, Taylor spun completely around. "Look at this kitchen! I wish we were staying longer. I'd love to cook." She turned her smiling gaze toward Phil. "See what you do to me. That's not something I ever thought I'd say."

He wrapped her in his arms and pulled her toward him. "There's a restaurant at the main mansion that also delivers." He shrugged. "I also saw a small grocery store about ten minutes from the resort."

Phil scrunched his nose. "Do you know how to cook?"

She slapped his shoulder. "Yes! Just because I haven't done it in a while doesn't mean I've forgotten how to do it."

Taking a step and then two, he backed Taylor against the refrigerator pressing his body against hers. "Hmmm, speaking from experience, lack of recent activity has been no indicator of your level of expertise." He ran his palms down her arms until their fingers intertwined. "As a matter of fact, I think I like being the one who's fortunate enough to experience your return to previous activities."

"Oh, you do?" she murmured, as she leaned closer, lifted her chin, and kissed his lips.

Phil nodded as their lips lingered. His chest pressing against her breasts, as the connection of their kiss remained unbroken. The thin material separating their skin did little to conceal the hardening of her nipples. Though the air conditioner roared, the temperature of their cottage rose with each passing moment. Her need filled his senses while her hands released his and began to pull his shirt from his jeans.

He reciprocated and when his touch found the soft skin of her waist, Phil asked, "Shall we find the master bedroom?"

Taylor didn't speak; instead she reached for his hand and led him through the archway toward the adjoining room with the large king-sized bed. Beyond the unblocked windows, the small lake glistened with the last rays of the evening sun. The earlier redness had bled from the sky, pooled behind the large trees and left lingering purple wisps floating above the horizon as dusk offered the dimmed illumination of only the moon and stars.

Phil didn't need Taylor's words to recognize her hunger. The appetite he witnessed wasn't for food, but for connection. The path before her was more daunting than she wanted to admit. It would take strength and support. As their bodies became one and the world beyond the window darkened, Phil wanted to give her everything she needed. His desire wasn't purely carnal, though that element's presence was unquestioned. He wanted to be the one she could lean upon, to applaud her inner strength, and also to catch her if she fell. The woman below him wasn't a damsel in distress. She was every bit as fierce as he, yet even he craved the knowledge of not being alone. Until Taylor, Phil had never known how badly he desired that connection.

Her beautiful eyes stared into his as her body clenched and her moans subsided. He loved how she didn't close her eyes, but watched him constantly as they united. Perhaps that too was a sign of her strength. Never did it feel as if she surrendered herself to him. On the contrary, she gave, a gift that only he was blessed to receive.

Collapsing next to her, Phil pulled Taylor near. "Shall we get dressed and head up to the mansion for dinner?"

The sweet aroma of Taylor's shampoo wafted through the air as she shook her head against his shoulder. "No, I meant what I said about cooking. I saw a grill outside, past the screened porch. Let's drive to that little grocery." She lifted her head and filled his hazel eyes with crystal blue. "I want to cook that dinner for you."

"You don't have—"

Her kiss stopped his words. "I know. I want to. Let me spend tonight thinking about other things, like salad, and steak, and maybe some wine."

Flipping their world, Taylor's hair fanned out on the pillow and her smile grew. "Well," Phil replied, "if keeping your mind occupied is my main mission, I'll do my best not to fail."

Taylor's back arched, confirming their connection. Unlike

before, they were skin to skin. "You've already done a great job. But don't get too comfortable. I think it could be a long night."

Sighing contently, Phil replied, "You know me, always a workaholic. I strive for perfection."

Finding himself lost in her aura, Phil realized what he'd just said—*you know me*—and the tips of his lips moved upward. Such a simple statement, truer than anything else he could utter, and more powerful in meaning.

Chapter 16

August 2018

Claire

———◆———

**The present moment is filled with joy
and happiness. If you are attentive, you will see it.
—Thich Nhat Hanh**

"HOW DO YOU like having two children?" Julia Simmons asked Claire, as they walked with their sons back to the screened porch from the nursery.

"Now that this little guy is sleeping through the night, I like it a lot more."

Julia smiled. "Yes, Christopher started doing that around five months. At first, I'd wake up to make sure he was all right. Caleb had to convince me not to wake him."

Claire laughed. "I know the feeling."

"And Nate sure isn't little," Julia assessed. "Goodness, he's grown."

"Yes," Claire replied as she juggled her son on her hip. Making her way to the sofa, wisps of her hair blew in the breeze of the ceiling fan as it circulated the warm summer air about the porch. As she sat, she heard squeals of delight coming from the backyard and pool. "He's over doubled in size since he was born. The doctor said that he's over the one hundredth percentile in height."

"Well, look at Tony, Claire," Courtney chimed in. "Of course Nate will be tall."

"But look at Nichol," Claire replied. "She's not nearly as tall. I mean, they say to double your height at age two. By age three she was only thirty-two inches."

Emily shrugged. "She's petite, like her momma."

"But a fireball like her father," Courtney added.

Claire grinned. It was true: someday despite her petite size Nichol Courtney Rawlings would be a force to be reckoned with, just like her father. Even now, Claire heard her daughter's voice above the glees and splashing coming from the pool.

"Look at them," Emily said. "It's like a daycare center here."

Claire scanned their backyard. For only a second she remembered the serenity and stillness of the estate when she was first brought here, maybe not serene but lonely. Now the pool and deck were filled with people she loved. Not only were Tony and Nichol in the pool, but so were John, Michael, Tim and his two sons, Shaun and Steven, as well as Brent and Caleb sitting on the deck. The sight was heartwarming as the children and fathers played and laughed.

Shaking her head, Claire agreed. "Like a *daddy* daycare."

"Well, that's fine with me. The boys love having time with Tim," Sue said.

Emily smiled, watching her daughter walk from lady to lady, petting the babies. "I think she thinks she's hot stuff."

"Well, she should," Claire confirmed. "She can walk. Nate and Christopher are still content to watch the world. Although, Nate is rolling all over the place. It's so funny. The first time I laid him down on the carpet and a few seconds later he was missing, I was shocked—he'd rolled himself under the coffee table."

"Well," Julia continued, "Christopher isn't that content. He'd rather be crawling all over the place."

"You can put him down. He can't get off the porch."

The bright sunshine warmed the air throughout the afternoon as the shrill laughter turned to pangs of hunger. Eventually, all made their way into the house for dinner. Shannon took Nate as Claire helped Nichol change out of her bathing suit. Once they were in her room, there was a knock on the door.

"Come in," Claire called as she worked to convince Nichol that her shorts and top were better dinner clothes than her Disney princess costume.

"But, Momma, it's dinner. I want to dress up."

"Honey, these are very nice shorts. You'll look beautiful."

Her lips pouted and dark eyes narrowed. "Not as butiful as I do in my princess dress."

Emily entered.

"You can wear the dress after dinner. You don't want to get it dirty with food, do you?" Claire asked.

With a sigh, Nichol agreed.

"What's up?" Claire asked turning to see her sister.

"I wanted to tell you something in private," Emily replied.

Claire's green eyes widened. "Okay."

The three chatted as Claire combed Nichol's wet hair. Once she was presentable, Claire said, "Honey, why don't you go find the other children? I'm pretty sure that Shannon and Becca have a special table set up for you, Michael, Shaun, and Stephen."

Her shoulders fell. "Why do I have to sit with all boys?"

"Because you're the princess and they're your court," Emily volunteered.

Nichol's eyes brightened. "Oh, yeah."

Moments later, Nichol was gone, happily ready to find her court.

"What do you want to speak to me about?" Claire asked.

"It's not that big of a deal. I just wanted to tell you John and I spoke with Harry the other day."

Claire took a step back. She hadn't thought of Harrison Baldwin in quite a long time. Well, she had when she'd been told about Amber. The whole story made her sad. But honestly, she'd been too preoccupied with her own family to give him much thought. After all, it had been over five years since she'd left California.

"Wow, that's out of left field."

Emily shrugged. "Not really. John and I have stayed in contact with him. We got to know him and Amber while we were living in Palo Alto."

"Really, Em, this doesn't need to be in private. Tony couldn't care less about Harry, and to be honest, I think I'm still upset that he lied to me."

"He's been through a lot. Besides, were you totally honest with him?"

"Excuse me?" Claire's volume rose. "What does that mean?"

Emily shook her head. "Nothing, never mind. I just mean that when you were out there, you weren't over Anthony."

"Emily, that was a long time ago, and I don't want to rehash it. Say what you wanted to say."

"I wanted to tell you that he's doing well."

"Good."

"He told us that he's seeing someone and he's happy."

"Well, I'm happy for him. I always wondered if he and Liz got back together."

Emily smiled. "See, you have thought about him."

"Not recently, but I wondered that." Claire thought back. When had she wondered that? Too many things had happened.

"They did," Emily replied, "for a while. But a few years back, when he left the FBI, he moved to North Carolina to be close to his ex-wife and daughter. Liz stayed in California."

Claire gasped as her eyes widened. "What did you just say?"

Emily reached for her arm. "Oh jeez, Claire, I thought you knew that."

Her head moved from side to side. "H-How would I know *that*?" She paused and sat on Nichol's bed. "He has a daughter and an ex-wife? Is that new?"

"No. I think his daughter is about eight or nine years old."

"Well, isn't that interesting." Claire's eyes narrowed. "No matter what my feelings for Tony were while I was in Palo Alto, I told Harry I had an ex-husband. Harry never mentioned an ex-wife or a daughter!"

"I didn't tell you this to upset you," Emily explained. "I told you, well, because I thought you'd be happy for him. I mean, you're happy. At least you seem to be. Don't you think he should be too?"

Claire nodded. She was happy and of course she wanted Harry to be happy too, but this was a lot to digest. Not only had he misled her with his job and initial intentions for their friendship, he never told her he was married. Emily's words interrupted her thoughts.

"Claire, I don't think I ever told you, but Harry came to see John and me, while you were... sick. He wanted us to know the truth about his job and about you. He's the one who told us that you and

Anthony left your island to save us from Catherine. I'm not sure I would've believed it coming from anyone else. What he did helped to open our eyes."

Claire stared at her sister as words failed to form. Memories rushed forth too rapidly to decipher. She suddenly remembered the Harrison Baldwin who took her to buy a cell phone and a used car. She hated that those memories were tainted by his undercover work. At the same time she recalled how happy she'd been. Those small things meant the world to her. Now to know that he'd gone out of his way to explain things to her family, she did want him happy. Then she remembered Amber.

"Em, I do want him to be happy. I can't imagine what he went through with Amber and the revelation about Simon. I still have trouble comprehending all of that. I'm glad he's found someone. Is he remarried? Does he see his daughter?"

A smile graced Emily's lips. "It sounds like he has a great relationship with his ex-wife, and because of that he's gotten very close with his daughter. I forget the woman's name, but they're not that serious. I guess she was Jillian's—that's his daughter—teacher. So at first they kept it quiet. Now that a new school year is coming and Jillian has a new teacher, they've made their dating status public."

Nichol's door opened and dark questioning eyes peered around the frame. "There you two are. Dinner's ready."

Claire smiled toward her husband. "We'll be right there."

He opened the door wider. "The natives are restless. Thankfully Shannon and Becca have the little ones eating."

Claire reached for Emily's hand. "Thanks for telling me. I *am* happy."

She saw the question in her husband's eyes and knew without a doubt this was a conversation she'd be retelling once they were alone.

"Where's Phil, Taylor, or Eric?" Emily asked as they made their way back downstairs.

Claire shrugged. "They're here. It's like I told you before, even though they're here, they don't hover."

"I miss Madeline and Francis."

"I do too," Claire admitted. "I understood their desire to get back to their home, but I know Nichol misses them too. We'll definitely need to plan a trip to visit them in the future."

LATER THAT NIGHT, the conversation Claire had anticipated came up for discussion as she and Tony readied for bed. She'd just settled onto the soft sheets with a sigh when Tony asked, "What was the big secretive meeting with Emily all about?"

Claire had contemplated this conversation every which way since Tony entered Nichol's room. However, she didn't expect him to be so forward. Well, fine. She'd be just as forward.

"She wanted to tell me something about Harry." When Tony didn't respond, Claire clarified, "Harrison Baldwin."

"Yes, I'm well aware of who you meant."

"All right, that's it," Claire said, as she laid her head on the pillow. "I'm exhausted."

"I'm thinking not."

She rolled to face her husband. "You're thinking I'm not tired?"

His chest expanded and contracted. "I'm thinking that's not *it*." He emphasized the word. "What did she want to tell you about Mr. Baldwin?"

She worked to suppress a smile. "You know you're cute when you're jealous."

"I'm not jealous." His dark eyes widened in a ploy of innocence. "I'm merely curious."

Sitting back up, Claire scooted closer, close enough to feel his radiating warmth. She reached out to touch his chest. "You're warm. I think you got a lot of sun today with the kids."

Tony grasped her hand and looked her in the eye. "Curiosity, Mrs. Rawlings. Could you please help me out?"

"You know what they say about curiosity, don't you, Mr. Rawlings?"

"You're playing with me right now, and I'm not in favor of it."

Claire giggled. "Would I do that? Maybe I should get you something for the burn. You should've worn sunscreen..."

Before she could finish, Tony's lips were on hers and she was back on her pillow. When he broke their kiss, his nose lingered millimeters from hers. "Thank you for your concern. Perhaps you could be as considerate of my mental health."

"Emily told me that Harry's in a relationship and he's happy." She lifted her lips to his. "See? No big deal."

"Why?"

"Why what?"

"Why does she think you need to know that?"

Claire pulled away from the weight of his chest and sat back up. "Honestly, I don't know. I guess she wanted me to know that he's doing well."

Tony shook his head. "Well, fine. He's living in North Carolina near his daughter and in a relationship. I know I'll sleep better tonight."

Claire tilted her head to the side. "Wait a minute. How did

you know about his daughter?"

"You knew too. Didn't you tell me?"

"Noooo." She elongated the word. "I didn't know anything about him being married or having a child until this afternoon."

Tony shrugged. "I'm not sure then." He feigned a smile. "He's happy, you're happy, I'm happy—we're all happy." He lifted a brow. "Now, where were we? Oh, yes, you wanted to get me lotion."

Claire's neck straightened. "Don't do that. You asked me a question and I answered it. Now I want to know how you knew about Harry. I was shocked when Emily told me that he'd been married. Obviously, you've known it for a while but never felt the need to tell me."

"Why would I tell you that? What possible reason do I have to bring up your ex-boyfriend?"

"It was a long time ago. You know how upset I was when I learned he was FBI."

"Roach told me."

Claire contemplated his response. "Phil told you I was upset? Because yes, he was with me when I found out. Or... Phil told you about Harry and has kept you up to date on him."

"Claire, you're making this into more than it is. Emily shouldn't have—"

"Don't you dare turn this around on her. Answer my question. If you don't, I'll ask Phil tomorrow."

"Yes," Tony admitted. "Roach has kept me up to date on Mr. Baldwin as well as Ms. McCoy. She's still in prison, by the way."

Claire crossed her arms over her chest. "Is there anyone else you two are investigating? Any other secrets you'd suddenly like to share?"

"Yes," his tone mellowed. "I have a burning secret I'd like to share." As he spoke, he inched closer. "Are you ready?" When Claire didn't answer, he lowered his lips to her neck. After a few butterfly kisses, he breathed heavily with each word. "Here's. My. Secret."

Goose bumps materialized as Claire waited for his revelation.

"I love you more than life itself." His kisses moved from behind her ear to her collarbone. "I didn't investigate Mr. Baldwin for any other reason than curiosity." His lips continued to roam. "I'm insanely jealous of the time you two spent together, but..." He brought his head up and looked directly into her eyes showing her the chocolate swirls of desire and regret. "...I don't blame anyone for the pain you were in when the two of you met, other than me."

This was more than Claire wanted to hear. She looked away, knowing she too was guilty.

"Look at me."

Slowly, she turned.

"Tony, stop. I'm not innocent."

"Nor am I. We've moved beyond all of this. I'm sorry that I didn't tell you. I didn't want to have this conversation, for no other reason than when it comes to that man my feelings are irrational."

Giving up her pretense of anger, Claire reached for his cheeks. The warmth of his face as well as the abrasiveness of his five o'clock shadow electrified her hands, sending shockwaves through her body. "I'm sorry. I admit that I thought it was cute that you were jealous. I shouldn't have baited you. I haven't thought about Harry in years. That may make me a terrible person, but I haven't. I'm too happy and satisfied with everything that I have right here to spend my time thinking about the past." her eyes filled with tears. "I've lost too much time in the past. I want the now."

Tony

AS TONY CARESSED Claire's cheek her eyes closed causing a tear to fall. Shit, this wasn't what he wanted. When would he learn to keep his mouth shut? Without thinking, Tony leaned nearer and kissed away the salty moisture.

"We both have. I'm sorry."

"Stop apologizing. I should've answered you. I knew you'd want to know."

Tony looked down into the sea of emerald green. "How? How did you know?"

A slight grin materialized on his wife's face. "I saw it when you opened the door."

"Am I that easy to read?"

Her hands on his cheeks pulled his lips toward hers. "You are to me," she answered. "You have been for as long as I can remember."

As their lips united, their bodies molded together. They were like pieces of a puzzle: one made especially to fit the other. They moved in sync, their caressing hands sending warmth and energy from one to the other. Their tongues danced, creating a waltz of give and take. Within minutes Claire's nightgown was gone, lost to the abyss of the carpet below only to quickly be accompanied by Tony's shorts. Tucked safely behind the security of their locked door, it was only the two of them moving as one.

Claire's back arched as they united, inviting him not only to enter her warmth but also to tease her taut nipples. Each time he sucked or taunted her hard nubs, moans of desire filled the suite. Their rhythm increased as the room around them disappeared.

She had been right. Too much time had been lost in the past. Their eyes were rightfully set on the present, and as they settled into one another's arms and the night air stilled, Tony's mind was not in their history, but filled with what he had in the here and now: his family, his wife in his arms as well as his children sleeping soundly in their rooms.

Though many may question the choices they'd made, as Tony and Claire neared sleep they both knew that every second of their past had been worth it. They wouldn't spend their lives rehashing it, but they also wouldn't regret it. For without their past, they wouldn't have their present, including the two young Rawlingses who would change the legacy of the Nichols-Rawls families forever, because tomorrow held the possibility for only the best of consequences.

A Parting Note from Aleatha

———◆———

Theirs was a long, complicated story with a monster and
a knight. What made their story unique was that these
two players were the same person.
—Aleatha Romig, CONVICTED

Dear Reader,

Your love and appreciation for Tony and Claire's story made this book possible, as well as each one post-Consequences. I've tried too many times to say that I'm done writing about this family. I won't say that again.

What does that mean? I make no promises. Someday I may explore the lives of Nichol and Nate. How did they grow up? What did they become? How did their parents influence them? What was it truly like to grow up Rawlings? Perhaps Phil will want a story of his own or maybe Harry?

However, for now, I'm content in knowing that Claire and Tony overcame their impossible beginning and love prevailed through impossible odds. I hope you'll not only allow me that reprieve, but perhaps also join me if the story ever decides to continue in my mind. For if that happens, for my own sanity, I must share it with you.

Thank you for spending your valuable time reading BEYOND THE CONSEQUENCES. If you've enjoyed this peek into the future, please tell your friends, leave a review, and shout it from the rooftops!

If you'd like to take a different dark journey with a little more heat, I recommend my new TALES FROM THE DARK SIDE series. Each book in the series is a stand-alone. INSIDIOUS, my first erotic thriller, is now available.

I ask you to take a look at my new romantic suspense, with a hint of dark, series INFIDELITY. It isn't what you think. The series consists of: BETRAYAL, CUNNING, DECEPTION, ENTRAPMENT, and FIDELITY and will all be released by early 2017.

The newest addition to the world of Aleatha Romig is my new thriller/suspense series THE LIGHT. It is my first traditionally published books coming from Thomas and Mercer. INTO THE LIGHT will be released June of 2016 and AWAY FROM THE DARK is projected for later in 2016.

All my books are listed following the Consequences glossary and timeline.

Thank you again.

Sincerely,

~Aleatha

Glossary of CONSEQUENCE SERIES Characters

-Primary Characters-

Anthony (Tony) Rawlings: *billionaire, entrepreneur, founder of Rawlings Industries*

Anton Rawls *(birth name): son of Samuel, grandson of Nathaniel (birth name)*

Claire Nichols Rawlings: *meteorologist, bartender, woman whose life changed forever, wife and ex-wife of Anthony Rawlings*

Aliases: *Lauren Michaels, Isabelle Alexander, C. Marie Rawls*

Nathaniel (Nate) Sherman Rawlings: son of Claire and Anthony Rawlings

Nichol Courtney Rawlings: daughter of Claire and Anthony Rawlings

Brent Simmons: *Rawlings attorney, Tony's best friend*

Catherine Marie London (Rawls): *housekeeper, friend of Anthony Rawlings, 2nd wife of Nathaniel Rawls, Anton Rawls' step-grandmother*

Courtney Simmons: *Brent Simmons' wife*

Emily (Nichols) Vandersol: *Claire's older sister*

Harrison Baldwin: *half-brother of Amber McCoy, president of security at SiJo Gaming*

John Vandersol: *Emily's husband, Claire's brother-in-law, attorney*

Liz Matherly: *personal assistant to Amber McCoy, love interest of Harrison Baldwin*

Meredith Banks Russel: *reporter, sorority sister of Claire Nichols*

Phillip Roach: *private investigator hired by Anthony Rawlings*

-Secondary Characters-

Amber McCoy: *Simon Johnson's fiancée, CEO of SiJo Gaming*

Derek Burke: *husband of Sophia Rossi, great-grandnephew of Jonathon Burke*

Eric Hensley: *Tony's driver and assistant*

Nathaniel Rawls: *grandfather of Anton Rawls, father of Samuel Rawls, owner-founder of Rawls Corporation*

Patricia Miles: *personal assistant to Anthony Rawlings, corporate Rawlings Industries*

Aliases: *Melissa Garrison, Charlotte Peterson*

Sophia Rossi Burke: *adopted daughter of Carlo and Silvia Rossi, wife of Derek Burke, biological daughter of Marie London, and owner of an art studio in Provincetown, MA*

-Tertiary Characters-

Abbey: *nurse*

Allison Burke: *daughter of Jonathon Burke*

Amanda Rawls: *Samuel Rawls' wife, Anton's mother*

Ami Beech: *office manager of the Diamond law firm in Olivia, Minnesota*

Andrew McCain: *pilot for Rawlings Industries*

Anne Robinson: *Vanity Fair reporter*

Becca: *Vandersols' nanny*

Bev Miller: *designer, wife of Tom Miller*

Bonnie: *wife of Chance*

Brad Clark: *wedding consultant*

Caleb Simmons: *son of Brent and Courtney Simmons*

Cameron Andrews: *private investigator hired by Anthony Rawlings*

Carlo Rossi: *married to Silvia Rossi, adoptive father of Sophia Rossi Burke*

Carlos: *house staff at the Rawlings' estate*

Dr. Carly Brown: *Claire's primary doctor at Everwood*

Cassie: *Sophia's assistant at her art studio on the Cape*

Chance: *associate of Elijah Summer*

Charles: *housekeeper, Anthony's Chicago apartment*

Christopher Simmons: *son of Caleb and Julia Simmons, grandson to Brent and Courtney Simmons*

Cindy: *maid at the Rawlings estate, adopted daughter of Allison Burke and her husband*

Clay Winters: *bodyguard hired by Anthony Rawlings*

Connie: *Nathaniel Rawls' secretary*

Danielle (Danni): *personal assistant to Derek Burke*

David Field: *Rawlings negotiator*

Elijah (Eli) Summer: *entertainment entrepreneur, friend of Tony's*

Elizabeth Nichols: *wife of Sherman Nichols, Claire and Emily's grandmother*

Elizabeth (Beth) Vandersol: *daughter of John and Emily Vandersol*

Dr. Fairfield: *research doctor at Everwood*

Agent Ferguson: *FBI agent*

Francis: *groundskeeper in paradise, married to Madeline*

Mr. George: *curator of an art studio in Palo Alto, California*

Agent Hart: *FBI agent*

Officer Hastings: *police officer in Iowa City*

Heather: *co-worker at Diamond Law Firm in Olivia, Minnesota*

Hillary Cunningham: *wife of Roger Cunningham*

Ilona (Baldwin) George: *ex-wife of Harrison Baldwin, mother of Jillian*

Agent Jackson: *FBI agent, Boston field office*

Jan: *housekeeper, Anthony's New York apartment*

Jane Allyson: *court-appointed counsel*

Jared Clawson: *CFO Rawls Corporation*

Jerry Russel: *husband of Meredith Banks Russel*

Jillian (Baldwin) George: *daughter of Harrison Baldwin and Ilona (Baldwin) George*

Judge Jefferies: *court judge, Iowa City*

Jim: *therapist at Yankton Federal Prison Camp*

Mr. and Mrs. Johnson: *Simon Johnson's parents*

Jonas Smithers: *Anthony Rawlings' first business partner in Company Smithers Rawlings (CSR)*

Jonathon Burke: *securities officer whose testimony helped to incriminate Nathanial Rawls*

Jordon Nichols: *father of Claire and Emily Nichols, married to Shirley, son of Sherman*

Julia: *Caleb Simmons' wife*

Kayla: *nurse*

Keaton: *love interest of Amber McCoy*

Kelli: *secretary, Rawlings Industries, New York office*

Kirstin: *Marcus Evergreen's secretary*

Mr. Leason: *administrator of Everwood*

Dr. Leonard: *physician*

Dr. Logan: *physician*

Madeline: *housekeeper in paradise, married to Francis*

Marcus: *driver for SiJo Gaming*

Marcus Evergreen: *Iowa City prosecutor*

Mary Ann Combs: *longtime companion of Elijah Summer, Tony's friend*

Maryn Simmons: *daughter of Courtney and Brent Simmons*

Michael Vandersol: *son of Emily and John Vandersol*

Sergeant Miles: *police officer, St. Louis*

Monica Thompson: *wedding planner*

Naiade: *housekeeper in Fiji*

Chief Newburgh: *chief of police, Iowa City Police Department*

Officer O'Brien: *police officer, Iowa City Police Department*

Miss Oliver: *Jillian (Baldwin) George's teacher*

Patrick Chester: *neighbor of Samuel and Amanda Rawls*

Paul Task: *court-appointed counsel*

Quinn: *personal assistant of Jane Allyson, Esquire*

Judge Reynolds: *court judge, Iowa City*

Richard Bosley: *governor of Iowa*

Richard Bosley II: *son of Richard Bosley, banker in Michigan*

Roger Cunningham: *president of Shedis-tics*

Ronald George: *second husband of Ilona (Baldwin) George*

Ryan Bosley: *son of Richard II and Sarah Bosley*

Samuel Rawls: *son of Nathaniel and Sharron Rawls, husband of Amanda Rawls, father of Anton Rawls*

Sarah Bosley: *wife of Richard Bosley II*

Shannon: *Nichol Rawlings' nanny*

Sharon Michaels: *attorney for Rawlings Industries*

Sharron Rawls: *wife of Nathaniel Rawls*

Shaun Stivert: *photographer for Vanity Fair*

Sheldon Preston: *governor of Iowa*

Shelly: *Anthony Rawlings' publicist*

Sherman Nichols: *grandfather of Claire Nichols, FBI agent who helped to incriminate Nathaniel Rawls. FBI alias: Cole Mathews*

Sherry: *assistant to Dr. Carly Brown*

Shirley Nichols: *wife of Jordon Nichols, mother of Claire and Emily*

Silvia Rossi: *married to Carlo Rossi, adopted mother of Sophia Rossi Burke*

Simon Johnson: *first love and classmate of Claire Nichols, gaming entrepreneur*

Dr. Sizemore: *obstetrician and gynecologist*

Sue Bronson: *Tim Bronson's wife*

Taylor Walters: *member of Rawlings' estate security*

Judge Temple: *court judge, Iowa City*

Terri: *nurse*

Tim Bronson: *vice president, corporate Rawlings Industries*

Tom Miller: *Rawlings attorney, friend of Tony's*

Tory Garrett: *pilot for Rawlings Industries*

Valerie: *assistant to Dr. Fairfield*

Dr. Warner: *psychologist at female federal penitentiary*

Judge Wein: *court judge, Iowa City*

SAC Williams: *Special Agent in Charge of the San Francisco FBI field office*

THE CONSEQUENCES SERIES
Timeline

-1921-

Nathaniel Rawls—born

-1943-

Nathaniel Rawls—home from WWII

Nathaniel Rawls marries Sharron Parkinson

Nathaniel begins working for BNG Textiles

-1944-

Samuel Rawls—born to Nathaniel and Sharron

-1953-

BNG Textiles becomes Rawls Textiles

-1956-

Rawls Textiles becomes Rawls Corporation

-1962-

Catherine Marie London—born

-1963-

Samuel Rawls marries Amanda

-1965-
FEBRUARY 12
Anton Rawls—born to Samuel and Amanda

-1975-
Rawls Corporation goes public

-1980-
JULY 19
Sophia Rossi (London)—born/adopted by Carlo and Silvia Rossi
AUGUST 31
Emily Nichols—born to Jordon and Shirley Nichols

-1983-
Sharron Rawls exhibits symptoms of Alzheimer's disease
Marie London starts to work for Sharron Rawls
Anton Rawls graduates from Blair Academy High School
OCTOBER 17
Claire Nichols—born to Jordon and Shirley Nichols

-1985-
Nathaniel Rawls begins affair with Marie London
Marie London loses baby
Sharron Rawls dies

-1986-
Rawls Corporation falls

-1987-
Anton Rawls graduates from NYU
Nathaniel Rawls found guilty of multiple counts of insider trading,
misappropriation of funds, price fixing, and securities fraud

-1988-
Nathaniel Rawls marries Catherine Marie London

Anton Rawls graduates with Master's degree

-1989-
Nathaniel Rawls—dies

Samuel and Amanda Rawls—die

-1990-
Anton Rawls changes his name to Anthony Rawlings

Anthony Rawlings begins CSR-Company Smithers Rawlings with Jonas Smithers

-1994-
Anthony Rawlings buys out Jonas Smithers and CSR becomes Rawlings Industries

-1996-
Rawlings Industries begins to diversify

-1997-
Sherman Nichols—dies

-2002-
Claire Nichols—graduates high school

Claire Nichols—attends Valparaiso University

-2003-
Simon Johnson begins internship at Shedis-tics in California

-2004-
Jordon and Shirley Nichols—die

-2005-
Emily Nichols—marries John Vandersol

-2007-
Claire Nichols—graduates from Valparaiso, degree in meteorology
Claire Nichols—moves from Indiana to New York for internship

-2008-
Claire Nichols—moves to Atlanta, Georgia, for job at WKPZ
Simon Johnson begins SiJo Gaming Corporation

-2009-
WKPZ—purchased by large corporation resulting in lay-offs
Jillian Baldwin is born

-2010-
MARCH
Anthony Rawlings—enters the Red Wing in Atlanta, Georgia
Anthony Rawlings—takes Claire Nichols on a date
Claire Nichols—wakes at Anthony's estate
MAY
Claire Nichols—liberties begin to increase
Anthony Rawlings—takes Claire Nichols to symphony and
introduces "Tony"
SEPTEMBER
Meredith Banks' article appears—Claire Nichols' accident
DECEMBER 18
Anthony Rawlings—marries Claire Nichols

-2011-
APRIL
Vanity Fair article appears

SEPTEMBER

Anthony and Claire Rawlings attend a symposium in Chicago where Claire sees Simon Johnson, her college boyfriend

NOVEMBER

Simon Johnson—dies in airplane accident

-2012-

JANUARY

Claire Rawlings drives away from the Rawlings estate

Anthony Rawlings—poisoned

Claire Rawlings—arrested for attempted murder

MARCH

Anthony Rawlings divorces Claire Nichols

APRIL

Claire Nichols pleads no contest to attempted murder charges

OCTOBER

Claire Nichols receives box of information while in prison

-2013-

MARCH

Petition for pardon is filed with Governor Bosley on behalf of Claire Nichols

Petition for pardon is granted; Claire Nichols is released from prison and moves to Palo Alto, California

Tony learns of Claire's release, hires Phillip Roach, and contacts Claire

APRIL

Claire and Courtney vacation in Texas

Tony travels to California. He and Claire have dinner and reconnect

MAY

Claire meets with Meredith Banks in San Diego

Claire and Harry connect

Claire and Harry visit Patrick Chester

Claire attends the National Center for Learning Disabilities annual
gala where Tony is the keynote speaker

Claire takes a home pregnancy test

JUNE

Caleb Simmons weds his fiancée, Julia.

Tony asks Claire to accompany him to the wedding

Claire is attacked by Patrick Chester

Claire moves back to Iowa

JULY

First mailing arrives to Iowa addressed to *Claire Nichols-Rawls*

SEPTEMBER

Tony leaves for a ten-day business trip to Europe

Claire leaves Iowa

OCTOBER

Claire moves to paradise

Phil Roach takes Tony to paradise

OCTOBER 27

Anthony Rawlings and Claire Nichols remarry

DECEMBER

DECEMBER 19

Nichol Courtney Rawlings born

-2014-

MARCH

Tony and Claire Rawlings return to the United States

Incident at Rawlings estate

Claire Rawlings suffers a psychotic break

Tony and Claire are arrested

Anthony Rawlings is booked for crimes against
the state of Iowa and the United States

Claire Rawlings is booked for attempted murder

Catherine Marie London is booked for crimes against the state of
Iowa and the United States

A protective order is filed against Anthony Rawlings

JUNE

Anthony Rawlings pleads guilty to kidnapping and is sentenced to four years at Yankton, Federal Prison Camp, Yankton, South Dakota

JULY

Michael Vandersol is born to Emily and John Vandersol

NOVEMBER

Catherine Marie London's case goes before a grand jury

-2015-

JULY

Catherine Marie London is convicted of crimes against the state of Iowa and the United States

AUGUST

Amber McCoy is arrested for crimes against the state of California and the United States

-2016-

SPRING

Anthony Rawlings fires his assistant, Patricia

Tony begins construction on new home

JUNE

Meredith Banks approaches Emily Vandersol in park

Meredith Banks goes undercover at Everwood to learn about Claire Rawlings

JULY

Harrison Baldwin retires from FBI and moves to North Carolina

SEPTEMBER

Claire Rawlings begins to speak

Tony starts petition to terminate the marriage of Anthony and Claire Rawlings

Courtney Simmons meets with Meredith Banks and sees Claire

OCTOBER

Anthony Rawlings' early release from Yankton Federal Prison Camp
is approved

FIFTEEN DAYS LATER

Anthony Rawlings is released from Yankton Federal Prison Camp

Tony signs Claire out of Everwood

Tony gives Claire the Rawlings estate and asks her for a divorce

Tony and Claire go to see Nichol for the first time in 2 ½ years

Tony and Claire reunite

DECEMBER

Nichol Rawlings' third birthday is celebrated in
paradise with family and friends

-2017-

JANUARY

Taylor Walters is hired by the Rawlings family

APRIL

Elizabeth (Beth) Vandersol is born to John and Emily Vandersol

OCTOBER

Harrison Baldwin meets Miss Oliver

Christopher Simmons is born to Caleb and Julia Simmons

-2018-

FEBRUARY 7

Nathaniel (Nate) Sherman Rawlings is born to Tony and Claire
Rawlings

What to do Now...

LEND IT: Did you enjoy BEYOND THE CONSEQUENCES? Do you have a friend who'd enjoy BEYOND THE CONSEQUENCES? BEYOND THE CONSEQUENCES may be lent one time. Sharing is caring!

RECOMMEND IT: Do you have more than one friend who'd enjoy BEYOND THE CONSEQUENCES? Tell them about it! Call, text, post, tweet... your recommendation is the nicest gift you can give to an author!

REVIEW IT: Tell the world. Please go to the retailer where you purchased this, as well as Goodreads, and write a review. Please share your thoughts about BEYOND THE CONSEQUENCES on:

*Goodreads.com/Aleatha Romig

Stay Connected with Aleatha

Do you love Aleatha's writing? Do you want to know the latest about Infidelity? Consequences? Tales From the Dark Side? and Aleatha's new series coming in 2016 from Tho+mas and Mercer?

Do you like EXCLUSIVE content (never released scenes, never released excerpts, and more)? Would you like the monthly chance to win prizes (signed books and gift cards)? Then sign up today for Aleatha's monthly newsletter and stay informed on all thing Aleatha Romig.

Sign up for Aleatha's NEWSLETTER:
http://bit.ly/1PYLjZW
(recipients receive exclusive material and offers)

You can also find Aleatha@

Check out her website: http://aletharomig.wix.com/aleatha
Facebook: https://www.facebook.com/AleathaRomig
Twitter: https://twitter.com/AleathaRomig
Goodreads: goodreads.com/author/show/5131072.Aleatha_Romig
Instagram: http://instagram.com/aletharomig
Email Aleatha: aletharomig@gmail.com

You may also listen Aleatha Romig's books on Audible.

Books by
NEW YORK TIMES BESTSELLING AUTHOR
Aleatha Romig

THE LIGHT SERIES:
Published through Thomas and Mercer

INTO THE LIGHT
To be released June 14, 2016

AWAY FROM THE DARK
(Release TBA)

TALES FROM THE DARK SIDE SERIES:

INSIDIOUS
(All books in this series are stand-alone erotic thrillers)
Released October 2014
DUPLICITY
(Completely unrelated to book #1)
Release TBA

THE CONSEQUENCES SERIES:

CONSEQUENCES
(Book #1)
Released August 2011

TRUTH
(Book #2)
Released October 2012

CONVICTED
(Book #3)
Released October 2013

REVEALED
(Book #4)
Previously titled: Behind His Eyes Convicted: The Missing Years
Re-released June 2014

BEYOND THE CONSEQUENCES
(Book #5)
Released January 2015

COMPANION READS:

BEHIND HIS EYES—CONSEQUENCES
(Book #1.5)
Released January 2014

BEHIND HIS EYES—TRUTH
(Book #2.5)
Released March 2014

Aleatha Romig

Aleatha Romig is a New York Times and USA Today bestselling author who lives in Indiana. She grew up in Mishawaka, graduated from Indiana University, and is currently living south of Indianapolis. Aleatha has raised three children with her high school sweetheart and husband of nearly thirty years. Before she became a full-time author, she worked days as a dental hygienist and spent her nights writing. Now, when she's not imagining mind-blowing twists and turns, she likes to spend her time with her family and friends. Her other pastimes include reading and creating heroes/anti-heroes who haunt your dreams!

Aleatha released her first novel, CONSEQUENCES, in August of 2011. CONSEQUENCES became a bestselling series with five novels and two companions released from 2011 through 2015. The compelling and epic story of Anthony and Claire Rawlings has graced more than half a million e-readers. Aleatha released the first of her series TALES FROM THE DARK SIDE, INSIDIOUS, in the fall of 2014. These stand-alone thrillers continue Aleatha's twisted style with an increase in heat. In the fall of 2015, Aleatha will move headfirst into the world of dark romance with the release of BETRAYAL, the first of her five-novel INFIDELITY series. Aleatha has entered the traditional world of publishing with Thomas and Mercer with her SAVED series. The first of that series, INTO THE LIGHT, will be published in 2016.

Aleatha is a "Published Author's Network" member of the Romance Writers of America and represented by Danielle Egan-Miller of Browne & Miller Literary Associates.

INSIDIOUS

TALES FROM THE DARK SIDE

Dark desires... Deadly secrets... Devious deceptions... Nothing is exactly as it seems in INSIDIOUS, the new erotic thriller from *New York Times* and *USA Today* bestselling author ALEATHA ROMIG!

When a powerful man is willing to risk everything for his own satisfaction, only one woman can beat him at his own game: his wife. Or so she thinks...

> *"Let's start with you calling me Stewart.*
> *Formalities seem unnecessary."*

Stewart Harrington is rich, gorgeous, and one of the most powerful men in Miami. He always gets what he wants. Anything is available to him for the right price.

Even me.

Being the wife of a mogul comes with all the perks, but being *Mrs. Stewart Harrington* comes with a few *special requirements*. I've learned to keep a part of myself locked away as my husband watches me submit to his needs. But the more he demands of me, the more beguiled he becomes and that's to my advantage. So I keep fulfilling his fantasies and following his rules because he doesn't know that what he's playing is really *my* game. And winning is everything, right?

INSIDIOUS is a stand-alone novel and the first *Tales from the Dark Side* title by ALEATHA ROMIG.

**Due to the dark and explicit nature of this book, it is recommended for mature audiences only. **

TALES FROM THE DARK SIDE are a series of standalone erotic thrillers. Each book will have new characters and a new storyline. Though the story will conclude, with Aleatha's signature twists and turns, each book will leave you with a bang!

Can you handle more from Aleatha? Can you handle TALES FROM THE DARK SIDE? Book #1, INSIDIOUS, released October 2014.

63211442R00160

Made in the USA
Lexington, KY
30 April 2017